GONE
to the
DOGS
Mysteries

BOOK 4

T0104110

The BARK of ZORRO

Gone *to the* DOGS *Mysteries*
BOOK 4

The BARK of ZORRO

KATHLEEN Y'BARBO

BARBOUR
PUBLISHING

The Bark of Zorro ©2023 by Kathleen Y'Barbo

Print ISBN 978-1-63609-517-2
Adobe Digital Edition (.epub) 978-1-63609-518-9

Scripture quotations taken from the King James Version of the Bible.

This book is a work of fiction. Names, characters, places, and incidents are either products of the author's imagination or used fictitiously. Any similarity to actual people, organizations, and/or events is purely coincidental.

Cover Illustration by Victor McLindon

Published by Barbour Publishing, Inc., 1810 Barbour Drive, Uhrichsville, Ohio 44683, www.barbourbooks.com

Our mission is to inspire the world with the life-changing message of the Bible.

ecpa Member of the
Evangelical Christian
Publishers Association

Printed in the United States of America.

DEDICATION

"Happiness is a warm puppy."—Charles Schulz

This book is dedicated to Baxter Boo II—
you were a very good boy.
And to Baby and Fifi, the cats that tolerated him.

What Gramps couldn't fix couldn't be fixed, so he was a popular guy with the broken lawn mower and farm equipment crowd. Since Mama was a secretary at an insurance agency and Daddy worked at the Blue Bell Ice Cream plant, every summer I became his sidekick. With his dark hair and features and my mop of red curls, we made quite a pair.

Gramps had customers all along this road. When I was a girl, the giant oil pump had looked terrifying—like a mosquito bobbing up and down toward the earth. It didn't help that the Venable brothers who lived across the way loved to tell me scary stories about how the pumping equipment came alive in the dark and went after little girls like me.

Now the site was nothing but an eyesore. Once I admitted the source of my fear of the old pump and the reason for it, Gramps made me stay in his truck and read or work on my stories when we made a pickup or delivery from the Venables.

I was that kid who always had a book or was writing one, even at the tender age or eight or nine. Since I was such a fan, I made up my own *Scooby-Doo* mystery stories. Funny, they always featured a villain who was basically one of the Venable clan disguised as a scary farmer or a weird professor or whatever villain du jour my little brain came up with.

Occasionally I considered writing a real mystery novel. The idea always burned bright for a day or two but flamed out hard when I actually had to put words on a blank computer screen. But if I ever did, I'd throw a Venable in for sure.

Not known for their honesty or for paying Gramps on time or in cash, the various members of the family drifted in and out of the county jail with regularity. Still my grandfather continued to do business with the clan, though I never could understand why.

I turned my mind toward the task at hand. Finding a pup on a night like this wasn't going to be easy. The description had been vague: *large, dark dog. Smudge of white on its side. Seen near the abandoned pump site on Post Road.*

"I'll get you, little guy. The rescue van is on its way," I said aloud to the empty van. "Now, if you'd just slow down this rain, Lord, I'd be extremely appreciative."

I leaned forward and began looking for the handwritten sign that advertised yard eggs and quilts for sale. A flash of lightning cut across the horizon just in time to let me know I was about to pass it up.

Yanking the wheel to the right, I managed to make the turn. However, the sounds coming from the back of the van told me I'd probably have a mess to clean up once I arrived at my destination.

Since I needed the larger crate, I'd had to do some creative rearranging of supplies. I tried not to think what might be rolling around back there. Next time I'd take the time to strap everything down like Parker did.

I hit a pothole that jarred my bones. Maybe I needed to be strapped down. Beyond a seat belt, of course. I am nothing if not a safe and law-abiding driver.

The van bounced down the gravel road past Ursula's Quilts and Eggs on the left and a peach orchard on the right. Ursula's was a favorite stop for my grandmother. She went for eggs when her hens weren't laying but always came home with something to add to her collection of quilts. I often wondered if she did something to make those hens give her an excuse to shop.

Anyway, the turn was just up ahead. I kept my eyes on the road and wrangled my thoughts back to the present.

After a few minutes, I reached the location. In contrast to the thick woods all around, the abandoned pump site had been paved over with concrete and enclosed with a high chain-link fence. I could see from the headlight beams that I was all alone here.

The gates were open just enough to allow the passage of the rescue van. I continued on, easing my way past the red No Trespassing—We Prosecute signs that papered the fence.

Lightning flashed again, confirming there was no evidence of a stray animal—or human—nearby. Maybe coming out here tonight was a mistake.

But here I was. If a pup was out in this weather, then I needed to find it.

I shifted the van into PARK and turned off the engine, silencing the music and leaving the drumming of raindrops on the roof in its place. Now to get this show on the road. Or, rather, to commence the rescue.

The back of the van wasn't in as much disarray as I expected. I moved the crate around close to the back doors and returned the supplies that had landed on the floor during the ride back to their places.

After rummaging around in the van, I found an umbrella, a flashlight, and a bright yellow raincoat and a pair of rain boots that were large enough to belong to Parker. I shrugged into the oversized coat, then slipped off my sneakers and stuck my feet into the boots.

I considered grabbing both the umbrella and the flashlight, then quickly changed my mind. I needed the flashlight to see, but I'd never be able to catch a frightened dog while juggling an umbrella.

At least I wasn't following Mari into a drainage pipe to chase down a rescue. We'd done that more than once and almost been arrested. But we'd rescued that dog, just as I would rescue this one.

Tugging the hood of the rain jacket over my head, I climbed back into the driver's seat and reached for the sandwich I'd hastily wrapped before I left my apartment. According to Parker, a juicy burger is guaranteed to soothe any beast, savage or not.

The rescue crew usually stopped to grab a burger to get the attention of the animal in need of rescuing. However, tonight's rescue would have to settle for a sandwich because that's what I'd had in front of me when the phone buzzed with the notification.

Ignoring the urge to contemplate the sadness of dining alone on a sandwich on Valentine's Day, I tucked the thing into my pocket along with my phone. Likely the little guy was hungry enough to appreciate anything edible.

Then I slipped the van keys into the other pocket, turned on the flashlight, and stepped out into the rain. Vague recollections of the Venables' terrible tales arose, but I pushed them back. There was nothing to fear here. Just an old abandoned oil pump site with rusting pump equipment and possibly a lost and frightened dog.

I shuffled across the clearing in my oversized coat and boots, sweeping the arc of light across the perimeter as I plodded along. Rain poured down my face in rivulets, making it almost impossible to see without swiping at my eyes.

Something darted across the far edge of the flashlight's beam just inside the fence that surrounded the abandoned machinery. I swung in that direction and spied a big ball of dark fur with a white spot on one side just before it disappeared behind the rusted machinery.

"Are you stuck, little guy?" I called out as I looked around for a way to get inside to save the poor pup. "I'm here to help you."

I made the circle all the way around the enclosure, trying to ignore the signs that matched the ones on the gate. I wasn't trespassing, was I? I was rescuing. There was a difference.

Unfortunately, no matter where I stood, the dog would position himself on the opposite side. We were at an impasse. At least rain had slowed a bit and the lightning had ceased.

Reaching the gate to the enclosure, I tugged on the lock. Nothing. It was rusty, as was the chain that had been looped through the gate and the fence.

Lightning cracked.

Thunder boomed.

The poor pup yipped in fear.

I had to do something.

CHAPTER TWO

I retraced my muddy steps and opened the back of the van to rummage around the best I could. After moving things around, I found one of those second-floor fire escape chain ladders rolled up behind a box of supplies and considered using it. What I couldn't work out was once I got in, how would I get out holding a medium-to-large extremely terrified dog?

Casting the ladder aside, I spied a tire iron. It was old and rusty and, as it turned out, heavy. Likely this thing was what had made the most noise as the van bounced along the back roads.

I lugged it across the back of the van and weighed my options. I could quit now and go for help. But where would I go? Calling Mari and Parker was out of the question, at least until I had exhausted all other options. And although the Venables were still living across the street, I sure wasn't going there on a dark and stormy night.

"Think, Cassidy," I muttered under my breath. "What can I do besides try to break that old lock and chain with this tire iron?"

While rescuing a dog might require a little harmless trespassing now and then, the volunteers at Second Chance Ranch Dog Rescue were trained not to break laws. And everything about the plan to smash a lock and chain with a tire iron felt illegal.

I mean, the signs everywhere practically declared it was.

The dog yipped. I let out a long breath and swiped at my wet face with the back of my hand. I was cold and wet, and I had the benefit of a slicker suit and waterproof boots. That poor pup had nothing but his soaked fur.

Something had to happen, and soon.

It was all down to me, so off I went. As it turned out, with two swings of the tire iron, the lock and chain gave way. It was then that I realized I didn't have the crate.

I did have the sandwich. I was reminded of this when the terrified pup darted toward me the moment I stepped inside the enclosure. I thought he was heading for the open gate.

Nope. The dog buried his nose in my pocket and rooted around looking for the sandwich.

"Hold on there," I said as I managed to snag his collar. "Let's go back to the van, and then we'll discuss the dinner menu."

The dog was the size and color of a small bear cub. Even though there hadn't been a bear sighting in Washington County in longer than I could remember, I'd run my flashlight over his face to make sure. You never knew what people kept as pets out in the country.

Nope. This wasn't a purebred chow chow, but it was definitely that breed mixed with something else to give it a darker fur and less stocky build.

Walking hunched over with one hand on a dog's rain-soaked collar, the other hand holding a tire iron, and a flashlight squeezed into your right armpit is even harder than it sounds, especially when your shoes and rain slicker were made for someone much larger. When I got to the van, I leaned the tire iron against the tire, grabbed the flashlight, and then opened the back door. While I was trying to figure out the best way to get this heavy animal into the van, it slipped out of my reach and jumped inside.

My mouth opened in surprise as I watched the animal shake the rain off himself—and onto every surface in the back of the vehicle—and then settle down inside the crate as if he owned the place. I retrieved the semi-soggy sandwich from my pocket and handed it over.

"Okay, fella—enjoy."

By the time I'd closed the crate door, the dog was sniffing the air and eyeing me as if I might be hiding another sandwich in my slicker. Then he whimpered.

"Sorry, Spot," I said. "I'll get you something more to eat and a bath, but first we've got to get out of here."

Closing the door, I retrieved the tire iron. That's when I heard footsteps on the gravel. Even through the drizzling rain, I could see in the van's side mirror that a dark figure was approaching behind me.

My heart lurched.

Had one of the Venables seen me? Maybe wanted to scare me for old times' sake?

Unlikely given the weather and the fact that I was almost unrecognizable in my current garb. Or at least I assumed I was.

I dropped the tire iron and raced to jump into the van and turn the key in the ignition. The man in the mirror picked up speed.

Venable or not, I was out of here.

No way was I going to try to figure out what a guy sneaking up on me at a dark, abandoned pump site had to say. A moment later, the pup and I were leaving the old pump site behind in a hurry.

With my heart thumping, the music blaring, and the raindrops once again beating against the windshield, I made it only as far as the gravel road leading to Ursula's Quilts and Eggs before I had to pull over behind the sign and turn off the engine.

There were no lights on at the building that served as a home in the back and retail establishment in the front. If there had been a security light on the premises, it was either long gone or the bulb needed replacing.

Spot whimpered as the interior of the van went dark. "Hang on, little buddy," I told him as I kicked off the oversized rainboots and tossed them onto the passenger side. "We'll get going again as soon as I get myself out of this slicker suit."

I'd just wriggled out of the jacket when the sound of a siren split the silence. Spot took up howling as I sat bolt upright to see what was causing the commotion.

Immediately I thought of the creepy man at the pump site. What if he was a crook hiding from police? Or worse, what if he was a murderer looking for a place to stash a body?

"Okay, Cassidy, you've been listening to one too many true crime podcasts. This is Brenham, Texas. Nothing like that ever happens here."

Yet I was probably the creeper's only witness that he'd been out at the pump site. Not that I saw his face. I sure hope he didn't see mine, because he was also the only witness to my crime.

The last thing I needed tonight was to be in the middle of a criminal investigation. Or worse, the subject of one if the creeper found me. I could see it now: *Single Vet Clinic Employee Caught in Valentine's Day Crime Spree.*

However, if this was an episode of *Scooby-Doo*, the bad guy would certainly be giving chase. Or at least plotting his revenge.

"Oh come on," I muttered. "Stop with the overthinking, Cassidy."

I fumbled in the dark to make sure the doors were locked as the siren grew nearer. If that guy was in these woods, the cops needed to find him before he found me.

Never mind that I'd driven a full quarter of a mile away from the pump site since I'd seen him, and he was on foot. I still needed to be sure I stayed as invisible as possible, at least until the cops caught him.

The siren grew louder, and now I could see the faint flicker of red and blue lights shining off the treetops. I'd inadvertently hidden the van behind Ursula's sign and out of the view of anyone on the road, something I now realize was likely the Lord helping those who didn't have the sense to help themselves.

I lifted my eyes and sent a prayer up through the van's roof and all the rain hitting it, giving thanks. "And help me stay hidden until the danger is gone," I whispered before adding my amen.

My phone buzzed, lighting up the interior of the van. I grabbed for it, knocking it onto the floor where it slid under the seat. By the time I finally retrieved it, the ringing had stopped. A moment later, the voice mail notification sounded.

I glanced at my screen. It was Mari.

I listened to her voice mail asking if I needed help on the rescue call, then quickly responded with a text telling her I did not.

I was not about to let them drop their plans. I could do this.

The siren's wail intensified until it sounded like the patrol car was only a few feet away. Likely it was, though Ursula's sign kept me from knowing for certain.

A moment later, one set of taillights rushed past, then faded as they disappeared down the road. I didn't plan to stick around to find out if there might be anyone on foot hiding from that cop.

I reached for the key as the dog whimpered again, then added a little yip for good measure. "Sorry, Spot. Hang on for a little longer. I promise it'll be worth it."

We often gave temporary names to our rescues if inspiration struck us. This sweet dog with his big blob of white on his side certainly seemed like a Spot to me.

Rather than taking Spot to the rescue tonight, I decided to take him home with me. Other than being wet and hungry, he seemed fine.

After all, tonight was Valentine's Day.

I turned the key in the ignition, and the van's engine roared to life. So did the radio, only this time I fumbled around until I managed to turn the volume down. Spot and I rode back to my apartment with me singing along to Trina Potter's greatest hits and him loudly snoring in the back.

"What better way to spend National Singles Awareness Day?" I muttered under my breath as the snores got louder. At least tomorrow would be more fun. Dr. Kristin was scheduled to speak with a class of fourth graders for career day at a local elementary school. I'd be going along to document the occasion for our social media accounts.

But first I had a wet and hungry dog to get situated. Since I had an early morning, I'd have to make arrangements for Spot as well.

Normally one of the rescuers would take the pup home until it was either returned to its owners or adopted. When that option wasn't available, we either kenneled the dog at the rescue facility or placed it temporarily with a foster, with preference given to the second option.

Once we arrived, I gathered up the wet towels and left the rest of the mess to deal with later. Then I went around to the back of the van, opened the crate, and slipped a leash on the drowsy dog.

"All right," I told him, thankful the rain had slowed to a light drizzle, "let's go see what we can do about dinner and a bath—for both of us."

Spot followed me across the parking lot and up the stairs to my apartment as if we were old friends. Someone was surely missing this sweet creature. I'd do everything I could to see that pup and owner were reunited.

After offering him a treat and promising him a bowl of kibble once he was clean, I deposited Spot into my tub and started scrubbing him. That's when I discovered that the spot of white fur on his side was actually a smudge of white paint.

I ran my fingers over the paint, noticing that parts of the saucer-sized stain had more white color on them than others. It was almost as if something had been painted on this dog and then the design was smudged.

Looking closer, I could see exactly what had been painted on sweet Spot: the letter Z. Now, that was odd. I'd used the app on my phone to check for a chip before his bath. The app located one, but it hadn't been activated. Maybe this detail could somehow identify his owner.

After I got Spot fed and settled in for the night on a dog bed that I kept for situations just like this, I took a quick shower. With the pup once again snoozing away, I heated up a bowl of leftover soup, located a foster who could take Spot in the morning, and then padded over to my computer.

There were several mentions of animals in the Houston area showing up with the letter Z painted on them. But why? No one knew.

Which meant I was bound and determined to find out.

Spot lifted his head and looked up at me with sleepy eyes. "Who did this to you, sweetheart?" I asked softly. "Since you can't tell me, I guess I'll just have to solve this mystery myself."

CHAPTER THREE

Wednesday, February 15

The next morning, I dropped Spot off at a foster home. I usually bring the rescues with me to the clinic if they're well socialized, which Spot definitely was. However, I had the first team meeting for the Brenham Spring Festival planning committee today, and I didn't want to be distracted.

Lone Star Vet Clinic had been a sponsor of the festival for several years. When an opening came up on the planning committee after one of the members dropped out, the committee came to the clinic to round out their group. I was nominated by the veterinarians to add festival planner to my list of duties.

Of course I happily accepted.

My phone buzzed with a text as I was climbing into my car. I glanced down to see it was my friend Nora Hernandez.

Until last October, Nora had been the area sales rep for the high-quality pet food our clinic stocked, but she'd also been a friend of mine since junior high and our *abuelas* had known each other since they were girls.

Have I mentioned that Nora also owns a dog that sniffs for truffles? Truffles she was growing on her family's land in rural Bastrop County and selling to local restaurants, of all things.

Suffice it to say, I was in awe of her.

With yesterday being Valentine's Day, surely her boyfriend, Lane, had finally popped the question. He'd be a fool not to.

I steeled myself for the obligatory engagement ring photos. I would be thrilled for her, truly. But one more friend engaged meant one less friend to commiserate on the single life with.

I exhaled and opened the text. Instead of a ring photo, there was just one line: No ring for Valentine's Day.

I frowned. Are you okay? I typed back.

The dots appeared on the screen, disappeared, and then appeared again. While I was considering what to say next, my phone rang. It was Nora.

"Cassidy," she said before I could even say hello. "I'm great. I only texted you because I figured you'd be bracing yourself for the photos."

She paused, and I heard a chuckle. I guess Nora really was okay about Lane being so commitment phobic.

"The reason I called is I think I've found the perfect spot for my restaurant."

"Okay," I told her. "So we're not talking about Lane anymore?"

"We can talk about Lane another time. We need to talk real estate right now. I think I've found the one."

After deciding her long-term boyfriend, a professor of veterinary medicine at Texas A&M, wasn't going to propose anytime soon, she stepped out in faith and followed her dream of opening a farm-to-table restaurant named Simply Eat.

Unfortunately, the restaurant was still in the concept stage because Nora had the same problem as me. She still hadn't settled on the right property at the right price.

"That's wonderful," I told her. "I can't wait to see it."

"Actually, I'm about to take a look, and I wondered if you might be able to meet me there. I've got a reason for asking."

"And that is?" I asked.

"The location is downtown, and it's part of a two-property deal." She paused. "The owners are selling the commercial space downstairs and an upstairs residential loft that might make the perfect new home for you. Each measures a little over 2,500 square feet."

I sat back against my car's cold seat and blew out a long breath. Thus far I'd only been looking at homes in the suburbs, and none of them came close to 2,500 square feet. But my job was downtown. And who wouldn't want to have the restaurant of Nora's dreams downstairs? Not to mention, the idea of living in a loft did sound kind of cool.

I looked at the clock. The meeting wasn't for another three hours. If I limited my time at the property, I should be fine.

"Okay, I'm interested," I said as Nora squealed. "*But*," I emphasized, "I need to know more, starting with the price."

She quoted an amount that had me smiling. Then a thought occurred. "What's the catch?"

"Other than you'd be stuck with me close by more than you probably want?" she said. "From what my real estate agent told me, it's a warehouse-type conversion. Basically, the upstairs was storage for the storefront downstairs back in the late 1800s."

"What kind of storefront?"

She laughed. "Not that it matters, but the building used to house the old funeral home."

"Really?" I joined her laughter. "You want me to live in a place where they used to store the bodies? No thanks."

"Cassidy, you've got it all wrong. They didn't store anything upstairs but caskets, and I'm skeptical they even put those up there. The ad shows fourteen-foot ceilings, original wood floors, and brick walls. I'd live there myself if I didn't already own my own place."

It sounded like more than I ever imagined I'd be able to afford. I still wasn't sold on the idea of living anywhere but on a little plot of land. Still, it would be convenient to walk to work instead of driving. And downtown was where I spent most of my time. Then there was the issue of buying all those yard tools to keep the grass from looking like a pasture.

Another thought occurred. "Where'd they put the bodies if not upstairs?"

"I don't know for sure where they put the bodies, but I've seen the stairs, and there's no way anyone carried anything heavy up there unless they had to."

"So that's negative point number two, I guess?"

"What? Steep stairs? Not at all. Think of it as a built-in step machine. And if it makes you feel better, my real estate agent showed me the perfect spot in the back of the building to add an elevator that would be just inside the door that leads to your stairs. If I get the storefront, I'd be happy to deed over that old storage closet to you for your swift-trip-upstairs option. Oh, and did I mention the floor-to-ceiling windows that face the square? Four of them, to be exact. And a little balcony that is absolutely adorable."

"You've thought of everything, haven't you?"

"I try. So, what do you say? Can you stop by now? I'm literally parked out front with the key code to the lockboxes. I won't make you too late to work. I promise."

She would, but I was intrigued. I sent Dr. Kristin and Dr. Tyler a text saying I would be a few minutes late because I was looking at a property. My ongoing home search was well known among the staff, so I knew no one would mind.

A few minutes later, I pulled up in a parking space next to Nora's ancient red Suburban. Both hands still on the wheel, I couldn't help but smile as I spied the bronze plaque that indicated the brick building had been built in 1888. Unless there was something very, very wrong with this place, I just might be interested.

I spied Nora grinning at me from the other side of the massive plate glass windows that decorated the length of the downstairs. I stepped inside, courtesy of an oversized pair of wooden doors.

Nora met me at the doors and squealed. "Two pieces of good news in one phone call, Cassidy. First, the building was not the funeral home. My real estate agent was wrong. They sold buggies here. And then later, the first cars in Washington County were sold right here."

"That's great," I said. "No reason to worry whether there are bodies in the attic."

She shook her head. "That's always a risk in a used home. Just kidding." Then she laughed. "I haven't told you the other good news. The seller wants to make a quick deal. He's offering a lower price if we can take immediate possession."

"Immediate possession?" I stared at her. "As in today?"

"Sort of," she said. "He is willing to lease the two properties to us until the actual sale goes through. He'll give us keys as soon as we sign the paperwork."

I was speechless. While I was currently paying rent at my apartment on a month-to-month basis now that my lease had expired, I hadn't given any serious thought to the idea of actually moving out. Until now.

Then she told me the new price. And the monthly cost to rent the place until we could close. Again, I was speechless. It was half the amount I was paying at my apartment complex.

"This is it, Cassidy," Nora said, interrupting my thoughts. "This is where Simply Eat will finally happen. I'm so excited."

"I can see it," I told her. "And I am super excited for you. But what I need to see now is the upstairs property."

She took me back outside and nodded toward a door set into the brick wall on the right-hand side of the window. "That's your entrance. I've already unlocked it. Let's go check it out."

The door was heavy but opened on well-oiled hinges. Stairsteps made of polished wood marched upward to disappear around a curve in the ancient red brick wall. A massive window allowed sunlight to pour into the space, turning the stair treads the color of golden honey. An old brass chandelier hung halfway up, dangling from the wooden ceiling on a matching chain.

"After you," Nora said.

I stifled a gasp. Then, once I gathered my wits, I hurried up the stairs.

To my surprise, there was no door at the top. Instead, the honey-colored wood flowed into a space that was so much bigger than I expected.

An ancient brick wall formed the opposite side of the room. To the left was the wall facing the square. Three windows that matched the one over the staircase filled the wall from floor to ceiling. Overhead was ceiling covered in narrow strips of wood that had been painted white.

I turned to my right and spied a half dozen small windows just below the ceiling. Taking a guess, I decided these were probably designed to let the heat out during ancient Brenham summers.

Heat. I noticed that it was nice and warm. I looked up to discover the very modern HVAC ducts that had been disguised with white paint that matched the ceiling.

Nora grinned. "The appraisal says the owner replaced the heating and cooling units in both properties two years ago. Plumbing was redone at the same time. I don't want to brag, but my industrial kitchen also got a redo." She nodded to the back wall. "Yours looks new as well."

I moved across the space to stand in the area designated as the kitchen. In contrast to the keep-it-original theme of the loft, the kitchen sparkled with modern stainless steel appliances, marble countertops, and antique pendant lights that glowed like jewels.

The bathroom had a similar modern yet vintage vibe with marble tile everywhere, double vanities, and two giant silver mirrors that captured the light streaming in from the little windows at the roofline. At the other end of the room behind an antique door with an etched glass window marked PRIVATE OFFICE was a decent-sized closet that would easily hold my meager wardrobe with space left over.

"I'm in love," I managed. "It's so beautiful, Nora. Nothing like I thought I wanted, and yet I can totally see myself living here."

"It is perfect for you," Nora said. "Although if it were me I'd probably carve some space out for a bedroom. I'm just not the everything-in-one-room type of gal."

"Oh, good idea." I scanned the room and found just the spot. "What if I had a wall put up in the corner to create a bedroom that has just the one window in it?"

"All the way to the ceiling or just a partial wall?" Nora asked. "Like eight feet or so?"

From there the conversation veered into renovations and design choices. We were in the middle of a discussion of whether to change the drawer pulls on the kitchen cabinets when my phone buzzed with a text message from Dr. Kristin.

You're going to have to handle the elementary school visit today by yourself. We had an emergency come in a few minutes ago. Tyler needs both of us in surgery, so I can't leave.

My fingers hovered above the keypad. I wanted to remind her that I had a committee meeting to attend during the time the school visit was scheduled, but I knew she wouldn't ask me to skip that to attend the event unless she absolutely had to.

I typed a response to Dr. Kristin, then sent a message to the committee to let them know I would have to miss the meeting due to work-related duties.

Finally, I turned to Nora with a sigh. "I've got to go. But Nora," I said with a sigh, "let's make this happen. If the inspection turns out okay, that is."

"Agreed." She reached over to hug me, then took a step backward. "Yes, let's do this. I'll get my real estate agent on it." Then she grinned again. "Is this even real?"

I laughed. "If it's not, then I don't care."

CHAPTER FOUR

The minute I got back in the car, I took a photo of the building and texted it to Mari. THIS COULD BE THE ONE. CAN'T WAIT TO TELL YOU ABOUT IT!

Mari's response was swift. CAN'T WAIT TO HEAR ABOUT IT!

I put away my phone, then headed to the clinic to pick up the treat bags the veterinarians handed out at events like this. Since I managed the social media and promotional materials for the clinic, the bags were stored in a closet in my office. I'd just retrieved them when a sound in the hallway caught my attention.

I whirled around expecting Mari or Parker. Instead, there stood Dr. Cameron Saye in all his six-foot, blond-haired, brown-eyed, handsome-man glory. Yes, I might have had a crush on the veterinarian when I first met him, but that fizzled away when I realized we had absolutely nothing in common except the vet clinic.

Since January, Cameron had been working Mondays, Wednesdays, and Fridays at the vet clinic. His part-time employment came as a surprise to me since I knew that Cameron had a long and not-so-great history with Dr. Tyler Durham, the owner of the clinic.

But the practice had grown past what two veterinarians—Dr. Tyler Durham and Dr. Kristin Keller—could handle, and the need was there. Because I'm the office manager, I'm probably the only other employee besides the two veterinarians who know that Tyler offered Cameron a full-time job here, but Cameron declined because he didn't want to give up the days he volunteered at local shelters and rescues.

A guy who loves animals enough to give up paid work to treat them for free? A real-life hero.

Even so, he was someone else's hero, not mine, and I was fine with that. As Mari liked to remind me, mine was on the way.

Right. Seems like he was held up in traffic.

"Good morning." Dr. Cameron offered me a thousand-watt smile. "Big night last night?"

"You could say that," I responded, knowing full well I was letting him think I had a date with a man rather than a date with a lost dog at a soggy pump site. "How about you?"

A shrug as he leaned against the wall. "Not me. It was my night at the shelter, and things were busier than usual. I did end up with a Subway sandwich and a bag of chips somewhere around midnight. I'd forgotten how tasty their meatball sandwiches are." He straightened and nodded toward the other end of the hall. "Oh well, I'd best go see what kind of trouble I can get up to. Have a great day, Cass."

Cass.

Cameron was the only person at the clinic who called me Cass. It was the same name that the neighborhood bullies loved to use. You'd be surprised at the number of insulting words that rhyme with Cass.

I should have told him eons ago that I preferred he call me Cassidy. Unfortunately, the window of opportunity for correcting him on this had closed. To say something now would just be awkward.

I chalked it up to one more reason why the man was not for me.

"You too," I said as he brushed past me, leaving a trail of soap-and-shampoo-scented air in his wake. Then I remembered I had a question, and he might have the answer.

"Dr. Cameron, do you have a minute? It's about a stray that the rescue picked up last night."

"Sure," he said as he turned back to face me. "Medical issue?"

"No, medically he's fine. But I'm wondering if you've had any dogs come though the shelters that have been painted."

His brows gathered. "Painted? You mean like covered in paint? Because that happens a time or two when an animal has knocked over a paint can."

"No, I mean intentionally painted," I said. "More specifically, painted with the letter Z on one side or both of the midsection."

"Oh," Dr. Cameron said slowly. "No, I don't recall anything like that. Is that what happened to your stray?"

"I think so," I told him.

He ran a hand through his hair and let out a long breath. "Did you bring the dog with you today?"

"No, but I'll have him here this afternoon." I shrugged. "He was happy when I dropped him off with the volunteer this morning. Not so much last night when it was thundering, but I get that."

"Yeah, the thunder and lightning kept me up too," he said, resuming his walk to the end of the hall.

As soon as he disappeared behind the door that led to the doctors' offices, I let out a long breath. He might be easy on the eyes, but Dr. Cameron Saye was not the man for me.

I wish I was wrong, but I know I'm not. No matter how hard I try to get past the fact that he absolutely bores me to tears, I just can't.

I don't mind a guy who is obsessed with sports. I mean, I do love a good Brenham High or Texas A&M football game. I even confess to watching baseball and hockey games long after a former boyfriend who played both was no longer in the picture.

However, Dr. Cameron Saye never talks about any of these sports. If he's not chatting about something related to veterinary medicine or the weather, the man has one thing on his mind.

Golf.

Yes. That stupid cousin of hockey, tennis, and ping-pong, where you hit a ball with a club repeatedly until it lands in a cup, is all he wants to discuss.

I fell asleep once while he was explaining the difference between a birdie and a bogie. When I woke up, he was still talking. I don't think he even noticed I'd taken a power nap during his enthusiastic speech.

So, if he was meant for me, wouldn't I manage to remain awake during our conversations? The answer to that question is why I absolutely, positively know that handsome animal-loving Dr. Cameron Saye is not for me.

Maybe I ought to begin praying for him to find someone who is right for him. My prayers for myself sure weren't producing any results.

I carried this question back into my office where I settled back in my chair. I pulled up the schedule and discovered that Mari had taken the morning off. Only then did I recall that she and her aunt Trina were meeting with a wedding planner to go over the details of her aunt's wedding.

Soon enough Mari would be having her own wedding. I needed to get used to that. Mostly I have.

And for the record, I'm so happy she's marrying Parker. She's my best friend, and I'm the one who tried my best to throw her and Parker together because it was obvious from the start that they were meant for each other. I even skipped going out on rescues with them so it would be just the two of them in the van.

Van.

I cringed. Parker should be told sooner rather than later that the rescued pup and I made a muddy mess of his rain gear.

I picked up my phone and realized I hadn't turned the page on my Word of the Day calendar yet. I bought it in hopes it would inspire me to take up my novel writing again. So far all it had done was give me anxiety worrying about whether I'd miss a day or forget to use it in a sentence.

I turned the page and spied February 15th's word: *obsequious.* "Giving unusual attention; fawning."

I sighed. This was an easy one.

"At least I am no longer obsequious in the presence of Dr. You-Know-Who," I muttered under my breath as I began working on my text to Mari. "The very thought of that ended with our first conversation about golf."

I glanced at the clock. I'd need to leave in fifteen minutes or so to get to the school on time. After typing out a quick summary of last night's events, my finger hovered over the SEND icon.

I hadn't mentioned the creeper who'd scared me half to death (no need to interrupt a lovely morning with something frightening) or the fact that I'd made a muddy mess of Parker's rain gear (my problem to fix, not theirs). I did tell them that the dog seemed healthy and was more likely lost rather than abandoned.

I hit SEND knowing I would catch Mari up on the loft and Spot's rescue this afternoon. Then I called Parker.

CHAPTER FIVE

H ey Cassidy," Parker said, sounding breathless. "What's up?"

"Are you running?" I asked.

"I might be," he said. "Okay, yes, but not because I want to. The short version is that Suzy, one of the rescues, thinks I'm having a grand time playing chase. Meanwhile I need to scrub in for surgery with Dr. Cameron in half an hour. Thank goodness she'll go to her new home on Saturday."

Since he only lived ten minutes from the clinic, I decided not to tell him Dr. Cameron was already here. Instead, I forged on with my confession.

"So, you probably know I went out on a rescue last night."

"Yeah, I heard. Gnarly night. I hope it turned out all right." He paused, and I heard, "Gotcha, Suzy."

"It did," I said. "Spot and I made it home just fine. He's with a foster right now. Suffice it to say the van suffered a bit."

"Were you in an accident?"

"No, but there's a mess inside," I hurried to say. "It was still raining when I went to bed, so I thought I'd get up early and clean it, but then I had a rough night keeping Spot from whining, and well. . ."

"It's still muddy inside?" he offered.

"And wet," I added. "I drove it over to the rescue since I'd left my car there last night. I absolutely don't mind picking it up after work and cleaning it out. I'll clean up your rain gear too. I'm sorry."

Parker chuckled. "No problem. I'll handle it." I heard a door open and close on the other side of the phone line. "Okay, I'm on my way. If you see

Dr. Cameron, let him know I'll be there in plenty of time to scrub in. It cost me an extra treat, but it worked."

"Parker to the rescue. And I'll try never to leave a mess again."

"I'm just glad you were there, especially on a stormy night and without any help. Hang on. Let me put the phone on hands-free." A moment later he was back. "Okay, on my way to the clinic. Seriously, Cassidy, if you hadn't taken that call last night, that dog would still be out there. Any idea who he belongs to?"

"Not yet, but I'm working on it. He's got a chip, but it isn't activated. Just one of several mysteries surrounding our newest rescue."

"Why do I think you're already working on solving them?"

"I might be," I admitted. "Along with all the other things I'm supposed to be doing."

"Then I'll let you get back to whatever's next on your list," he said. "And I'll be there soon."

Parker and I hung up, and I could hear Isabel, our groomer, chatting with Brianna, the clinic's receptionist.

When the text had come in about the rescue in need of picking up, the three of us were having our own observance of National Singles Awareness Day. By mutual agreement, Isabel, Brianna, and I were binge-watching *Downton Abbey* while eating popcorn and carrying on a running commentary on a text loop we'd titled "Lone Star Ladies" while the other two members of our group—Mari and Dr. Kristin—enjoyed their Valentine's Day dates with their significant others.

Though I was tempted to join them in conversation, it was time for me to leave. Plus, Mari was my best friend. I couldn't tell Isabel and Brianna about the loft before I told her.

I snatched up the box of treat bags filled with those crazy balls that bounce high and some really cute rubber bracelets shaped like dog collars with the Lone Star Vet Clinic logo on them. Balancing the box and my purse, I slipped out the back door. Ten minutes later, I pulled into a parking space next to a large green truck with a Washington County game warden logo painted on the side.

Apparently Lone Star Vet Clinic wasn't the only invitee this morning. Or maybe the game warden's kid forgot his lunch.

After checking in at the front office, a woman with a badge that proclaimed her to be Brenda, School Secretary handed me a sticker with a black-and-white image of my driver's license. I'd been the last one called at the DMV the day that license was renewed, and it showed. What might look like a cute messy bun on someone else was anything but cute on me, and the black-and-white version accentuated the racoon-looking circles under my eyes.

I gave Brenda a pleading look. "Don't you have one that just says visitor?"

"Sorry," she said. Her expression looked anything but. "And you'll need to fill out these forms. Once they're complete, let me know. I'll witness your signature."

I frowned. "That seems like a lot for a classroom visit. We've never had to do all of that at the other schools the clinic has presented this to."

"I don't make the rules." Brenda gestured to a chair in the waiting area, causing a riot of silver bracelets to jangle on her wrist. "Fill out the forms there, then come back here to sign."

I looked down at the stack of documents, then back up at Brenda. "This says television taping."

She nodded.

"So my presentation could be on television?" I asked.

Another nod.

I shrugged. "Well, I guess somebody's parent is well connected."

"Lights, camera, presentation," Brenda said dryly.

I wasn't sure if she was being sarcastic or funny. Apparently both looked the same on her. I shrugged. "I guess it's okay."

She shrugged. "If it makes you feel better, the parents had to sign for their children before they could participate."

"Goodness," I said. "When I was a kid we didn't have to do anything like this."

Another shrug. "Are you signing, or do I need to ask for the badge back?"

"I'll sign," I said.

After what seemed like an eternity, I completed the paperwork and returned to the desk. The secretary looked up from her laptop, then slowly rose to close the distance between us.

"Just one question," I said. "Why do I have to sign a release to be filmed? I'm just giving a little presentation on what it's like to work in a vet clinic."

"I don't make the rules," she said. "Are you signing or not? You can't go into the classroom unless you sign."

"Yes, of course."

I signed, she witnessed, and then she moved the papers to her desk. "Go down the hall, turn right, and it's room 301." She nodded to the spot where I'd left the box from the clinic. "They may want to look over the contents, but that's up to them. Just don't come back to me to complain if they do."

Before I could respond, Brenda had already turned away to answer a ringing phone. With her free hand, she waved me away.

"Okay, then."

I snatched up my box and navigated the maze of halls until I found room 301. A sign taped to the door stated that filming was taking place inside.

"Hence the release," I said, though it still seemed a little silly to require a release when it was probably just the teacher or possibly parents who were invited to attend. Sometimes schools would do that. Other times the audience was limited to just the students.

I heard voices inside as I reached for the doorknob. Glancing at the clock, I saw that my ordeal with the paperwork had made me seven minutes late. At this point, I probably shouldn't interrupt whoever was speaking—the game warden from the sound of the deep male voice—so I opened the door and stepped inside as quietly as I could.

Okay, not exactly stepped. More like stumbled, though in my defense I didn't expect a tangle of cords snaking across the floor in front of me and a spotlight aimed right at my face.

The box I'd been holding went flying as I spiraled forward and my arms flailed in an attempt to keep me upright. Bouncy balls danced in my peripheral vision, and rubber bracelets flew up like confetti as the box landed with a thud.

As if in slow motion, a floor covered in blue-and-white-plaid industrial carpet rose toward me. Or so it seemed.

I closed my eyes and braced for impact. Then, in an instant, everything stopped.

I opened my eyes to see a khaki-covered bulletproof vest with the words Texas Game Warden embroidered in black across the top. Beneath the vest, he wore a matching khaki shirt, trousers, and a thick black belt that held a service revolver and a number of other gadgets.

My gaze lifted to a clean-shaven chin and a smile. Then I looked into a pair of very familiar and very brown eyes.

Dr. Cameron?

Not exactly but almost.

Where Dr. Cameron's expression defaulted to a smile, this man's decidedly did not. Rather, it was somewhere between a curious stare and the beginnings of amusement.

With the same firm grip he'd used to catch me, the game warden steadied me on my feet. I wobbled sightly but remained upright.

"Hello," he said in a gravel-deep whisper. "I'm Jason."

"Hello, Jason."

There. I'd managed to say something without sounding like a fool. I punctuated the response with my best attempt at a smile.

Indeed, this was not Cameron Saye, but I didn't mind at all. He was better looking—if that was possible—in a rugged, I-can-survive-in-the-wilderness kind of way.

Plus, he was a game warden. And ever since I got hooked on the *Texas Law: Real Life* show on television, I was intrigued with game wardens. Okay, I think they're cute.

Not that I'd admit that to anyone, not even Mari.

This one, however, was beyond cute. He was. . .I had to think hard to come up with the right word. He was gorgeous.

"Cassidy?" he said in that oh-so-masculine voice.

"Yes, Jason?" I awaited his response while trying to remain cool. And upright.

THE BARK OF ZORRO

Jason the Gorgeous Game Warden—I decided to call him that since I didn't have a clue what his last name was—glanced down, then back up at my eyes. "Your driver's license is expired."

Someone shouted, "Cut!" A chorus of cheers and clapping followed.

CHAPTER SIX

The time that had shuddered to a stop during my plunge toward the floor sped up again, leaving me breathless. And maybe just a little embarrassed. I could also admit to behavior that was more than a little obsequious in regard to the man still holding tight to my arms.

Not that I'm proud of using that particular word of the day in describing myself.

I took a step backward, out of the arms of Jason the Gorgeous Game Warden. This time I made sure there were no cables in my way.

"You should really get that renewed," Jason said. "It's illegal to drive with an expired license in the state of Texas."

"Right," I managed.

And then I walked away.

So much for having one of those meet-cutes like I love to watch in the movies. Not only had I stumbled my way into the room, but I'd also acted like an idiot. Since when did a man render me unable to successfully complete a sentence?

Since I met Jason the Gorgeous Game Warden, apparently.

While he conferred with a man wearing a headset, I found my way over to a desk made for a fourth grader. I was surrounded by noisy children competing to see whose bouncy ball could hit the ceiling the hardest and arguing over the color of dog collar bracelet they'd ended up with. One of them had climbed into the box and was being pushed around by a classmate.

THE BARK OF ZORRO

With nothing else to do, I figured I'd document the moment for the clinic's Instagram page. I retrieved my phone from my pocket and snapped a few photos and short videos of the chaos.

People with clipboards chatted with people adjusting microphones and lighting. The slender woman with a blond ponytail, dressed in jeans and a pale pink T-shirt, who I'd assumed was the class teacher, turned out to be the producer on the set. This I figured out when I heard her say to one of the crew, "Because I am the producer, and what I say goes—all right?"

Despite my mortification at my how it happened, I had literally stepped—okay stumbled—into the filming of an episode of *Texas Law: Real Life*. With nothing else to do, I documented all of it, including a boy using his dog collar bracelet like a basketball hoop for the bouncy balls that were flying around.

His success at managing to loop a ball midair was impressive. I was about to tell him so when I spied the producer heading my way with a determined expression.

"You'll have to delete those," she said, tersely. "No photos on set. It was in the paperwork you signed. Or should have signed."

I obliged her by deleting the pictures while she supervised, then looked up and smiled. "Sorry about that. I was in a hurry to get here for my talk. I must have missed that part."

"Your talk," she echoed. Then she nodded, a smile rising. "Yes. Let's go ahead and get that done. It might make a good B reel moment. Oh, and ignore the cameras. We'll bring the kids into the frame, so you'll just be focused on them."

Ignore the cameras? I glanced around the room at the equipment crowding each corner as well as the overhead lighting and microphones suspended in several places.

Then reality dawned.

"You're not going to put me in the show, are you?" I shook my head. "I'm just an office manager / social media manager / animal rescuer. I really don't do anything interesting, just talk about what a vet does." Then I looked down at my jeans and blue Lone Star Vet Clinic pullover. "And if I'd known I'd be filming something, I would have dressed a little nicer."

"You look fine," the producer tossed over her shoulder as she walked away. "Just remember, don't look at the cameras."

Not looking at the cameras is the hardest part of filming. This I discovered when I had to be reminded of it more than once.

I finished to mild applause and a polite invitation by the teacher to return anytime I wished. Next came the star of the show.

I took a seat in the nearest desk and watched while an unbelievably handsome man was fussed over by what I'd learned was the tech team. His radio and phone were silenced, and then the microphone was attached to his shirt collar. When a woman approached him with a makeup brush in her hand, he grimaced and shook his head.

Not that he needed anything to help him look better.

Okay, I am not obsessed with looks, I promise. But when a man is that handsome, it's hard to miss.

He stood very still as lights were adjusted and the microphone tested. Then it was go time.

While the fourth graders were attentive to my presentation, they were much more interested in Jason the Gorgeous Game Warden's presentation on types of snakes and what to do if confronted by one. He was absolutely adorable as he quizzed the students on what he'd taught them. Then, for his grand finale, he brought out a massive green snake for them to pet.

Personally, I think all snakes should be considered enemies to humanity. Thus, I wasn't thrilled with the topic. The children, however, couldn't get enough of him or his slithering friend as they passed the creature from one to the other under the watchful eye of the game warden.

Had the cameras not been aimed at the only door in the room, I might have slipped out and gone back to work. As it was, I had to wait until the snake-a-palooza was done.

I dared not retrieve my phone lest the producer think I might be trying to take videos or photos again. So, I sat quietly and watched the seconds then minutes tick by on the clock above the door.

I was just contemplating the loft I'd visited that morning and whether I would put curtains or shades on the windows when I heard Jason the

Gorgeous Game Warden call my name. I looked up to see the snake curled around one of his muscled biceps.

"Cassidy, would you like a turn?" he said with a grin as he disentangled the snake from his arm.

"I'll pass," I said, proud that the words actually came out sounding like I wasn't terrified of snakes and entranced by the man currently holding one.

Jason took a step toward me. "He won't bite."

I squelched an internal squeal and remained stoic. "I might if you come any closer with that creature."

The class laughed. I didn't.

So much for impressing Jason the Gorgeous Game Warden. I glanced back up at the clock. Surely the bell would ring soon. What time did these kids go home, anyway?

Finally, the teacher called for the students' attention. "Class, please thank Cassidy and Jason for coming to visit today."

A chorus of high-pitched thank-yous echoed across the room, punctuated by applause. The spotlights dimmed. The director and several crew members circled around the game warden and were soon in deep conversation.

With the gifts distributed and the box I'd brought them in flattened and discarded in the back of the room, I grabbed my purse and headed for the door. All I could think as I headed for my car was that Dr. Kristin was going to be sorry that she missed this one.

I'd just used my remote to unlock my car when I heard my name being called. I turned around to see Jason the Gorgeous Game Warden sprinting toward me with that stupid snake in its box under his arm.

Literally sprinting.

For a tall man, he sure was fast. He beat me to my car and stood between me and the door. I took a step backward, not so much to put distance between me and the game warden but to put distance between me and that nasty slithering reptile.

He reached into his pocket and slipped on a pair of aviator sunglasses. As he lowered his hand, I noticed the gold ring that marked him as a graduate of Texas A&M.

"I'm sorry, Cassidy," he told me. "But I can't let you drive that car with an expired license. You're going to have to find another way to get wherever you're going next."

I looked down at the sticker I'd been required to wear when I checked in with Brenda at the school's front desk. Then I returned my attention to him, intending to protest. I remember now that he'd mentioned it early on in our disastrous first conversation.

He was right. Thanks to my penchant for procrastinating when it came to a trip to the DMV to renew my license, I was indeed past the renewal time.

I peeled off the sticker, then made a face as I looked up at him. "Couldn't you just let me drive back to work? I'll renew my license online the minute I get back."

Jason the Gorgeous Game Warden shook his head. "I can't do that. If you drive out of this parking lot without a valid driver's license, the law says I'll have to cite you."

I tried again. "Isn't there just a little wiggle room in that law?"

His expression made it obvious that my question had offended him. "There's never any wiggle room in the law. Not as far as I'm concerned," he said, his tone brooking no further argument.

I thought of my transgression last night while chasing Spot. "I disagree."

His brows rose. "Do you now?"

"What if you have to break a law that's not a big deal but you do it for a good reason?" I challenged.

"Cassidy, are you trying to confess to something?" he said.

"No," I told him. "I'm just saying that sometimes you have to decide whether it is more important to not break the law or to save a life."

"Okay, now I'm really curious," Jason said. "Be more specific."

This was not going well. "I'm just saying," I tried, "that sometimes you need to keep the end goal in mind."

"Again," Jason told me, "specifics."

I gave the request a moment's thought. I could confess to trespassing and likely win this argument. Or I could give up. I chose the latter.

"Fair enough," I said on an exhale of breath as I retrieved my phone and punched the icon to pull up my contacts. "I'll call someone at the clinic to pick me up."

"And your argument about saving a life?" he pressed.

"Just a theoretical question," I said. "Forget I mentioned it."

I got the impression he wasn't sure how to respond. Then he shrugged. "I've got to stop by the courthouse next," he said, his tone all business. "I don't mind dropping you off at the clinic."

I suppressed a sigh of relief. He'd let me off the hook, but I had learned an important lesson about Jason the Gorgeous Game Warden. He went strictly by the rules.

"I appreciate the offer, Jason." I looked down at the box containing the reptile. "But I'd rather not ride with your friend there."

"Not fond of snakes?" he said.

"They should all die," I told him. "And do not lecture me about how the king snake keeps rodents under control. I don't care."

When I was a child, a massive king snake had been given a home under our porch. Daddy thought it was the best thing in the world to have what he called a "little helper" to keep the critters away.

I, on the other hand, refused to go in and out of the front door until my father showed me proof that the nasty reptile had died of old age or whatever kills snakes. It was years later that my mama let it slip that the dead snake in the box we buried in the backyard was a trick rubber snake from the magic shop.

I'd never recovered from the deception. Nor had I changed my mind about snakes.

Just one more reason why living in a second-floor loft with no yard to harbor slithery creatures was a good idea.

"What if I made him ride in the back?" he offered.

"Back seat or back of the truck?" I said warily, my eyes on the box still tucked under his arm.

Jason the Gorgeous Game Warden walked over to his truck and pulled down the tailgate. Then he secured the box into a crate in the bed of the truck and closed the tailgate again. "Satisfied?" he asked.

I gave the situation a cursory glance, then returned my attention to the game warden. "Is he in danger of flying out of there while you're driving?"

"I've got the crate tied down, so no," he told me.

"Too bad," I muttered.

He gave me a look and then laughed. Actually laughed.

CHAPTER SEVEN

O n the drive back to the clinic, I took the opportunity to tell Jason about Spot. Though I carefully left out how he got to the rescue, I did mention that we were looking for his owner as well as any clues as to who might have painted the letter Z on his side.

I also told him about my brief foray into internet research about painted dogs. "There have been a few sightings but none that could be pinned on anyone. And no one seems to know why."

"I'll check on all that," Jason said. "Where did you say you found Spot?"

"Out at the old pump site," I said reluctantly, hoping he didn't ask for more details.

He kept his attention on the road, but his fingers drummed on the steering wheel. "Last night? In the storm?"

"Yes and yes." I tried to sound casual, but I shifted positions and prayed for all traffic lights between here and the clinic to be green. "The poor guy was terrified. He was fine once I got him home, though. A hot bath and a good meal will do that."

I was babbling, but I couldn't help it. The last thing I wanted to do was stay on the topic of where I found Spot. Better to concentrate on the mystery of that painted letter.

Or to distract him with another topic altogether.

I warmed to the idea when we were forced to stop at yet another red light. Sliding Jason a sideways glance, I said, "So, what's it like to film a television show?"

He grimaced. "I like it about as much as you like snakes."

"Really?" I said. "That bad?"

The light turned green and the truck was in motion again. "I didn't say it was bad. It's important that people learn what we do. If a kid sees the show and decides to become a game warden, that's great. I'd just rather do my job and let somebody else stand in front of the spotlights."

The radio crackled, and Jason answered. The conversation that ensued was mostly one-sided with whoever was speaking on the radio saying a whole bunch of words that sounded garbled to me.

"I'll go check that out," he said.

"How do you know what they're saying?" I asked when the conversation ended.

He shrugged. "I spent my first month of warden training in a little room listening to a radio until I could transcribe the conversation."

"Really?" I gave him a sideways look. Goodness but he was handsome. "A month of that?"

Jason chuckled as he made a turn. "No. I was teasing you. It's just something we have to learn. Some dispatchers are easier to understand than others. After a while, we mostly know what they're going to say. It's just the details we're looking for."

"And you got details from that?"

"Yep. I've got a lead on a case I'm working on." He paused. "Actually I may be able to connect it with your dog mystery."

My hopes rose. "Really?"

"Too soon to be sure, but it's possible. I've just got to run down a lead, and then I'll let you know."

"Great." The clinic appeared up ahead. "Pull into the employee parking in the back, please." I wasn't ready to explain to the ladies who'd be watching out the front window why I was arriving in the game warden's truck.

Jason stopped in a parking space and shifted into PARK. Then he swiveled toward me. "I'll need your number so I can let you know what I find out. Or should I just call the clinic?"

Let me see. . .give the cute game warden my number or let him call my work? The obvious answer took absolutely no time to determine.

I gave him my number, then opened the door. Before my feet reached the ground, Jason had hurried around to help me out. "Thanks for the ride," I said through the swirl of crazy emotions that being near him caused.

Jason answered with a nod of his head and a quick, "I'll be in touch."

I had almost reached the door when I heard him call my name. I turned around to see him walking toward me.

"Hey, you were a good sport at the school." He adjusted his aviators. "I doubt you were expecting your presentation to be on camera like that."

I laughed. "Especially since I'm only the backup presenter. One of the veterinarians usually does the talking."

There was that grin again. "I doubt they would have been as good." A pause. "So, Cassidy, would you like to get coffee sometime?"

Coffee? I hated the stuff. I know—totally unpopular opinion. But hey, I'd sip the burned bean juice if it meant this cutie was across the table from me.

"Sure," I said as casually as I could. "That would be nice."

"Okay, great. I'll call you and we'll set that up, okay?" He paused. "Once I know what my filming schedule is and all."

"Sure." I was repeating myself, but conversing with a guy who had to consult his filming schedule before he could make a coffee date with me was new territory.

We stood there like a couple of awkward teenagers for what seemed like an eternity. Then I nodded to the door. "Okay, well, I need to get back to work."

"Yeah," he said, relief showing on the part of his face that wasn't covered by those mirrored sunglasses. "Me too. You, um, have a good rest of your day."

"You too."

I was already anticipating that call as I settled back at my desk to begin work on the lengthy list of tasks facing me that day. A few minutes later, Dr. Cameron plopped down in the chair across from me. He pressed his palms down on my desk and grinned.

In that moment, I thought of my encounter with the Dr. Cameron almost-look-alike. I still saw a similarity, but Jason the Gorgeous Game Warden was the absolute winner in the gorgeous man contest. I really needed to find out what his last name was so I didn't have to call him that.

I cleared my throat. What in the world was I thinking? One conversation with the game warden and one brief ten-minute ride to the clinic—which, to be fair, included giving him my cell number—and I was becoming obsequious. This wouldn't do.

"Cass?" Dr. Cameron said. "Did you hear me?"

I shook my head. "Sorry. No. would you tell me that again?"

He gave a good-natured nod. "So, this dog you found with the paint on it? I put out an APB on it."

"APB?" I shook my head, again thinking of the lawman who'd helped me in and out of his truck in such a courtly manner. Who'd adjusted the ice-cold temperature on the air conditioner to suit me and who'd. . .

Enough of that! Focus, Cassidy. "Isn't an all-points bulletin just for people?"

"All-Paws Bulletin," he said with a grin that reminded me why I had once considered having the hero of my novel based on him. Until the unfortunate golf conversation.

"I've never heard of an All-Paws Bulletin? What is it?"

Dr. Cameron grinned. "Great name, right? Basically, there are a bunch of us volunteer vets who recently decided to combine forces to communicate needs or send out requests for information. We mostly put out the call when we need supplies or volunteers. Second Chance has been well supplied and staffed since the beginning with no trouble placing their rescues, so I'm not surprised you haven't come across us."

Thanks to Mari's aunt Trina, the shelter had a well-supplied permanent home. Word of mouth and an active social media community had been key in either returning our rescues to their pet parents or finding new forever homes for them. This blessing was beyond amazing. We were very grateful.

"Anyway," Dr. Cameron said, "you'd be surprised how fast information travels on the grapevine. Plus I've got a guy in law enforcement I've got on alert."

He retrieved his phone from the pocket of his scrubs and thrust it toward me. Predictably his wallpaper was a giant white spinning golf ball on a field of neon green. A couple of clicks later, the screen showed a text response from someone named GWJ.

NOT THE FIRST TIME I'VE HEARD OF THIS. I'LL DO SOME CHECKING.

"Okay good. He's heard of this. They've got a database he can search," Dr. Cameron said. "I'll let you know if I hear anything back from him or anyone else."

"Thank you. That would be great."

"Did I miss a meeting?" Dr. Tyler Durham, owner of the clinic, now stood in my doorway. He grinned as he checked his watch, then looked over at Cameron. "And aren't you scrubbing in with me this morning?"

"Just helping Cass out with the rescue from last night."

Dr. Tyler turned to me. "Does the dog need medical care?"

"No, Spot is fine," I told him. "But his chip was never activated, and I think someone tried to paint something on him."

"Is someone painting dogs?" Dr. Kristin asked from the hallway a moment before she squeezed past Dr. Tyler and into my office.

I caught her up on what happened with last night's rescue, omitting the part with the weird stranger.

Dr. Kristin shook her head. "I guess we'll have to be on the lookout for painted dogs now. What's the world coming to?"

Dr. Tyler frowned. "I hope this is an isolated incident."

I wanted to tell him I didn't think it was. Or at least according to the small amount of research I'd done last night, it didn't seem to be an isolated incident. It just hadn't happened here yet.

Other than Spot, of course.

CHAPTER EIGHT

B efore I could say anything about my online search for painted dogs, all three veterinarians were discussing the afternoon's surgeries while filing out of my office. Dr. Kristin stuck her head back in a moment later.

"Try rubbing olive oil on Spot's spot." She shrugged. "You don't want to know how I know it works."

Considering it wasn't all that long ago that Dr. Kristin moved into a new-to-her home and adopted a rescue dog, I could imagine any number of scenarios where dog and paint might meet.

"Oh, and how did the presentation go this morning?" she asked.

"So much to tell," I said with a chuckle. "The presentation went fine, but wow, do I have a story to tell you and the other ladies. But not now. You've got a surgery."

"Okay, later, then." Dr. Kristin's brows rose. "Hold on. Did you meet your dream man at the elementary school?"

"Again," I said, "too much to tell."

She laughed. "Oh, this is going to be good. Now I must run. Tyler adores me, but he won't be happy if I scrub in late for his surgery."

"Definitely!" I called as she hurried away.

I had conquered most of my mountain of work by the time Mari came in with Spot, two salads, and a broad smile. "This guy is the cutest," she said, nodding at Spot, who she'd picked up from the foster for me so we could photograph. "He's so sweet. If we don't find his owners, there will be no problem getting him rehomed. I'm sure of it."

I scratched the pup behind his ears. "I think he's got a family out there. I've been posting on social media about him, so maybe we'll get some information soon."

"I hope so."

Mari placed the salads on my desk, then settled in the chair across from mine. I returned to my chair and watched as Spot sniffed around the room, then plopped down beside Mari.

"Okay, so let's talk about that text you sent this morning," Mari said as she opened the lid on her salad. "I'm so excited that you may have found a new place."

"Me too!"

I texted her a link to the real estate site, then sat back and made room for my salad on the messy desk. "It's absolutely perfect. I mean, not completely perfect, because there are some changes I'd like to make, but they're minor and I cannot wait to seal the deal and get the keys."

While I took a bite of my salad, Mari scrolled through the pictures. When she looked up again, there were tears in her eyes. "You're right. It's perfect."

"Oh Mari." I stood and walked around the desk to place my arms around her. "What's wrong?"

"We won't be neighbors anymore," she said, her voice quavering. "And I absolutely know how dumb it is to cry over that considering when Parker and I get married it will be me moving. I guess I just never thought about that part of it." Mari sat her phone on the desk and swiped at her cheeks. "I'll miss you."

I took a step back and wiped at the tears in my eyes. "You will not. You'll be happily married to your happily-ever-after man, and we'll see each other every day at work. Plus I'll be doing rescues with you."

Mari nodded. "I know. And it will be great. When will you know if you got the place?"

"Nora practically had me moving in this morning. I doubt it will be that simple. However, her real estate agent is working on it, so I guess when he has more details, I'll have more details."

She grinned. "In the meantime, we plan the decorating and renovating. Tell me what you're thinking of doing to it."

I told her my ideas and she added hers. We were almost finished with our salads when Mari shook her head. "Wait. How could I forget? I also heard you've got big news about something that happened this morning."

I gave her a sideways look. "Who told you that?"

"Brianna, who heard it from Isabel, who heard it from Dr. Kristin, but none of them had details. So spill," Mari said. "I'm your best friend, so I need to hear it first." She paused. "Besides, Brianna is at a dentist appointment, and Isabel is covering the phones while Brianna is out."

"Okay," I said slowly as Mari settled across the desk from me. "When I got to the classroom to give my presentation for the fourth graders, I walked—stumbled actually—right into a filming of *Texas Law: Real Life*."

"You did not!" she exclaimed.

"I did." I proceeded to tell her all about the morning, including the fact that Jason the Gorgeous Game Warden drove me back here because my driver's license was expired.

"Did he ask for your number?"

"He did, actually," I said. "But it was to follow up on the painted dog issue. He's going to follow up on a lead that might be related to Spot."

I paused, looking somber. Then I grinned.

"Then he asked me if I'd like to go for coffee."

Mari squealed. "Of course he did. And you said yes, right?"

"You know I hate coffee," I told her, my expression serious.

"Yeah, but you said yes anyway."

"You know it." I paused. "He's going to call me once he knows his filming schedule."

"He did not say that," Mari exclaimed.

"He did," I said, and we both fell into laughter.

Then Mari sobered. "Cassidy, do you like him?"

Her question confused me. "Sure, I like him. I mean, I've known him almost no time, but he doesn't appear to be a serial killer or anything. He's nice. And definitely cute. Why do you ask?"

A shrug. "I don't know. Just wondering if he's the one."

"Mari," I said slowly, "do not have me married to a guy before I've had coffee with him, okay? But yeah," I said, leaning back in my chair. "I do like him."

"Okay," she said, but her smile told me she had plenty more she wanted to add. "I'll just say this: you hate coffee."

Before she could go any further into our discussion of the game warden, I changed the subject to the spring festival. "I had to miss the meeting, but I've got lots of ideas."

"What part are you handling?" she asked.

I shrugged. "I don't know. They're supposed to send me an email with the minutes of the meeting."

The topic moved on until we'd finished our salads and it was time to go back to work. Mari gathered up the salads and stuffed them into a bag, then rose. Spot, who'd slept through our lunch, opened sleepy eyes to regard her but made no move to stand.

"He looks comfortable," she said.

I smiled. "Leave him with me. I'll go grab a bed out of the back, and he can snooze the afternoon away."

"I'll send Parker with it. How's that?"

"Thanks."

I opened the email from the spring fair committee and was greeted by a picture of a dachshund in a straw cowboy hat and red vest and matching boots. Somehow she had managed to make it look like the pup was playing a little guitar.

The text said: I'M SO GLAD WE'LL BE WORKING TOGETHER. CALL ME WHEN YOU GET A CHANCE SO WE CAN STRATEGIZE.

It was signed GRANDMA PEACH.

I groaned. Peach Potter Nelson was Mari's grandmother, and as we say in the South, she was a character. In addition to being mother to the country singer Trina Potter and Mari's late mama, Grandma Peach was known for the pies she baked. Her latest endeavor was an online designer dog clothing boutique offering a full range of everyday wear and costumes for the pampered pet.

Oh, and did I mention she was a newlywed and a pastor's wife?

Grandma Peach picked up on the first ring. "I knew you'd call," she said, chuckling. "Isn't that the cutest cowboy costume you ever saw? I had spurs on those boots but had to take them off when I realized the dogs were scratching themselves to bits with them. Not a good look."

"No, I would think not. So, Grandma Peach," I said, "this is my first year working on the festival, so I'm not clear on what my role is on this committee. Or, for that matter, I'm not clear on what committee I'm on."

"You're on my committee, honey," she said. "We do a little bit of everything so that the festival is a success."

Okay. That was a broad definition. "Can you be more specific?"

"No."

"All right," I said, reminding myself that this was my best friend's grandmother. "What is the first thing we need to do?"

She sighed. "I'd like to sit down and plan some things with you, but you've got that pesky day job, so I guess we'll have to do this another way." I heard a cat wailing behind her. "Hush up, Hector."

"Would you like me to work up a publicity plan for the festival?" I offered. "Or maybe create some social media posts?"

"Actually," she said as the cat continued to make noise in the background, "I wonder if you might know anything about a television production that's filming in town right now."

"Why?" I said as casually as I could manage.

"Well, it'd be nice if they'd do some filming at the festival. It might do us some good for next year. And of course, I'd provide the pet costumes free of charge." She paused. "I usually rent them out for events, but I'd make an exception in this case."

"Okay," I said. "Anything else?"

I bargained on her not realizing that I hadn't actually answered her question. No way was I going to get lured into a conversation that would have me admitting to Grandma Peach that I might have been filmed for a television show. She'd want to hear every detail, and I wouldn't get anything done. And if I refused to answer, she'd be pestering Mari.

"Just one more thing," she said sweetly. "Tell me about that young man who dropped you off at the clinic a little while ago. Do we have a new game warden?"

"Yes, we do," I said.

"Well, since you know him, I'd like you to have him stop by so I can get a good look at him."

Several responses crossed my mind. "Grandma Peach," I finally said, "you're a newlywed."

She cackled with laughter, which made her cat howl. "I just want to make sure I get the uniform right for the game warden costume I'm planning to make. Nothing better than going to the original to make the pattern."

"Yes ma'am," I said, glancing up at the clock.

"Oh, one more thing, and then I'm going to have to let you go. Marigold said someone found a dog up at the old pump site."

"Yes, I did," I told her.

"The reverend and I were down that way yesterday afternoon. It was just before the bottom fell out and the storm started up."

I sat a little straighter. "Really? Did you happen to notice anything unusual going on at the pump site?"

"I saw someone chasing a dog."

"Could you describe this someone?" I asked. "Or the dog?"

"No, honey," she told me. "Well, not the person. It was dark, and he was wearing dark clothes. I remember the dog, though. We had to swerve to keep from hitting it."

She went on to offer a description that would easily fit Spot. Then she mentioned the blob of white on the dog's side.

"Yes, that sounds like the dog I rescued," I said. "Now, what about the person? Could you tell if it was male or female, tall or short? That kind of thing."

"My eyesight at night isn't very good. Other than the dark clothes, I couldn't say." She paused. "Oh, I do remember that it looked like he was on a bicycle." Another pause. "But I could be wrong about that. He might have just been a fast runner. Anyway, I'll ask the reverend if he remembers anything."

"Thank you," I told her.

"Now about that game warden," she said.

My office phone lit up with an incoming call. "I'm sorry, Grandma Peach. I've got a work call coming in. We'll chat later, okay?"

Then I hung up and picked up the phone on my desk. "This is Cassidy," I said.

"Cassidy, Camille Finley here."

I sat up straighter. "Camille, yes. The producer. Hello."

"I'll get right to the point," she said, ignoring my greeting. "I've been going over the dailies from the elementary school. You and Jason have on-screen chemistry. I want to see more of you on the show."

I opened my mouth to speak, but no words would come out. Finally, I managed to squeak out, "You do?"

"Yes. But we need to work you in somehow. You're a veterinarian, so that's an obvious connection, and you volunteer at a dog rescue, but I wonder if that's enough. You're not dating him, are you?"

"Dating him?" I sputtered. "Jason? No. I'm not." No need to mention the offer of a future coffee at this point. Especially since he hadn't yet called to make good on that offer. "And actually, I'm just the manager of the vet clinic, but I do volunteer at Second Chance Ranch. I could connect you with one of the veterinarians, though."

"No, it needs to be you."

"But I don't want to be on camera," I told her.

She paused. "Okay, well, I'll figure something out, but it does really need to be you."

Then she was gone. No goodbye. Nothing. Just gone.

"Okay, then," I said. And then I laughed.

CHAPTER NINE

Friday, February 17

The door flew open, and Brianna stuck her head in. "Cassidy, what have you done?" she said in a loud whisper.

"How did you know I was here? I'm just finishing up a few last-minute things before I go home and finish packing."

"I'm good at knowing who's here. But forget about that. You've done something," she said, her voice now trembling. "There's a cop out there, and he's got an attitude. He's demanding to speak to you."

"Me?" I thought of the No TRESPASSING signs and the lock I had ignored at the pump site. I won't deny that I also thought of Jason for a brief second. But he was going to call about coffee, not come back to the clinic and demand to see me.

So it was down to the trespassing. "Surely not."

"Surely yes," Brianna said, and then she paused. "I can create a diversion if you want to make a run for it. I mean, he's super cute, so I could chat him up while you—"

"That won't be necessary," a familiar male voice said from somewhere behind Brianna. "But thank you for the compliment."

The receptionist moved out of the way. A moment later, the doorway filled with a familiar sandy-haired man in a khaki uniform. Jason had ditched his bulletproof vest and now wore a black sleeveless fleece jacket with the words State Police embroidered over the pocket. I had learned from watching *Texas Law: Real Life* that in Texas the game wardens were a division of the state police.

"Hello, Jason," I said with a smile. As heroes go, he was more GI Joe than Mr. Darcy. And that was fine by me. "This is Brianna. Come in and join us."

Maybe Jason the Gorgeous Game Warden would end up as the protagonist in my mystery novel. One more sweeping glance of the lawman confirmed the thought.

"Cassidy Carter," he said, not moving from the door.

A statement, not a question.

"You know that already. You've seen my driver's license, remember? Well, the expired one, anyway." I upped my grin. "I wasn't expecting you to drop by, but I'm glad to see you. Do you want to set a time for coffee?"

Jason's stern expression slipped, and for a moment he looked kind of sad. "Sorry, Cassidy. I have to do this by the book. I can't talk to you about that right now." His gaze swept over me one more time. "State police. I'm going to need you to come with me."

"That sounds more like you're putting me under arrest, Jason," I said, my smile slipping. "I promise I haven't driven anywhere. You can check. My car is still at the elementary school. I confess I haven't had a chance to order a new license, though."

"You're not under arrest, but I prefer to talk about this outside. It's police business. Come with me, please."

"What for?" Mari demanded from the hallway with Parker standing behind her. "Has she done something wrong?"

"It's fine," I told her. Then I turned my attention back to Jason. "It is fine, right?"

After all, I had trespassed at the pump site and then almost confessed this to the no-wiggle-room-in-the-law lawman. My heart sank. Had he done some investigating and figured out the person who smashed that lock was me? Or had I confessed to that already? I couldn't remember.

"I'd rather we speak outside."

"You don't have to go with him," Mari said.

I glanced over at her. "This is the game warden I met at the elementary school."

"I can come with you," she said, undeterred.

"No," Jason told her. "You'll need to stay put, ma'am." He looked up at Parker. "You too, sir."

"It's fine, Mari. He's helping with the Spot case. I'll be back in a few minutes."

I followed Jason down the hall and through the lobby, past Isabel and Brianna, who didn't bother to hide their interest or their pointed stares. As he stepped out into the parking lot, he donned the Stetson.

"Let's talk in my truck."

"Is the snake in there?" I asked to distract my thoughts as we walked toward the truck.

I might have heard a grunt, but I wasn't sure. So I tried again. "Jason?" No response.

Instead, he walked ahead of me in silence and opened the passenger side door, then helped me climb inside. "Seat belt, please," he said.

Hmmm. . .something was obviously wrong.

"Okay." After I complied, Jason closed the door, then walked around the front of the truck to the driver's side.

I didn't have time to react before I spied Dr. Cameron racing out of the clinic's front door. He wore operating room scrubs and an angry expression. He'd obviously been called out of surgery, for he still wore his cap and his mask hung from one ear.

"Seriously, Jason?" he shouted across the distance between them. "You're arresting our office manager? What comes next? Handcuffs?"

Jason was now standing in the doorway of the driver's side of his truck. His spine was straight as an arrow, his shoulders broad and his expression unreadable behind mirrored aviator sunglasses.

The men stood almost nose to nose now.

"Sorry, Cass." He returned his attention to the game warden. "She found the dog. She didn't paint anything on it. Do you arrest everyone who reports a crime?"

"No," he said evenly. "Only the ones who have committed crimes."

"Oh please," Dr. Cameron said sarcastically. "She was rescuing a dog. Once she had the animal, she found evidence that someone had intentionally painted on it. I am the one who reported that to you. That is your department, isn't it?"

A muscle worked in his jaw, and for a moment the game warden didn't respond. Finally, he nodded. "It is."

"Then let the woman tell you what she knows instead of arresting her. She's invested in getting to the bottom of this mystery of who is doing this."

"I know that," Jason said.

"He does," I echoed. "We talked about it."

Everyone had poured out of the clinic and was watching. As they all hurried toward the truck, I sighed.

"She's not a criminal," Dr. Tyler said from his position behind Dr. Cameron. "She's our office manager."

"I smashed a lock, and I am willing to attest to that in court," I told Jason in hopes I could end the argument. "Can we just get this over with? I have a lot of work to do before I can go home today and pack."

Not exactly what I ever thought I'd tell Jason if I ever saw him again. However, it did serve the purpose of distracting the two of them.

Dr. Cameron's expression showed surprise while Jason's was unreadable. I couldn't see Dr. Tyler's face, but I'm sure he hadn't expected any of this either.

"Cassidy, be more specific," Parker warned. "You were on a rescue. You did what you had to do for the dog. Tell the game warden the details."

I shifted positions. "The only way to get to the dog was to smash the old rusty lock," I began matter-of-factly. "He'd gotten himself stuck inside, and I was afraid if I didn't smash it, he'd hurt himself before I could get help. It was wrong to break the law, but I did what I felt was best for the dog. I'll sign whatever you want me to sign if we can just get this over with."

"Cassidy, no," Mari said, phone in hand. "I'm calling Todd."

Todd was Officer Todd Dennison of the Brenham Police Department. He'd not only been a supporter of the pet rescue, but he'd also adopted the cutest rescue pup. The last thing I wanted to do was to put him in the middle of a situation where he might be required to side with the game warden over me.

Because when it came down to it, I did break the law. "Please don't involve him, Mari," I pleaded.

"Come on, Jason," Dr. Cameron said, his tone surprisingly gentle. "You work with animals too. You would have done the same thing."

"Stand down, Cameron," he told the vet. "Take a step back. We're leaving now."

He shook his head and grasped the door. "Not until you let Cassidy go."

"Keep in mind that handcuffs are protocol for any suspect I think might try to escape. And she certainly has plenty of possible accomplices to an exit from my truck standing here in this parking lot." Jason paused to focus on Dr. Cameron. "Don't make me use them, because unlike you, I follow the rules. Right now I'm only taking her in for questioning. I've had a report, and I need to follow through with it."

Dr. Cameron stepped back as if he'd been slapped.

"It's okay, Dr. Cameron," I told him. "Just let me take responsibility for what I've done."

"You don't have to do that," Dr. Kristin said.

"I know, but it's the right thing to do." I shifted my attention to Mari. "Would you check and see how Spot is doing?" Then I added, "I'll be fine."

"Of course," Mari said, still clutching her phone. "I'm so sorry, Cassidy. Parker and I should have been out there at the rescue with you. I'll call Wyatt. He'll fix this."

"Mari's right," Parker said. "And for the record, we would have done exactly the same thing Cassidy did."

This he said directly to Jason. Then everyone started talking at once, each of my sweet colleagues arguing for my freedom. During this barrage, the game warden remained silent and stone-faced.

"You've always been stubborn," Dr. Cameron said, his voice loud enough to silence the rest of the Lone Star Vet Clinic gang.

"Stand down, Cameron," the game warden said again. "We're leaving."

"Who is this guy?" Dr. Tyler said.

"He's my brother," Dr. Cameron told him before looking past him to the rest of the Lone Star Vet Clinic crew. "Everyone, meet Jason Saye, my brother and your newest Washington County game warden."

CHAPTER TEN

Jason climbed into the truck and slammed the door, then started the engine. Then he placed his hat upside down on the console between us and ran his hand through his hair.

So Jason the Gorgeous Game Warden had a last name and it was Saye. That took a second to process.

"You're Dr. Cameron's brother?" I said, incredulous. "I didn't even know he had a brother."

"Half brother," Jason corrected.

I was a little worried that Dr. Cameron might not move. When Jason shifted into Reverse, my coworkers scooted backward and took Dr. Cameron with them.

A moment later, we were driving away. We didn't get far.

Jason pulled into a parking space around the corner and out of sight of the clinic and shifted the truck into Park. He pulled a small leather notebook and silver pen out of his pocket, then shifted positions to face me.

Silence. With both hands on the wheel, he stared straight ahead.

When the silence grew uncomfortable, I nodded toward the door of Wyatt Chastain's law office directly in front of the truck. "Did you park here so I could hire a lawyer?" I asked, only half kidding.

"Do you want to hire a lawyer?" he asked, no hint of teasing on his face.

"No," I said. "Unless you're about to charge me."

"Right now I'm just trying to get the facts. At any point while I'm questioning you, you're free to stop me and ask for an attorney. Okay?"

"Okay. And just so we're clear, you do not have that snake with you, right?"

That almost made him smile. Almost but not quite. "I do not." He paused. "You've admitted to being at the pump site." He squared his shoulders and glanced over at me. "Tell me what happened. Start at the beginning. And before you say anything, I have had a tip come in from a person who claims knowledge of this case."

I frowned. "A tip?"

"Stick to the question I asked, please," he said, not terse but not exactly using an overly friendly tone either.

"Okay, yes, as I told you, I got a call and went out to the pump site to rescue Spot, and for no other reason. Someone called in a tip on the rescue line. Since Mari and Parker were on a date, I took the van and went out to see if I could find the dog. I did find him inside a fenced enclosure. After trying to figure out how to get him out of there, my conclusion was the only way was to smash the lock."

I told him the rest of the story with as much detail as I could recall. When I mentioned the person with the hoodie and how I was afraid one of the Venable clan might be after me, he winced and stopped writing. "Why did you think it was a Venable?"

"Proximity," I said. "They own the land across the street."

He paused and seemed to be considering his next question carefully. Finally, he spoke. "The person who you said came up behind. Could you positively ID him or her in a lineup?"

"No," I said. "It was too dark, and it was raining. Plus the slicker suit I was wearing was too large, and the hood kept falling into my eyes."

Jason nodded, then wrote something down. "Did the person say anything to you?"

"The person—I think it was a man—shouted something, but I couldn't hear anything over the sound of the rain hitting the van's roof. It was so loud, and I was scared. So was the dog." I shrugged. "I know I made stupid choices out there, but I just wanted to take Spot home where both of us would be safe."

"And you didn't feel safe?"

Surely he was joking.

"Have you not been listening to my story, Jason? I hate driving in the rain; it was cold; the dog was scared. Despite the fact that my driver's license expired and I forgot to renew it, I am not a person who breaks even a speed limit, but I had to decide to break the law or not save the dog, and on top of all that, some dude in a hoodie thinks it's fun to come up on me from behind? Of course I didn't feel safe."

I tamped down my anger. That certainly wouldn't help me get out of this mess.

"Look," I said slowly, "I get that you don't have a favorable impression of me. I just admitted to driving with an expired license—twice, actually—and trespassing. But that is truly not who I am. I'm a by-the-rules girl."

Then a thought occurred. "Oh. A man in a hoodie. On a bicycle. Of course."

He shook his head. "I don't follow."

"Right, well, I spoke with Peach Potter Nelson, that's Mari's grandmother, and she was out on the pump site road before the storm hit. She saw a man in a hoodie, possibly on a bicycle, chasing a dog. Or at least she thinks she did. She's going to ask her husband for more details, if he has them."

"The pie lady?"

"Yes, only now she makes pet costumes." I left it at that instead of mentioning Grandma Peach's desire to get Jason in her clutches so she could create a little canine game warden costume.

Jason wrote something in his notebook, then tucked it into his pocket. Then he reached behind his seat and produced a tire iron that looked very much like the one that had been in the van. "Can you identify this?"

I let out a long breath. "It looks like the tire iron that was in the rescue van."

"Seems like this would make you feel pretty safe, whether it was a Venable or not."

"At the time, I wasn't thinking about fighting back, if that's what you're asking." I sighed. "I used it to break the lock so I could get to the dog, and that's all. I must have left it behind when the man scared me. It belongs in the rescue van."

"For now, it's evidence," he said, returning the tire iron to its place behind the driver's seat. He picked his notebook out of his pocket and started writing again.

"I'm ready to plead guilty," I told him. "So can we just go into the courthouse and get it over with?"

At that moment, Wyatt Chastain walked out of his office door, then stopped short and waved at me. "Hey Cassidy," I heard him call over the sound of the engine. Then he added in an almost questioning tone, "Jason."

I mustered a smile and returned his wave. My companion offered a curt nod, then went back to work. Wyatt stood there a moment longer, then nodded and walked away.

Jason was still writing in his notebook, so I sat back against the headrest and closed my eyes. I probably should have called Wyatt over. After all, he was a lawyer, and I'd probably need one. And bail money.

I sighed. I'd finally found what I hoped would be a home of my own. Unfortunately, whatever I'd need to pay for my legal defense would have to come out of my savings. I tried not to imagine the deal of the century falling apart because I could no longer afford to purchase the loft.

I opened my eyes in time to see someone approaching on a skateboard. I glanced over in that direction and spied Ben Tanner moving toward us. Several times over the past few months, the local skateboard designer had expressed an interest in adopting a dog from the rescue.

Ben had placed an application for Suzy, a high-energy pup, but Mari wasn't sure the dog would be a good fit. Unfortunately, this was hardly the time to mention it. I smiled as he waved on his way past us while Jason merely glared until the skateboarder disappeared around the corner.

Finally, he turned his attention to me. "Is there anything you want to add?"

"Plenty," I said. Like how I just wanted to do the right thing by Spot. And how I thought that being honest with him was the right thing to do. Also, how I really didn't want to lose the loft around the corner from where we were sitting.

Then I reconsidered. "No. I've told you everything. But I do have a question. What was the tip about?"

Jason studied me a moment. "You."

"Was the caller male or female?"

He paused. "Why?"

"I'm just curious."

"Male. And the caller who sent you the tip on Spot?" he asked. "Male or female?"

"No idea," I told him. "It was a text."

Jason nodded. "I think I have everything I need."

"Okay." I paused. "You didn't give me a chance to grab my purse, so I don't have my ID with me. I guess someone from the clinic can bring it when they bail me out."

Jason's expression softened. "I'm not taking you to jail, Cassidy. You broke the law several times, but I'll be issuing a warning this time."

Relief washed over me. "Thank you."

"I'm sorry I had to do things this way, but under the circumstances it would be just like my brother to interfere. He has his job, and I have mine." His eyes met mine. "I had to be clear on what your story was about the pump station incident, and I wasn't sure which of us you'd listen to. It needed to be me. Then there was the tip. Without going into detail, an allegation was made against you."

"Against me?" I said, louder than I intended. "For what?"

"Doesn't matter," he said. "I'm satisfied you didn't do anything wrong."

"It does matter, Jason. Why would anyone do that?"

"Because they saw the rescue van where it shouldn't have been?" he offered. "That's my guess."

"Okay, but I don't like that someone thought I did something bad." I paused as what he said about a warning sunk in. "So I wasn't under arrest?"

"I never said you were," Jason countered. "I said I was taking you in for questioning. That happens to be right here in this parking space. We could have gone to my office, but I thought that unnecessary."

I smiled. "Thank you for just giving me a warning. I know I broke the law by trespassing at that pump site."

He gave me a look I couldn't quite decipher. "Do you plan to trespass much in the future?"

I could have answered with an assurance that it would never happen again. Instead, I told him the truth. "Only if that's what it takes to capture a rescue dog."

"Well, at least you're truthful," he said, shaking his head.

"And I drive slow," I told him.

Jason's phone rang with the sound of the Texas A&M fight song. He answered it with a curt, "Game warden."

The notebook came back out. He balanced the phone between his shoulder and ear and scribbled something on the page. Jason's side of the conversation consisted of grunts and nods, but the person on the other end of the call had plenty to say.

Unfortunately, I couldn't make out a word of it.

"I'll get there as soon as I can." He hung up and put his phone away. "Sorry. I need to handle this," he said as he tucked the notebook back in place and consulted his watch. "Can we set a time next week for me to see the rescue? The dog needs to be there so I can examine him for my report."

"What about out at the Second Chance Ranch facility?" I suggested. "How about Tuesday? Mornings are busy for me. Would two o'clock work? I need to go out and film some videos for social media posts, so I can do that while I'm out there with you."

"As long as you don't try to video me, I'm good," he said, the beginnings of a smile lifting the corners of his mouth.

"Says the television star," I quipped.

Jason ducked his head. "Yeah, I did that only because my lieutenant specifically asked me to do it. Otherwise you wouldn't find me anywhere near a film crew."

I thought about mentioning my call from Camille Finley but decided against it. "Hey," I said slowly, an idea dawning, "I would love to interview you for the clinic's social media followers. You could give them some tips on, oh, I don't know. I'm sure there's something a game warden could advise pet owners on. It would be from a public service standpoint, of course. I'd never ask you to sell dog food or tell our listers how amazing our clinic is. I promise."

"Not what I like doing, but I'll check with my lieutenant and see what he thinks. Text me the address, and I'll be there on Tuesday, though." Jason paused. "I'll drive you back to the clinic."

I shook my head. "Thanks, but I'll walk. It's just around the corner."

Relief flooded his expression. "If you're sure."

"I am. You need to go, and I need a walk."

"Look," he said slowly, "I don't like this part of my job when it involves people I know, but I do it because I swore an oath to uphold the law. I won't apologize for that."

"And you shouldn't," I said. "I'd already broken the law when I trespassed, and I'll do it again if it means saving an animal. Also, there's the dual crimes of two days of driving with an expired license that I've admitted to."

Jason looked thoughtful. Then he met my gaze. "And the other month and a half of driving you'd been doing before you figured out the license was expired." He paused. "Or did you know?"

I laughed. "I truly did not. I mean, I knew somewhere in my brain that my license expires on my birthday, but since it isn't every year it's not like I check it. You probably don't either."

He frowned. "Actually I do."

"Of course you do," I said lightly. "Anyway, I should get back to the clinic. They're probably pooling their money to bail me out about now."

Jason cringed. "Not my finest moment. I don't know what it is about Cameron, but he and I are like fire and water. Always have been. He knows exactly how to push my buttons, but to be fair, I can do the same to him."

"So I noticed," I said.

He shifted positions to face me, one hand resting on the steering wheel. "So, Cassidy, about that coffee."

An awkward silence fell between us. Again. Like it was becoming a habit. I didn't really mind. Despite the fact he'd just scared me into thinking I was going to jail and losing my savings, I liked him.

"Yes?" I prompted.

"Could we make it dinner instead? Tomorrow night? Seven o'clock?"

Oh. Well.

"Of course." My response was as casual as I could manage considering the way my insides were quaking. "See you then."

I climbed out of the truck and closed the door. When I turned the corner, he was still watching.

And still smiling.

So was I.

CHAPTER ELEVEN

I returned to an office in chaos. While the clinic employees were outside watching me be taken into custody, one of the dogs had escaped from Isabel's grooming room and was currently eluding capture.

"There's a reason his owner calls him Houdini," Isabel said, then she spied me. "Cassidy! Hey, everyone, Cassidy is back."

"Cass," Dr. Cameron called. "I thought that idiot brother of mine arrested you. It would be like him to do that what with. . ." His expression told me he realized that to complete the sentence would be to give away personal information about me and his brother. "Well, anyway, it would be something that Jason would do."

"No," I said as the team reassembled in the waiting room. "He was very nice and polite. I just got a warning for trespassing."

Although now that I thought of it, Jason had never actually given me any paperwork to show that there was a warning issued. Then there was the part where he'd asked me out.

"I'm glad," Dr. Tyler said. "I wouldn't have wanted to have to have words with him or his supervisor, because you absolutely were in the right in what you did rescuing that dog. There were extenuating circumstances that involved possibly saving a dog's life."

"I think he knew that," I said.

Mari walked in with Spot in tow and joined the group. My coworkers peppered me with questions until Spot spied Houdini creeping down the hall and barked. Isabel scooped up her runaway pup and headed for the grooming room.

I looked up to see a car pulling into the customer parking lot. "That's probably someone's one o'clock appointment, so I'll make it quick," I said. "The short version is everything turned out okay, and I'm going to meet Jason at the rescue on Tuesday with Spot to talk about the painting issue."

"I'm going with you," Mari and Parker said in unison.

Dr. Cameron frowned. "I'm on call, or I'd go too."

"Probably not the best idea," I said gently. "But thank you. And again, your brother was very nice. He apologized for taking me into custody."

The vet snorted. "And probably said something about me."

No way was I answering that.

Instead, I smiled and hurried off to my office with Spot to await Mari and Brianna. I knew them too well to believe they'd just go on about their day without getting the scoop from me.

Ten minutes later, they arrived along with Dr. Kristin. All but one of the Lone Star Ladies were in the room. "We'll have to fill Isabel in later. She can't leave Houdini," Dr. Kristin said, patting her lap and urging Spot to climb up. When he did, she scratched him behind the ear.

"So," Brianna said slowly, "spill. Tell us all about that handsome game warden and your arrest and escape from his clutches."

Dr. Kristin's eyes widened. "Oh! It's the same guy you were filmed with?"

"Yes. Jason Saye."

"Okay," Dr. Kristin said, "am I the only one who didn't know that Cameron had a brother who was a game warden?"

"A hunky game warden," Brianna added.

"And although I am happily committed to my relationship with Tyler," Dr. Kristin said, "it is impossible to disagree with Brianna. He's cute, Cassidy."

Brianna looked over at me. "Okay, why are you being so quiet over there? What haven't you told us?"

"Oh," Dr. Kristin said, "she is definitely leaving something out."

"We've got the Lone Star Ladies promise of silence going on here," Brianna said. "So spill it, Cassidy."

The LSL promise of silence was invoked when no one other than those of us in the group could know whatever information was being conveyed. It was the highest form of secrecy, and none of us would ever think of breaking that promise.

After everyone had agreed, I went to my office door and looked both ways. With no one in the hallway, I closed the door and turned back to my friends.

"He asked me out. We're having dinner tomorrow night."

The ladies all spoke at once. Finally, Mari's voice rose about the chaos. "Where and when? We'll all hide out and spy on you. For your protection, of course."

I shook my head. "No you won't. You'll get the details when I decide to tell them to you."

We all laughed. They all knew the details would be shared and discussed.

"To be continued," Dr. Kristin said. "I think this may be the start of an interesting romance between you and Jason Saye."

"I'm not so sure about that," I said. "But I do like him."

Mari joined in. "Do any of you think it's odd that Dr. Cameron never told anyone he has a brother?"

"Honey," Dr. Kristin said, "I don't talk about my relatives either. I love them all to death, but I've got some real characters in my family tree, and I'd rather most people not know the full details."

"That's fair," Brianna said, "but I'm having a hard time figuring out why anyone would be ashamed to talk about the hunky game warden if he was their relative."

"His name is Jason," I said. "And who knows? Maybe the two of them are super competitive."

"That's possible," Dr. Kristin said. "They look sort of close in age. If I had to guess, I'd say Cameron was a year or two older."

My phone dinged with a text. I picked up my phone to look, then smiled. It was from Jason.

See you tomorrow.

I suppressed a smile, then tucked my phone away. "Okay, so you've heard the whole story. I'd appreciate it if you don't say anything to the guys, especially since Dr. Cameron doesn't seem to get along with Jason."

"Good idea," Mari said as the others nodded.

Just then, Dr. Tyler stuck his head in the door. "Why is it I keep missing meetings?" he joked. Then his expression went serious. "Just making sure you're okay, Cassidy."

"I'm fine," I assured him. "He got some anonymous tip about me and had to check it out, that's all. Apparently I was never in trouble. At least not much."

"I'm glad to hear it," he said. "Although I am concerned that someone would make allegations against you."

"I agree." Dr. Kristin jumped to her feet. "And I need to get back to work. Tyler, if you have a minute, I need a consult on the Pomeranian that came in this morning."

The two veterinarians left my office together. Brianna filed out behind them, leaving only Mari in the room.

"Okay," Mari said. "Just two words of wisdom, and then I won't say anything else."

"All right," I told her, "although you know you can always talk to me about anything."

"I do, but I think I'll stick with this. Just two words, Cassidy: be careful. I'm just worried that you're going to fall in love with him. Before that happens, you should find out why his brother isn't on good terms with him. There could be any number of reasons, and none of the ones I can think of are good. That's why I want you to be careful."

"I promise," I told her. "But what happened to me finding my forever groom?"

Mari chuckled. "I still want that for you. I'm just concerned after seeing how things went between those two brothers. I like Dr. Cameron. I want to like Jason, you know?"

I nodded. "Yes, I understand. Now stop worrying about me."

"When you stop worrying about me," she countered.

"Deal," I said. "Now don't you have to be somewhere?"

She laughed. "Okay, I'm leaving. But we'll talk more about this."

After Mari had gone, I retrieved my phone. First I completed the online application to renew my driver's license. Then, with a smile on my face, I responded to Jason's text.

SEE YOU TOMORROW. LEGALLY.

CHAPTER TWELVE

Saturday, February 18

Of course the phone always rings when I'm on the other side of my apartment in the middle of something that I can't stop doing without causing a disaster. In this case, I was applying tape to a box I had overfilled, which meant I was using most of my body to manage the feat.

I let go, and the stubborn cardboard flew open, expelling the towels and bedding I probably should've just donated to the shelter and sending Spot into a fit of barking.

"I'm coming," I called as Spot continued to sing the song of his people.

I picked up on the fourth ring and heard a familiar chuckle. "Bad time to call?"

"Jason," I said. "No, Spot's just protecting me from a cardboard box. What's up?"

"About tonight."

My heart sank. He'd changed his mind about the date.

"I know I said seven, but I'm wondering if we could move that to six," he said.

I glanced at the clock and noted it was not quite noon. I'd been at this packing thing for several hours and had lost track of time.

"Six is fine," I said as Spot wandered into the kitchen. He gave another half-hearted bark, then hurried to the dog bowls to see if I'd added any kibble since breakfast. That fact that I hadn't earned me a pitiful look.

I heard the now-familiar crackle of Jason's radio in the background. "Are you working today?"

"I work every day, pretty much," he said. "But yes, I'm out this morning. I got a call about a bull chasing cars out on Blue Bell Road. That was fun."

"Sounds anything but fun. How'd you manage to catch him?"

Jason launched into a story of playing matador to an angry Brahma bull. Spot whined at my feet, so I settled on the floor. He landed in my lap with a flop, and I scratched him behind his ear.

"It's quiet where you are," Jason commented when his story was done. "Are you safe from the box?"

"Apparently," I said as the pup rolled over and offered his belly for me to scratch. "Although there are some complaints regarding an empty food bowl. Imagine not getting anything to eat two hours after you've had your morning bowl of kibble."

"Sounds like Spot is trying to make up for not being fed for a while."

"I don't know," I said slowly as I rubbed Spot's belly. "He seems well fed and well taken care of. I think his owner must be missing him terribly. Brianna, that's the clinic's receptionist, has been doing callbacks on any tip with a phone number and is answering emails when she can, but so far it's all dead ends."

"We'll find his home," he said.

I liked how he said *we*. "I think so too."

"Will he be there when I pick you up? I'd like to meet him."

"No," I said. "You'll have to wait until Tuesday for that. He's going home with Mari this afternoon. I think she's going to bring him out to her aunt's ranch so he can run around and socialize with her aunt's dogs."

"Okay, Tuesday it is. So tell me about the Second Chance Ranch."

An hour later, we were still on the phone and I was still sitting on my kitchen floor. Spot had given up on his campaign for kibble and was snoring loudly in his bed.

And I still wasn't tired of talking to Jason.

We'd discussed everything from favorite movies to least favorite vegetables. Spreadsheets, which I was for and he was against, were hotly debated. We agreed on how we liked our steak but disagreed on eating cilantro and waking up early. He was in favor of both while I liked neither. We also agreed that of all the things we did well, we were both terrible cooks.

"My mother tried," I told him. "So did my abuela. Unless it's grilled cheese or an omelet, I'm hopeless. The upside to this is my grilled cheeses are stellar."

"I'm pretty good at hot dogs cooked on a campfire. My specialty is canned chili, though."

"You can't live on canned chili."

"True," he said. "I fill in the gaps with ham sandwiches and canned soup."

A debate on which of the *Scooby-Doo* characters was the most valuable to the team was in progress. I made a case for Velma Dinkley, which is, of course, the right answer. Jason had begun to defend his choice of Shaggy Rogers when someone knocked on my door.

I scrambled to my feet, then pushed past Spot who was yapping like crazy. Peering out of the peephole in the door, I spied Mari standing there. Then I looked at the clock.

"Jason, it's almost one o'clock," I said, shaking my head. "Mari is here for Spot."

He laughed. "It's not." Then he paused. "It is. I guess we ought to say goodbye, then."

"We should." But I didn't want to.

"Yeah, well, probably for the best. It gives me time to work up a spreadsheet on how Shaggy is by far the best character on the show."

"Goodbye, Jason," I said, laughing as I reached for the doorknob.

"See you in a few hours," he said.

By the time my doorbell rang at straight-up six o'clock, there was a stack of moving boxes along one wall that stretched halfway to the ceiling. Basically, I'd packed everything I didn't need.

As I walked toward the door, I wondered if I shouldn't just donate all of it and take only what I needed to my new place. I was contemplating this when I opened the door, which is why I was not prepared for what greeted me.

Or rather who.

It was Jason. That much I could tell by the grin and the sandy lock of hair that fell down on his forehead.

But the ever-present uniform, sunglasses, and aviators were gone. In their place was a white pearl-snap shirt, dark denim jeans with a starched center crease, and a pair of black boots that had definitely never been used for roping or riding horses.

"You look great, Cassidy."

I'd chosen an outfit of black jeans, black knee-high boots, and a black sweater. Nothing creative, but it was a great first date outfit that could fit in most situations and hide any evidence should I spill something on myself.

"Thank you," I said, grabbing my purse and stepping out onto the porch where he waited for me.

After locking my door, I turned around to see a puzzled look on Jason's face. "Are you moving?"

I was so busy trying not to stare at the man standing in front of me that it took me a moment to respond. "Yes."

"Not far, I hope," Jason said as we walked together toward the parking lot, then climbed into his vehicle.

"No. Closer to work, actually," I told him. "I'm buying a second-floor loft downtown in the Mercer Building. My friend Nora plans to put her restaurant in the ground-floor space."

"That's great," he said as he pulled out of the parking lot. "Soon?"

"I hope so," I told him. "We're both waiting on the paperwork, but I'm kind of a planner, so I've started packing. I guess you noticed the boxes. Anyway, I'm excited about being a homeowner."

"My only complaint about homeownership so far is that I have to cut the grass." He glanced over at me and smiled. "You won't have to do that."

"True." We fell into a comfortable silence. Then a thought occurred. "Are we allowed to talk about work tonight?"

He gave me a sideways look. "Whose work?"

"Ours," I said. "The painted dog case."

Jason stopped at a red light. "Sure. Did you find out something new?"

"No, I was just thinking about the tip you got."

"Cassidy, forget about the tip," he said. "It was probably someone's idea of a joke."

"Maybe," I countered, "but I don't think it's a coincidence that you and I were both out at that pump site because of an anonymous tip. Do you?"

He let out a long breath. "I've considered that. But you said yourself that you aren't usually the one who has the rescue phone. Did anyone know you'd be the one answering?"

I thought a moment. "The only ones who knew were Parker and Mari. We have volunteers, but they don't go on rescues. So anyone who knew after the fact that I rescued Spot would not have known when it was happening, or before that."

"That rules out all the employees."

I sighed. "Not all employees," I said reluctantly. "The Lone Star Ladies knew."

At his confused look, I continued. "The Lone Star Ladies are the text group for the women who work at the clinic. You remember Brianna. She's the one who greeted you when you came to arrest me. I believe she said you were cute."

"I never intended to arrest you," he countered, ignoring the rest of my statement.

"Isabel is our groomer, and Dr. Kristin is a veterinarian," I continued. "Those of us without dates—that would be me, Brianna, and Isabel, were watching a show together at each of our homes. When I had to leave, I told them where I was going."

He shook his head. "I'm not going to rule those two out, but if the topic of who would be handling rescues didn't come up until you were called out on one, then that doesn't prove anything either way. Unless they knew you always handled it when the other two weren't available."

"No," I said. "I had never gone out alone. That's one of the reasons I was so scared that night."

"So this unprecedented event was caused by someone calling out a tip on Valentine's Day." He paused. "No angry clients at the clinic?"

"None that I can think of. I'm just the office manager, so I rarely interact with anyone other than the staff and the vendors, and I haven't had any problems with any of them."

"Okay," he said slowly. "You didn't turn down a date or break up with a guy before the fourteenth, did you?"

Oh how I wish I could have told him there were any number of men vying for my attention or heartbroken because I did not bestow said attention on them. Unfortunately, I had to answer with the truth.

"No."

Was it my imagination, or did Jason look pleased with my answer? "Okay, we can rule that out, then."

"Are you asking me that because you want to know about my previous boyfriends or because you have a lead on someone?" I challenged.

"It doesn't matter why." As if my thoughts showed on my face, he hastily added, "Don't take it personally."

I had plenty of arguments for that statement. I could have told him that it mattered because if he wasn't asking out of personal interest, then that changed everything. Because if I was honest, it hurt my feelings a little to know there was someone out there who might have it out for me. But most of all, I just didn't like the idea that anyone I might speak to or pass on the street could be the person who made that call.

But I said none of that. Instead, I plotted how to make Jason tell me without him knowing he was telling me.

Suffice it to say, I had no real plan for this.

CHAPTER THIRTEEN

J ason signaled to turn into the parking lot of a super fancy Italian restaurant that I'd been dying to try. Unfortunately, it was one of those places where you went with a date and not a group of pals. Plus, it was pricey.

"Have you been here before?" he asked as he parked.

"Never, but I've wanted to," I told him, leaving out the no date part.

"Same," he said. "I've heard it's good. So let's go see what all the fuss is about."

We walked toward the front door together. If the luscious scents swirling around the parking lot were any indication, tonight's meal was going to be amazing.

The glass doors opened before we could reach them, courtesy of two pretty ladies clad all in black. A third woman greeted us from behind an ornately carved desk that was lit by a pair of gold lamps.

"You're here for the special event," she said, her voice silky. "Welcome."

While Jason spoke with her, I walked over to the massive mirror on the opposite side of the room to check my appearance. The all-black ensemble made me look like I was an employee, and I should have worn the cute gold earrings instead of the smaller gold studs. And a statement necklace would have been a good choice.

But it was too late. I'd have to live with the fashion decisions I'd made.

I turned to see Jason walking toward me. "They've got our table ready," he said.

The woman nodded for us to follow, so Jason and I fell in line behind her. She led us to a small room with four small tables. The decor was elegant with carved furniture and paintings of Italy on the red papered walls. Well, on three of the walls. The fourth wall was covered by a massive hunter green velvet curtain.

Jason pulled out a chair for me, then went around to take the remaining seat. A waiter delivered two glasses of water and a cloth-covered basket that I assumed contained the usual selection of breads.

"Alessandro will be with you momentarily," he said with a smile as he exited the room.

My stomach growled. I'd missed lunch while I was on the phone with Jason and hadn't taken time to do more than snack while I was packing. By the time I realized I was starved, Jason's arrival was imminent.

So here I was staring at the bread basket and wishing Alessandro would hurry. Whoever he was.

Had I not been on a date, I'd be perusing the choices under that cloth right now. Instead, I sat back and offered Jason a smile.

"This is fabulous," I told him. "I can't wait to try the food." I didn't add that I meant that literally. Well, almost. I could wait, just not very long.

Jason nodded. "Smells good too."

What a guy thing to say. And yet he was not wrong. It did smell amazing in here.

"Alessandro will be with you shortly," the woman tossed over her shoulder as she left the room.

So I heard, I wanted to say. But this was a first date, and being cranky about the slow appearance of whoever Alessandro was would not leave a favorable first impression on the man I was trying to impress.

The sound of violin music filled the room. I'd expected Dean Martin and Frank Sinatra, so this was nice. It's difficult to decide on menu items when you're singing along with "That's Amore."

I glanced around, then looked back at Jason, who was studying me. "This is nice, Jason."

He nodded. "Nicer than I'm used to, if I'm honest. I wasn't sure what to expect when they offered the couples special meal, but I figured why not? At least we don't have to cook it."

I joined him in his laughter. "True. That would be the worst. Can you imagine you and me making an Italian meal?"

"I don't know. You claim to make a mean grilled cheese. Could you do one up Italian-style? That might be good."

Before I could respond, the green velvet curtain snapped open. We both swiveled to see a dark-haired man in a chef's hat and jacket. Behind him was a glass wall that revealed the busy restaurant kitchen. In front of him, bowls and various foods were resting on an industrial-looking metal table.

I'd been in restaurants where a table in the kitchen was available to watch the chef prepare the meal. This would be the first time I'd actually had the experience.

Now to hope he wasn't slow about it.

"I'm Alessandro," he exclaimed with a flourish. "You must be Jason and Cassidy. Welcome to our lovely kitchen, my friends. Are you ready to begin?"

He spoke the words with an Italian accent that was dramatic and also a little difficult to understand. At our nod, he continued.

"Tonight's menu will be a traditional Italian five-course meal beginning with the *antipasto* and then the *primo, secondo, contorno,* and finally the *dolce.*"

I didn't have any idea what most of these things were, but I clapped enthusiastically. This earned a nod of approval from Alessandro.

"Specifically," he continued, "the techniques used tonight have been taught to me by my father who learned from his grandfather and he from his until the original is lost in time."

Jason leaned toward me. "He's a little dramatic, don't you think?"

"I think it's all part of the show." He was also talking when he needed to be cooking. I didn't mention that to Jason because, after all, it was our first date.

"Because the remainder of the meal will be more intensive, I have prepared the antipasto for you." He retrieved a tray from among the items on the table and beckoned us toward him. "Come and enjoy, please."

THE BARK OF ZORRO

We looked at each other. Then I nodded. "I guess it's self-serve," I whispered.

"Looks that way."

Jason rose, and I followed him to the table. The antipasto turned out to be a beautifully arranged charcuterie tray with mortadella roses and more types of meats and cheeses than I'd seen in a long time. I tried to be delicate, but it was all I could do not to snatch up a handful of deliciousness and enjoy it.

But I couldn't do that. Not with Jason watching.

First dates are hard.

While we hovered around the antipasto, Chef Alessandro was busy arranging things like flour and eggs in the center of the table. After a few minutes, just as I was beginning to think I might survive my hunger, he snatched the antipasto tray away with a flourish.

"Time for primo!" He gestured to us, then nodded at the ingredients in front of him.

I looked at Jason. He looked back at me. Neither of us knew what to do.

"Cassidy," the chef said, "you will stand here, and Jason, you are here. I will instruct, but you must do the work."

"Hold on," Jason said, confusion evident in his tone. "You're the chef. Aren't you the one who does the work?"

Chef Alessandro laughed, then turned his attention to me. "He is funny, your boyfriend. Come, you will start, Cassidy."

"Start what?" I asked.

"The primo. First we make pasta." He nodded at the ingredients again. "You'll begin."

"Me?" came out in a squeak.

He reached over to the other end of the table to grab something from the stack of cloth there. He held up two red chef's aprons and thrust one toward me. Then he handed the other to Jason.

"Tonight you are the chefs. So tie these on and let's begin."

Jason looked at me, the apron in his hand. His expression likely mirrored my own.

"Hold on," the game warden said. "This is the couples special meal. I was told it would be a dining experience."

"It is," the chef said. "The experience is that you'll be cooking the meal."

"But we can't cook," Jason protested as I nodded in agreement.

Chef Alessandro shrugged. "And yet you will tonight."

Somewhere between primo and dolce, we managed to get the hang of Italian cooking. Or maybe we were so hungry by then that we just thought it tasted good.

By the time Jason dropped me off at my apartment, I had laughed so hard my sides ached.

"Thank you for a memorable evening," I told him, grinning as I leaned against my door.

He matched my smile. "I had no idea what I was signing us up for. But hey, now we know how to make pasta from scratch. Go figure." Then he sobered. "Honestly, it's the most fun I've had in a long time. I really like you, Cassidy."

"I like you too." I looked up into his eyes. He looked back into mine. I know it sounds corny, but time sort of stood still like it does in the movies.

Then his phone rang.

Jason made a face and checked the screen. "Sorry, Cassidy. I need to get this." He punched the button and said, "Game warden."

He'd explained over dessert that a game warden was always on call. At least we'd been able to spend most of the evening without interruption.

A moment later, Jason hung up and tucked the phone back into his pocket. "I'm sorry. I need to go."

"Of course," I said lightly. "Thank you again for an unforgettable evening."

He smiled. "Next time let's go somewhere where we don't have to work for our meal, though."

"I would like that."

Jason nodded, then frowned as his phone rang again. "Sorry, Cassidy. But—"

"You need to go," I supplied. "Go. I'll see you on Tuesday at the rescue."

He smiled and then turned to leave, answering his phone as he went. My phone dinged with a text. I slipped inside and then opened the image Mari had just sent along with a message that said: TATTOO!

CHAPTER FOURTEEN

I enlarged the image until I could read a code of numbers and letters. Still, it didn't mean anything to me, so I called Mari.

"Why are you calling me?" Mari demanded. "You are out on a date with that gorgeous game warden."

"Jason got an emergency call, so he had to leave." I hurried to add, "It's fine. We were actually at the end of the date. He was seeing me to the door."

"Did he kiss you?" Mari asked.

"Too soon," I protested. "It would have been awkward."

But would it have been? I thought back to earlier in the evening when the two of us were trying to make a meal under the watchful gaze of Chef Alessandro. We'd had so much fun. It had really been. . .what?

"Cassidy?" Mari said.

"Oh, sorry. So anyway, what did you mean by tattoo?"

"There's a tattoo on the underside of Spot's belly near his back legs. Parker found it by accident when I was bathing him. All three of the dogs had been running around the fields and were a mess, so Parker and I decided to do a good deed for Aunt Trina and wash them."

"Are you home? I can walk down to your place and see it better."

"No, I'm still at Aunt Trina's place," she said. "But I'll bring Spot to work tomorrow and you can look at it then."

"So what does a tattoo mean?" I said. "Where do you start to find that out?"

As I was saying the words, the answer came to mind. "Oh, I know. I'll call Lane. He'd know."

Dr. Lane Bishop was a veterinarian, a professor, and a researcher at Texas A&M University. More specifically, at the Texas A&M University Teaching Hospital. He was also the son of well-known veterinarian Dr. Elvin Bishop and Nora's commitment-phobe boyfriend.

I looked at the time. Almost eleven. Too late to contact him tonight. So I made my way past the wall of boxes and retrieved my laptop. A few minutes later, I hit SEND on an email to Lane with the photo attached.

While the browser was open, I navigated over to check the social media sites for any information related to Spot or painted dogs. Before I got very far, my laptop dinged with a new email. It was from Lane.

I'm working late in the lab tonight. Nora is with me, or was. I think she slipped off to the doctor's lounge to take a nap. Anyway, if you're still up, give me a call.

I punched in his number and waited while it rang twice.

On the third ring, Lane picked up. "Cassidy," he said in a cheerful tone while dogs barked in the background. "Give me a second to get back to my computer, and I'll see if the information has arrived. I've got access to a database that may be able to locate the source of the tattoo and the owner of the dog."

"Wow, that fast!" I said, leaning back in my chair. "I'm impressed."

"Okay, I'm seeing a response. Let me read it to see what it says." He paused. "There's a match."

My hopes rose. "That's wonderful."

"Okay," he said slowly, "I'll have to make a call and get the details. The system locks that pending approval. It might be a day or two before I know anything. Sometimes it takes even longer. Red tape and all."

"That's fine. Spot is safe with us until his owner is located." I paused. "Lane, I really appreciate this. I know you're busy."

"Not too busy to reunite a dog and his owner." He paused. "Hey, Cassidy. I guess you know there's a game warden out of your area who's been looking for this dog's owner too."

"Yes," I said slowly, wondering where this was going. "We've been sharing information on my rescue case."

"Then you know it's very much like the case we documented here over the weekend," Lane said. "I know he was interested in the details. I sent him over to the campus PD to read the report. Not sure what happened after that."

A second case. Oh really? Jason didn't mention that. Just wait until I spoke to him.

"Remind me of the details again, please," I said as casually as I could manage.

"Someone set a dog loose over at the football stadium. Kyle Field groundskeepers caught the animal and brought it to us. She's an English bulldog with a microchip that led us to a student who claimed it was all just a prank."

"How are that case and Spot's alike?"

"Both owners have home addresses in Washington County," he said. "And both dogs showed evidence of paint on their midsections. Campus cops aren't releasing the name of the student because he's a minor."

"Interesting. Did your bulldog have a letter painted on her, or was it just a blob of paint?"

"It was definitely a letter Z, but instead of white paint, the guy used Aggie maroon." He paused. "Considering our university's mascot is a dog, we're not amused when someone plays a prank like this."

I decided against reminding Lane that the Aggies weren't always above such a thing. Eons ago a group of cadets had thought it was just fine to commemorate the school's 13–0 football victory over rival University of Texas by painting the score on the side of their longhorn bull mascot. Apparently the Austin school decided the best course of action was to turn that bovine graffiti into the word *Bevo*, which became their mascot's name.

Or at least that's how I heard it.

"Of course. Thanks, Lane."

"Glad to." He paused. "Hey, Cassidy, can I ask you a question?"

"Of course," I told him.

"You've known Nora a long time. How's she doing?"

"She's great. Busy getting ready to open the restaurant of her dreams. Why?" I said, putting extra emphasis on the word *great*.

"I know she's busy. But since she's not listening to me right now. . ." He paused. "Just wondering."

I wanted so bad to tell this guy to put a ring on my friend's finger. To just marry her already. If he was that clueless, then some clarification from me on the subject was needed.

Except that Nora would kill me. Not literally, of course. But still.

"You should probably ask her about that, then," I told him instead. "Maybe take her somewhere nice over in Austin."

Lane replied, "That's a good idea. Any suggestions on a place she would like?"

I gave the question some thought. "There are so many. Why don't you go on social media and look around to see where people are having their romantic meals?"

"Great idea," he said, "but you're the social media expert. How do I sort through all of those photos to find what you're talking about?"

"Well," I said sweetly, "are you familiar with hashtags?"

"I am."

"Excellent." I paused. "Then I would suggest you start with the hashtag #AustinRestaurantProposals."

I wasn't a bit sorry I said that. In fact, I was proud of myself.

After hanging up with Lane, I sat back in my chair to plan how to deal with the next problematic male. Why in the world would Jason decide not to tell me about an event similar to Spot's?

I frowned. Probably the same reason he couldn't give me the details about that tip that was called in about me. Details of official investigations could not be shared. I got that. But that didn't mean I liked it.

Oh, but I did like him. So there had to be a compromise, right?

CHAPTER FIFTEEN

Sunday, February 19

On Sunday, I drove over to Somerville to attend church with my family. After, Mama and Abuela served a feast, as they usually did when my brother and I were in attendance. Rob worked in IT in Austin, so the job of computer repair on my father's aging computer always fell to him. Meanwhile Mama and my grandmother were sitting on the front porch shelling peas and chatting.

I wandered out to join them. The weather was warming nicely with temperatures in the upper sixties and brilliant blue skies overhead. With the lake glistening off in the distance and the trees swishing in the late February breeze, the temptation to settle onto the oversized porch swing for an afternoon nap was strong.

"Something's on your mind," my mother said. A statement, not a question.

I'd been thinking about Spot and all of the things related to him since I'd spoken to Lane last night. I settled onto a porch rocker beside Mama and shrugged.

"It's this dog I rescued on Valentine's Day. We're close to finding his owner, which is great, but I want to know why he had a letter *Z* painted on his side."

"That is odd," my grandmother said. "Z like Zorro. You know the story, yes?"

"The story of Zorro?" I asked. "Vaguely. He's some masked Robin Hood character who does good but never gets caught and marks things with a Z to show he's been there?"

Abuela nodded. "That's the general idea, although the story is so much more than that. The premise is based on a book from the early 1900s called *The Curse of Capistrano*. You should read it sometime. Or watch the old movie version. It's the best."

"My mother the English teacher," Mama said with a chuckle. "She never stops educating, not that I'm complaining."

My grandmother shook her head. "Anyway, it's a good story. And what's the application for your dilemma? I think if your person is painting a Z on dogs as some kind of mark of Zorro, then I would suggest you look for someone hiding in plain sight. And this someone will not be as they seem."

Mama chuckled. "No, they'll be nuts. Who paints a Z on dogs? That's awful."

"Someone trying to make a point," Abuela insisted.

I wanted to make a joke about points and swords but decided to keep quiet as my grandmother continued.

"The person hides but leaves evidence behind that he wants to be found. Something that says clearly that he was there. The question is why? What does he stand to gain? For Diego Vega, the character who became Zorro in the story, it was to defend the downtrodden and right wrongs. You just need to figure out what your Zorro wants to gain."

And there it was in a nutshell. I just needed to figure out what my Zorro wanted to gain. I sighed. If only it were that simple.

Mama and Abuela had moved on in the conversation without me. Abuela was singing the praises of the original Douglas Fairbanks version and Mama was pointing out that it was believed the character of Batman was based on Zorro. Baby, Mama's ancient tabby cat, peered up at me from the steps as if to plead for me to make them stop talking.

"What if it was a joke?" I asked, inadvertently interrupting their conversation. "Sorry. I was just thinking aloud."

"Go on," Mama said.

"What if someone just thought it was funny? There's a case over at A&M where a student painted a *Z* on a dog and turned it loose on Kyle Field. I can't help but wonder if the two incidents are connected."

"You should check the TipTop," Mama said. "There's always a new challenge going around. Maybe dog painting is the new fad."

"TikTok," Abuela corrected. "And that's not a bad idea."

"I did," I said with a sigh. "Nothing on painting dogs is being promoted."

"So go meet this student in College Station," Abuela said. "Talk to him and see what you get from the conversation. Is he the one who's doing this? Possibly. Or maybe not. You'll never know unless you meet him face-to-face and ask questions."

"You sound like an investigator," I told her with a grin as I checked my watch. Just past two.

"She's reading a mystery series right now," Mama said. "Old folks who solve murders."

"And I'm learning a lot. So, why not go see if you can speak to this fellow?" my grandmother asked.

"Because I don't know how to find him," I told her.

"If the police were called, there should be a report," Mama said. "And unless I'm wrong, the police department never closes."

She was not wrong.

By half past three I was standing in front of a ramshackle rental on the outskirts of the city. The home next door was obviously student housing, as witnessed by the number of cars, the pizza boxes overflowing from the trash cans, and the lawn filled with pink flamingos, all of which were wearing Santa hats.

By contrast, Gavin Welch's house was relatively nondescript. A car was parked on the street in front—an older model beige sedan with the obligatory Aggie stickers—and a pricey-looking black sports car in the driveway.

I did spy a Texas A&M flag hanging inside a window on the front of the house. Otherwise, the pale green exterior and overgrown grass would not have drawn attention in this neighborhood.

I knocked on the door, and it inched open. Despite the fact it was the middle of a sunny afternoon, the interior of the home was dark. Off in the distance I could hear the *ping* and *pong* sound of an electronic video game.

"Hello? Is anyone here?" I called.

Silence.

I tried again. "Hello? I'm here to see Gavin."

A twenty-something guy dressed in baggy shorts and white T-shirt appeared in the doorway at the end of the hall. He had shaggy black hair and one of those virtual reality game set things on his head. He slid the headset up out of his eyes and stared back at me.

"Are you Gavin?" I asked. "Gavin Welch?"

"Nope," he said. "Gavin's at work."

He disappeared around the corner, but I called after him. "Where does he work?"

"Vet," he called.

"Can you be more specific?"

No answer.

Okay. I had not come all this way just to reach a dead end. I stepped inside as alarm bells went off. I had not been invited inside. Hadn't I promised Jason I would not trespass anymore?

Actually, I'd told him I probably would if a dog's life was at stake. While I couldn't argue that exactly, this was being done on behalf of a dog, so that was close enough.

Now that I think of it, where was that dog? I picked my way over piles of what appeared to be laundry, beanbag chairs, and books. Strangely, there seemed to be no evidence that a dog lived here.

When I reached the end of the hall, I tried again. "Hey, it's me again. Which vet?" I paused. "I need to know the name of the clinic where I can find Gavin."

Behind Headset Guy, the flashing lights of a video game went on pause. He turned around toward me, the headset still firmly in place. "Are you a cop or something?"

"No," I said. "I work at a clinic in Brenham. I just need to see him about something."

That seemed to reassure him, as he smiled. "Yeah, all right. He's at the big clinic. You know, the one at the vet college on the other side of the railroad tracks."

"The A&M College of Veterinary Science?" I said.

"I guess," was his answer as he returned to his game.

Okay, then. So much for roommates being best friends.

Twenty minutes later, I was standing at the information desk asking for Gavin Welch. I found him mucking out a stable at the equine medicine facility.

He wore dusty jeans and work boots with a maroon Texas A&M T-shirt. But then so did the others who were also mucking stalls. It must be the uniform for the job.

When I called his name, Gavin straightened and peered at me over a blue bandanna tied almost up to his dark brown eyes. Ginger hair almost the color of my own barely showed beneath the maroon baseball cap.

"That's me," he said.

"Do you have a minute to talk?" I asked.

He gave me a suspicious look. "Who are you?"

I introduced myself. "I work for Lone Star Vet Clinic in Brenham."

Gavin stuck his pitchfork into the ground and swiped at his forehead with the back of a gloved hand. "Okay. I don't mean to be rude, but what does that have to do with me? Are you an equine clinic?"

"Small-animal clinic," I said. "Your name came up in an investigation regarding a dog that was rescued in Brenham on the fourteenth." I paused and watched his eyes as I continued. "Our rescue dog was painted with a Z in white house paint."

And there it was. Recognition.

"So you're a cop."

This was the second time in less than half an hour that had come up. What were these guys afraid of?

"No, I'm not a cop. I told you, I manage Lone Star Vet Clinic in Brenham and volunteer at Second Chance Ranch Dog Rescue. We're just trying to figure out what happened to a rescue dog that we placed."

"I don't have anything to say about anything like that." Gavin reached for his pitchfork. "Sorry, ma'am, but I've got to finish this stall."

"I read the police report," I told him as he turned away. "Why did you paint the dog?"

He froze. Then, a moment later, he went back to his work as if I hadn't asked the question.

"Gavin," I said. "Like I said, I just want to find out why my dog was painted. And maybe keep that from happening to other dogs."

I thought of the conversation on the porch. I wasn't yet thirty, but to students like Gavin, I was practically middle-aged. Was there something going on online that my searches had missed? I decided to try again.

"Is this some kind of new trend on social media? Maybe a new dare?"

No response.

"Does the vet school know what happened on Kyle Field with that bulldog? I doubt that a cruelty to animals charge would go over well if you're wanting to work in any field related to veterinary medicine."

That did it.

Gavin turned around and stalked toward me. He looked more desperate than dangerous. "I told the cops it was a joke. That's the end of that. And nobody ended up being charged."

"I was at your house, Gavin," I said. "There was no evidence of a dog living there. So, whose dog was it? Should I try your parents in LaGrange to see if the dog was brought back there?"

He said nothing. I stared back, daring him to answer me.

"Look," I finally said. "I just want to get to the bottom of this mystery. Why a Z? Why that dog? Those are just a couple of the many questions I have. I'd really appreciate it if you'd help me answer them."

Finally, he glanced around, then shook his head. "I can't do that. Sorry."

"Look, Gavin. I'm not trying to get anyone in trouble. But you might have information that would be helpful to me." I retrieved a business card from my purse and handed it to him. "If you change your mind or think of something you'd be willing to tell me, please get in touch. You can call, text, or email."

He took the card and stuck it in the pocket of his jeans. "Yeah, okay," was his gruff response. "Now really, you have to go. I need this volunteer work on my résumé, and I don't want to get in trouble. The same goes for calling my parents."

"I would never want to get you in trouble," I said. "I hope to hear from you."

Gavin didn't reply. Instead, he went back to mucking the stable. I turned and walked away, pausing only when I reached the door to the barn. When I glanced back, he was watching me.

CHAPTER SIXTEEN

Monday, February 20

My first order of business on Monday morning was to attend the meeting of the Lone Star Ladies tell-us-about-your-date gathering. I hadn't planned this, but apparently they had. When I arrived at the office, Spot and the ladies were already waiting for me.

I gave them the highlights, and we were all laughing at my Italian restaurant cooking lesson. "I wish I could have seen you and Jason trying to make pasta."

"It was pretty funny," I said. "And it didn't help that I had missed lunch and was starving."

Isabel sighed. "It all sounds wonderful. And he's so cute, Cassidy. I know looks aren't everything, but girl. . ."

The ladies all murmured agreement. "I like him," I admitted. "But it's too soon to assume that there's anything there other than a friendship, okay?"

They exchanged glances. No one responded. Finally, Mari said, "Let's just see what happens, okay?"

The topic moved on, and eventually everyone but Spot left the office. I'd just begun to tackle the Monday morning email inbox when my office phone rang.

"Someone named Camille," Brianna said. "She said you'd know what it was about."

I sighed. It would be easy to have Brianna send the call to voice mail. "Okay, thanks," I told Brianna instead.

"Cassidy, thank you for taking my call. I know you're busy," the producer said in her businesslike tone. "But I would like to revisit our recent conversation."

"The one where I declined to be on camera anymore?" I said.

"That's the one." She paused. "There's been a development that I thought might change your mind."

"Oh?" I said, leaning back in my chair. "What development?"

Camille chuckled. "Now that I think of it, there are two developments. The most important of them is that after speaking with Jason's boss— Lieutenant something-or-other—he is going to urge Jason to continue filming despite the fact that Jason wasn't keen on doing more shoots. He likes that the game wardens are represented in the show. In previous seasons we've focused on cops mostly."

"I see," I said softly. "By the way you said that, I'm guessing Jason doesn't know this yet."

"Probably not, since I just finished my conversation with his boss. I'd think he'll know soon, though." She paused. "And that brings me to the second development. Since we focus on the real life of each person featured, Jason is about to have to agree to have dates with you filmed."

The air went out of me. "That's not possible," I managed. "We aren't dating. And if we were, we wouldn't want a film crew following us."

"You *are* dating, Cassidy," Camille said evenly. "You and Jason were seen making pasta at an exclusive Italian restaurant on Saturday night. Law enforcement aren't the only ones with tip lines."

I frowned.

"So here's the thing," Camille said. "I get it that you don't like your privacy invaded. You're probably fuming right now. But I have been hired to produce a good show, and your boyfriend has a presence on-screen that I haven't seen in a long time. Why not let him shine?"

"Because he doesn't want to?" I said, trying to keep my voice in check.

"Didn't want to," Camille said. "He may have changed his mind. All I'm asking is if he's changed his, will you change yours?"

"I don't know what to say."

"I think you do," she said. "And for the record, I'm just doing my job. I get it. But if you want to help Jason, you'll do this."

"Help him how?" I said.

"I shouldn't tell you this, but he's facing some strong pressure to participate. His boss isn't going to be happy if he says no. So," she said slowly, "if you were on board, then he would be."

"You want me to convince Jason to film episodes of the show?"

"Of course not," Camille said. "At least not unless you want to. I just don't want you to discourage it."

"I wouldn't," I told her.

"Right." She paused. "Okay, well, just one more tiny detail. If he's on, then we need you to be part of that. If you elect not to, then he'll have to wait until after the show stops filming to continue dating you."

"That makes no sense."

"Doesn't it?" she said. "Well, it's like this. Anytime Jason steps outside his house, he can be subject to filming per the terms of the contract with the show. So, if you're going out with him, then the cameras are tagging along."

"But we've only had one date," I said. "That's not fair."

"I know," she said with a sigh. "But it can't be helped. Jason is probably working on some interesting cases, and I have to say it—he's just too cute."

I couldn't argue with that part.

"Anyway, trust me," Camille said. "I'm on your side here. If I didn't have the studio executives who screen the dailies demanding more Jason, I'd absolutely not be making this call. I do respect your feelings. I want you to know that."

"Okay," I told her. "Thank you for telling me."

"What're you going to do?" she asked.

"I don't know yet." I paused. "It's up to Jason, I guess."

As we said our goodbyes, something Camille said caught my attention. *Jason is probably working on some interesting cases.*

"Like the case of the painted pup," I said softly. Spot's ears perked up as he cast a sleepy glance toward me. "That's right, boy. It wouldn't hurt to get you some attention, would it?"

His excitement level was much lower than mine. A moment later, he was back asleep.

I reached for the phone. Camille answered on the second ring. "That was fast."

"I just have a question," I told her.

"Okay, go for it."

"Do you think the studio executives would be interested in the mystery of who is painting the letter Z on dogs here in Brenham?"

Silence. Then she said, "How many dogs?"

"Just two so far," I said. "Only one in Brenham, actually. The other was in College Station and may or may not be related. That's part of the mystery at this point."

"I'll make a note of it," she said. "Thanks."

CHAPTER SEVENTEEN

Tuesday, February 21

I arrived early at Second Chance Ranch Dog Rescue, but Jason pulled in right behind me. "Let me guess," I said as we climbed out of our vehicles at the same time. "You grew up being told if you were on time you were late, didn't you?"

Jason grinned. "Something like that."

He walked over to my car to wait while I got Spot out. Spot took one look at Jason and his tail started wagging. Jason knelt down to greet the happy dog.

"He's a friendly guy," Jason said. "So whatever happened to him, it hasn't made him afraid of humans."

"Definitely not."

"Any progress on the tattoo?" he asked.

I'd told Jason about Lane's database search last night when he called. I filled him in on my trip to College Station to speak with Gavin. He'd listened without comment until I got to the part when I had provoked Gavin while he held a pitchfork.

"Don't ever do that again, Cassidy," he'd snapped, and his sharp tone had taken me by surprise. "That was a foolish risk."

The comment still stung a bit even thought we'd smoothed it over before we hung up last night. I brought my thoughts back to the present and shook my head. "I haven't heard from Lane—Dr. Bishop—yet. He said it could take a while to get a response."

"Right." He stood. "Now that I've seen Spot, I have to say something about him looks familiar. I'll have to think about where I might have seen him before. Right now I need to examine Spot and take photographs."

"I'll get out of your way, then," I told him.

"No, stay," he said. "I like having you around."

I smiled. "Okay, then I'll stay."

Once Jason had finished with his task, he stood and glanced past me at the rescue building. "How about showing me around?"

I gave him the grand tour. Along the way, Jason asked questions about different aspects of the facility and the rescue.

"Most rescues I've seen don't have this quality of facilities," he said, taking in the building adjacent to the fenced area.

"Thanks to Mari's aunt Trina—her home is on the other side of the property—the rescue dogs are well taken care of until they find their forever homes," I told him.

"I can see that," he said over the yips and yaps of the dogs.

The building had been renovated specifically for the purpose of keeping these lost pups safe. The interior featured bright white walls, washable painted floors, and windows on two sides that allowed for breezes on a nice day and for sunshine to fill the space. State-of-the-art heating and cooling kept the interiors just right.

Just inside the door was a massive bulletin board that was beginning to fill with photos of rescued dogs and their owners. I smiled as I glanced over the photos, then took a snap of the board. I had an idea to use the board in some social media posts later in the week.

Help us fill the board.

Do you belong here?

Something like that.

The windows were thrown open to the crisp afternoon air. The light in the room was absolutely gorgeous, so I lifted the phone up to take a few more photos of the two pups awaiting homes before I let them out to play in the fenced-in yard that adjoined the building.

"Hey, where's your film crew? The rescue could use the publicity," I said with a chuckle.

I'd heard nothing about Jason's return to filming. He hadn't mentioned it, and Camille hadn't called.

I wondered if he'd said no. But I didn't dare ask. Hence the joke.

Jason looked down at me and smiled. "Yeah, I'm a big star among the elementary school crowd." He paused. "About that."

I waited for Jason to continue, but he seemed to be having trouble deciding what to say. Much as I was tempted to help or at least tell him what I knew, I kept my mouth shut and let him tell me in his own time and way.

He gave me a look. "I'm sorry, Cassidy. My lieutenant didn't force me to agree to more filming, so I cannot blame it on him. But let's just say after the producer of the show called, I felt like I needed to say yes."

There came the worried look again. "There's just one more thing."

Again Jason seemed to be struggling to find the words. I decided to help.

"If you're outside your home, you may be subject to being filmed. Which means if I'm with you, then I could be filmed as well?"

Jason's brows rose. "You've just quoted the lady producer almost word for word."

"That's because Camille called me too."

He gave me a sheepish look. "So you knew when we talked on the phone last night?"

"She called me yesterday. Camille mentioned that she was trying to convince you to agree to more filming. If you agreed to do it, I figured you'd tell me about it eventually. I didn't want to influence you either way."

He looked down to study his boots, then shifted his attention up to meet my gaze. "I wanted to tell you last night, but I was afraid you'd say we couldn't go out as long as I was filming."

"Why would I say that?" I asked.

He made a face. "Because no normal person would sign up for being followed by cameras."

"Jason," I said slowly, "if I have to choose between being followed by cameras and not seeing you until the filming is over? There's no question. I'll endure the cameras if you will."

He let out a long breath. "You're sure?"

"I am," I said.

"Good." Jason let out a long breath. "Because the film crew is waiting to get permission from you to film the rescue."

I glanced around. "They are?"

"I had them wait down the road," he hurried to say. "They won't come here unless I call and tell them you're okay with it."

I shrugged. "I'll have to get approval from Mari, but I don't see why it would be a problem."

His worried look turned to a smile. "Are you sure?"

"Of course." I retrieved my phone. "I'll call her."

"And I'll go over there and play with the dog so you can have some privacy."

I grinned. "Thank you."

Mari was thrilled and gave an immediate yes. Then she giggled. "Cassidy, you're going to be on television, and with the cutest game warden in Washington County."

On the other side of the enclosure, Spot was racing to catch up to a ball Jason had thrown.

"He's the only game warden in Washington County," I said. "But yeah, can you believe it?"

"I'm happy for you," Mari said. "Really happy."

"I'm happy too," I said. "But I'm also not getting ahead of myself."

"I'd tell you if you were," Mari said. "Oh, and good news on a whole other topic. The Baker family from LaGrange is going to take Suzy home tomorrow. I let them know we'd chosen them, and they were thrilled."

"That's great news. Much as I wanted Ben to have her, going home with a family and a fenced yard makes more sense for her."

"And one more thing," Mari told me. "The local paper wants to run a story on Spot. Do you want to talk to Mollie, or should I?"

Mollie Kensington was a local reporter who'd supported the clinic and the rescue in the past. She would do a great job with the article. Still, I didn't want to be the one who spoke with her. Not when I'd skirted a few laws to rescue Spot.

"Would you mind?" I asked.

"Not at all."

We said goodbye, and then I tucked my phone back into my pocket. Jason seemed to be having a good time with our newest rescue. Spot dropped the ball at Jason's feet. Just as he leaned down to grab it, the dog snatched up the toy and took off.

"Looks like Spot's playing keep-away," I said as I walked toward the game warden. "Make your call. Mari's fine with the camera crew being here. I'll go let the other rescues out so they can play with Spot."

I turned to go, but Jason called out, "Hold on, Cassidy," as he closed the distance between us and reached for my hand. "So we're doing this, then. The filming, I mean."

"Sure, it will be fun," I said, looking up into his eyes. His hand was warm in mine.

"And we'll be on camera anytime we're together," he said. "So we will have to consider that before we go out anywhere."

Worry about being on camera with the man I was quickly losing my heart to? It was all so surreal. And yet that was absolutely what was happening.

"Yes, I suppose we do."

"Okay," came out in a long breath. "Then before I make this call, I need to say something, Cassidy." Jason released my hand and leaned in to gather me into an embrace. "Just us. No cameras."

"Okay," came out in a soft squeak.

"I know this seems fast. We haven't known each other long. But I think about you all day, and I could talk to you for hours."

My insides were turning to mush, but I managed to smile. "I'm having the same problem."

His smile lit up. "You are? I'm glad to hear it because there's just one more thing."

"What's that?"

"I want to kiss you, and I would very much like that kiss to be between just you and me and not put on any television show. Would you be okay with that?"

I grinned. "Very okay."

And oh, that kiss. Jason chuckled as we stepped apart. "Cassidy, you've stolen my heart."

"Are you going to arrest me again?" I managed through the emotions swirling around me like a warm breeze.

He laughed. "You were never under arrest, remember?"

Suzy, ever the energetic beagle-terrier mix, darted past, ruining the moment. Running was her special gift. She'd also been the one who'd given Parker a reason to run around his neighborhood the other morning. Apparently now she'd mastered the art of escaping from her kennel.

"How did you get out?" I demanded.

The family who'd be picking her up had lots of acreage for her to run and three boys to run with, whereas Ben had neither of these things. According to Mari, seeing Suzy with the boys when they came to visit the rescue had sealed the deal. I'd keep looking for Ben's best fit, but in the meantime, we all knew Suzy had found her forever family with the Bakers.

"You're a mischievous girl," I chided as she galloped past.

While Jason placed the call to the production folks, I went in and opened the other two kennels. Buster, the somber basset hound that always looked as if he'd been awakened from a nap, ambled out. He'd finally recovered from the back surgery he'd needed when we found him and was ready for adoption. I'd already created the posts and scheduled them to go out starting today.

Finally came Gramps, the black lab with the graying muzzle. He'd been found hidden in a patient's room at a senior center and might have lived out his days there if the residents hadn't been caught sneaking food off their plates to feed him.

He nuzzled my hand as he strolled past. I scratched him behind the ear, then followed him outside.

"What's his story?" Jason donned his aviator shades and nodded toward the lab that had moved only as far as a patch of sunlight before stretching out in the grass. "He's a nice-looking dog."

I told him the tale of the Sunny Days Senior Center and their stowaway. "He's only been here a few days. I think he's missing his people."

Spot trotted over and joined Gramps. "Looks like he might have new people," I quipped.

CHAPTER EIGHTEEN

L et's talk about Spot again before the cameras show up," Jason said. "Now that you've had time to think about it and you've done some research, what's your assessment of how he got where you found him?"

I leaned against the fence and watched Suzy running circles around the two more sedate canines. Neither appeared to be paying her any attention.

"I've given that a lot of thought. He was behind a locked fence. I didn't see a way in other than through the gate, but it was pouring. And to be fair, I couldn't exactly see well due to the rain and the oversized rain gear I was wearing."

"And it was dark," Jason offered.

I looked up at him. "Exactly. Although the lightning gave enough light for me to see glimpses."

"Standing in a clearing next to a metal pumper and fence is not the safest environment for a dog or a woman," he said. "But go on."

"Oh," I said under my breath as the implications dawned on me. "I was so busy worrying about breaking the law, catching the dog, and running from the creeper that I never thought about getting electrocuted."

"Might want to put that higher on the list next time," Jason said. "Not that there needs to be a next time."

I cringed. "Anyway, I just can't make sense of why a dog that looks otherwise well cared for was where he was during a blinding thunderstorm. If I had to guess, I would say that whoever started painting him didn't get to finish because he ran away. Maybe the thunder scared him and he took off."

"Or the person doing the painting scared him."

"Yes," I said, "that's definitely possible." A thought occurred. "Maybe the creeper put Spot behind the gate and locked him in. Could be that Spot wouldn't cooperate and he got mad about it."

"Nope," Jason said a bit too quickly.

"Nope?" I echoed. "So you're not even going to consider that theory?"

He met my gaze. "Nope. And actually, that's why I wanted to talk to you before the cameras start rolling."

I put my hand on my hip and gave him an incredulous look. "And why not?"

Jason's expression remained unreadable. "Because it isn't possible."

"It absolutely is possible," I said. "You may be the game warden, but I work with dogs both at my day job and here at the rescue. I think I'm a pretty good judge of what a dog might do in a rainstorm. If Spot tried to bite him because he was scared, the creeper definitely could have retaliated."

Jason chuckled. "It's possible that Spot retaliated against someone, but it wasn't the man you're calling the creeper."

Several responses to his audacious remark occurred. Instead of giving voice to my thoughts, I bit my tongue and shook my head. "All right, Jason," I said as calmly as I could manage, "exactly how do you know this?"

He looked down at me, lowered his aviators just enough to show his eyes, and then grinned. "Because I'm the man you saw out at the pump site, Cassidy."

"You?" I shook my head. "Surely not. He was trying to sneak up on me. He yelled, and I think he might have hit the van with his fist."

"It was me." Jason repositioned his aviators. "County dispatch got an anonymous call that there was someone out at the pump site. I was closest to the scene, so I took the call." He paused.

"Why did you wait so long to tell me?"

He let out a long breath. "Honestly," he said slowly, "I don't like how I handled that incident. I should have been clearer in who I was and approached from the front, not the back. In retrospect, I see that I frightened you, and I don't like that either. I assumed you were a perpetrator."

I shook my head. "I was, actually. I'd trespassed, broken into a secure fence, and was carrying a tire iron. That's pretty shady-looking, I'd guess."

"Yeah, true. But I should have told you immediately after I determined you weren't going to receive a citation."

"I guess I have to stop calling the guy at the pump site the creeper," I said, then laughed.

As Jason joined me in laughter, I recalled a message I'd intended to give him. This seemed like a good time to change the subject.

"Speaking of the case, I got a message on social media this morning that someone over in Chappell Hill might have had a painted dog last week."

Jason shook his head. "False alarm," he said. "I investigated that one myself. Cow dog got too close to a construction site and ended up with some cement on him that dried light. Wasn't a Z or any letter, just a big mess that the owner had to clean up."

"That'll happen," a familiar voice said.

Jason and I whirled around to see Wyatt Chastain walking toward us. His hound dog, Ed, was at his side. Since Wyatt would soon be marrying the owner of the property where the rescue sat, it wasn't unusual for him to turn up.

His gaze went from me to Jason, then back to me. "Trina's up at the house plotting a Christmas album with that producer fellow, so Ed and I decided it was a good time to take a stroll. When the topic of adding a boy band to sing backup comes up, I'm out. Ed agrees."

Gilbert "Sticks" Styler had recently set up a satellite office for his recording studio right here in Brenham. Technically on a ranch just outside of town, but that still counted as local. The transplanted Englishman had fallen in love with the city and now split time between here and his main offices in Nashville.

As soon as Ed spied me, he hurried over for belly rubs. While I knelt down to oblige the sweet pup, the men shook hands.

"Why is it I keep seeing you in the company of the game warden, Cassidy?" Wyatt said with mock sternness. "What kind of trouble have you been getting yourself into that the state police have a man assigned to keep you in line?"

"Trespassing, breaking and entering, and threatening an officer of the law," Jason deadpanned. "Then there was the pasta-making incident."

"Hey," I said, standing. "You told me I was just getting a warning."

"That's under judicial review," Jason said. "And I'm considering a felony on the pasta."

"If you need a good lawyer, I know one," Wyatt said with a wink.

"I just might." I walked over to join the men. "I was just showing Jason the rescue facility. He's investigating the painting on our newest rescue."

"I heard about that." Wyatt shook his head. "Not sure what to make of it."

"Neither am I, frankly." Jason retrieved a business card and handed it to Wyatt. "But if you hear of anything that you think might help the investigation, I'd appreciate it if you'd call me."

Wyatt accepted the card, glanced at it, and nodded before tucking it into the pocket of his flannel shirt. Then he let his attention drift over where Ed had joined the lazy dogs lying in the sun.

"There is one thing that occurs to me," Wyatt said. "I had your uncle Ken in my office just last week. He'd run into some trouble and needed me to straighten it out. Had to do with some missing paint. I didn't ask what color."

"Uncle Ken?"

"Ken Venable," Jason supplied. "My mother's brother."

Jason's mother, a Venable, was married to Cameron's father? That took a second to process. There couldn't be a more different type of person than the game warden I'd come to know and the Venables I knew from my youth.

I fumbled for a response. "Right," I finally said. "I didn't know that."

A muscle worked in Jason's jaw as he gave a curt nod. "Thank you, sir. I'll check into it."

Wyatt returned the nod, then whistled for Ed. The hound reluctantly joined him, bringing his new friend along.

"Hold on here, Ed," Wyatt said to his dog. "He's not ours."

But as the lawyer spoke the words, he was kneeling to scratch the old dog behind his ears. Gramps leaned forward to press his head against Wyatt's knee.

Wyatt looked up at me. "Ed and I might need to have a conversation about getting him a friend. Once Trina and I marry, he'll have her two to contend with. They all get along, but Trina's pair runs at warp speed while Ed here prefers to amble."

Patsy and Cline, English springer spaniels with a penchant for sneaking food off neighborhood barbecue grills, were an energetic pair. More than once I had arrived at the rescue to find the duo wandering the grounds, likely looking for their next meal to steal now that the next-door neighbor had moved to a jail cell in Huntsville.

But that was a whole other story.

"Just so you and Trina know," I said, "there will be a film crew down here any minute. They're filming Jason for a television program, so they're going to cover his visit to the rescue."

"Well how about that?" Wyatt said. "From Cassidy's bodyguard to television star. Congratulations."

"Not sure it's something I wanted to do, but here we are." He paused. "Get followed around by a film crew, that is."

"Right." Wyatt straightened and looked down at the two canines. "Time to go, Ed. Say goodbye to your buddy."

The hound dog yelped. The old dog joined Ed in voicing his objection.

"That's the first bark I've heard out of him," I told Wyatt.

Wyatt shook his head. "Apparently my dog is under the impression that we can check out dogs from the rescue like books from the library and just take them home with us."

I grinned. "That's not normally how it works, but I think I can make an exception."

"You sure?"

I nodded. "Absolutely."

"All right, then. Come on, crew," he said, and together they disappeared back up the trail that led to the main house.

"Is it my imagination," Jason said, "or was that old dog moving a lot faster when he left?"

"We see that a lot," I told him. "Some of these animals just need the right person to make everything better in their world. Others need more than that, of course. We get dogs with health issues and all kinds of things like that."

"But never anyone painting them in any way until now," Jason said.

"No, that's a new one." I paused. "What do you think of Wyatt's tip about your uncle Ken?"

There was that expression again. Finally, he gave me a direct look.

"Same as any tip," he said. "I won't have an opinion on it until I can follow up on it."

And yet I had a feeling that the game warden already had formed his opinion on whether or not Ken Venable had something to do with this crime. What I couldn't figure out was whether Jason thought his uncle was guilty or not.

Jason's radio squawked, and he reached for the mic and responded with "Game warden."

While the game warden spoke with his dispatcher, I strolled over to where Spot and Buster were sprawled out in the sunshine. Curious, Suzy bounded over to join us. A moment later, she was irritating the other two dogs by running in circles around them—and me.

"Come on, guys," I said to the trio. "Time for snacks."

All three happily followed me back inside. I'd already taken my place on the bench just inside the door and was tossing treats to the pups when Jason stuck his head in the door.

"Is your entourage here?" I asked him.

"I'm afraid so. They're doing B reels," he said. "I guess that's filming exteriors, because that's what it looks like they're doing. Camille asked me to bring you and the dogs outside so they can get some action shots."

I stood and smiled. "Okay, Woof Gang," I said to the dogs. "It's time for your close-ups."

CHAPTER NINETEEN

Wednesday, February 22

My chance to see Ken Venable came when Dr. Tyler asked for a volunteer to go pick up some supplies that were being kept in a storage unit at the Store More facility very near the Venable compound. I decided to go see Ken first and then complete my errand.

Driving up the long driveway leading to the Venable compound wasn't nearly as frightening as I recalled. When I was a kid, I could reach out and touch the tree limbs as my grandfather eased his truck along a rutted dirt road.

That had been then. Now the trees had been trimmed back and the gravel road was wide enough for two vehicles to pass side by side. As I drove into the clearing, another surprise awaited.

The old house with the sagging porch and poorly mended roof had been renovated. Now it looked like one of the homes in the historic section of town. The windows sparkled, ferns hung from the porch, and the entire home shone with a fresh coat of white paint.

My thoughts stuttered to a stop.

White paint.

Fresh white paint.

I glanced around, not sure what I was looking for. It wasn't like there would be evidence of dog painting here. Or would there be?

From what I recalled, this home was the original house on the land. Other homes, smaller and less grand, were built as needed until the expansive property held a half dozen residences for Venable family members.

I never stepped foot inside any of them, but before Grandpa banished me to the truck for his visits, I'd walked a step behind him as he traversed the path that led to the homes. I spied the path, now wide enough for a vehicle to travel and covered in the same material as the driveway and outlined with dark green miniature azalea plants.

The front door opened, and a woman in an oversized pink sweatshirt and pale gray yoga pants stepped outside. She wasn't much older than me, with her dark hair captured in a sleek ponytail and minimal makeup.

"Oh, I'm sorry," she said. "I didn't realize you were out here." Then she looked down at her clothing and back up at me. "Excuse my appearance. I was about to go for a run. Anyway, can I help you?"

I was so distracted by how nice she was. How perfectly, ordinarily nice. There was nothing scary about this place anymore, and I hadn't decided how to reconcile that with my childhood *Scooby-Doo* villain nightmares.

"Hi, um...," I began. "I'm Cassidy Carter from Lone Star Vet Clinic. I'm looking for Mr. Venable. Ken Venable," I added.

I must not have sounded too much like an idiot, because the woman smiled. "Ken is either at his office or at the storage units," she said. "Would you like me to call him?"

"That won't be necessary," I said. "I was heading to the storage units next."

At her nod, I moved to climb back into my car. Then I stopped. "It's so pretty now," came out before I thought about how it might sound.

The woman walked down the wide steps toward me. "Truly I don't know how anyone lived here. When I married Ken, I told him either we'd live elsewhere or there would be improvements."

"There certainly have been improvements," I said.

She extended her hand to me. I could see now that she was standing close to me that she was expecting. "I'm Delia, Ken's wife."

"Oh," I said, fumbling for the appropriate response while processing this additional surprise. "I didn't know he was married. But then again, I guess I don't really know much about the Venables except what I remember from childhood. My grandfather used to repair their lawn mowers and small-engine equipment, and he'd bring me along when he picked up or delivered here."

"Any child of mine would never have gotten out of the car," Delia quipped, cradling her expanded waistline. "Not if it looked anything like how I found it when we got married last year. I told Ken it was a complete overhaul of the house and grounds or he could buy me something new elsewhere."

I matched her smile. "Grandpa felt the same way back then. Anyway, I'm pleased to meet you, Delia. You've done an amazing job of renovating the home's exterior and the landscaping."

"Thank you," she said. "It's all still a work in progress. You should see the back of the house." She shook her head. "No, actually, no one should see it in the state it's in. But it will be beautiful just like the front. And I'm hoping it will be done before this little one arrives. That's the goal, anyway."

"I'm sure it will." A thought occurred. "Delia, do you happen to have a dog?"

"Not currently," she said. "I'd love to, though. When we're ready for one, that is."

I reached down into the car and retrieved a card from my purse. "If you decide you're ready for a dog, this is a shelter I volunteer for. We're always getting dogs looking for forever homes."

Delia took the card and read it. "I'll do that." She looked up at me. "Thank you, Cassidy. Let me know if you can't find Ken. I'll track him down for you."

I drove away feeling a pang of guilt. I'd gone to Ken Venable's home looking for evidence to prove he'd been painting dogs or, at the least, had terrorized Spot and locked him into the area surrounding the pump site. Instead, I'd found a lovely home, a lovely wife, and nothing at all to show for him being the *Scooby-Doo* villain I'd believed he was.

This thought followed me all the way down that lovely drive to the road. From this direction, I could see that behind the two garbage bins that had been set out for pickup there was a large box of something shiny. As I got closer, I could see it was silver cans with their labels removed.

I pulled to a stop beside the bins and walked over to the box. Sure enough, there were a half dozen or so empty paint cans. Though the lids were sealed shut, there were enough drips on the cans to see that the paint inside had been white.

On impulse, I snatched up one of the cans and walked back to the car. Opening the trunk, I retrieved an empty bag from the stack I kept there to hold my groceries and deposited the can inside. I might have removed the paint from Spot, but if another dog turned up, we would at least have evidence taken from Ken's home to determine whether there was a match.

After securing the evidence in my trunk, I continued on to the Store More facility. With Ken nowhere to be seen, I drove to the unit our clinic rented to retrieve the items on Dr. Tyler's list. I'd almost finished loading my trunk when I heard someone approaching.

"You must be Cassidy Carter," Ken Venable called from his golf cart. "Delia told me you were looking for me."

I slammed the trunk closed just in time to keep him from seeing that I'd retrieved one of his empty paint cans. "Yes, that's me." I walked over to where he'd stopped the cart. "She shouldn't have bothered you, though."

"No bother at all," he said. "Isn't your grandfather the man who used to repair our mowers and such?"

"Yes," I said.

"We were sorry when he retired. He was good, you know? Really good. No one we've hired since has had that magic touch."

I nodded. "He's still repairing things, but from his retirement home out at Lake Somerville. And only for my mom and my abuela. They all live on the same property with the grandparents in the back and Mom and Dad down closer to the lake. It keeps him busy, and he likes that."

Ken chuckled. "That sounds about right. Men like that never change. They always have to stay busy. But then I get it."

Men like that never change. I pondered that for a moment. From what I saw, Ken Venable had changed.

Ken Venable looked nothing like my nightmare version. He wasn't as tall, although I had to admit in my memories I was looking up at him from the height and viewpoint of a kid. His dark hair was still long and curly like it had been back then, but there were strands of gray that, along with the wrinkles at the corners of his eyes, reminded me of how long it had been since I last saw him.

"So what was it that you wanted?" Ken asked.

The reason for my visit was to determine whether he'd painted Spot or at least trapped him at the pump site. Seeing his wife and his home, I was less certain. Seeing him, I really wasn't sure at all that he had anything to do with the crime.

Still, I had to come up with something to answer his question. So I went for the first thought I had.

"I'm looking for the owner of a rescue dog that was found across the road from your property. I wondered if you were missing a dog, but your wife said you aren't. So I guess I'm just wondering if you knew if anyone else who lives around here is."

I punctuated the statement with a serious look that belied the butterflies in my stomach. What was it about the Venables that made me so nervous?

"Are you talking about that dog that's all over social media?" At my nod, he continued. "Ursula down the road had a dog that looked a lot like him. She closed up shop and moved to Chappell Hill to live with her daughter just before Christmastime. I don't suppose he could have come back here looking for his home."

"He might have," I said. "Do you happen to have the contact information for her or her daughter?"

"I'd have to hunt for it. My crew used to do the landscaping work over there after her husband passed. Ursula, she was particular about her front yard looking just so, what with the shop she had."

"I remember that shop," I said. "She sold quilts and eggs."

Ken chuckled. "I never understood why, so one day when I was out there trimming hedges, she came out to bring me a glass of sweet tea, and I asked her. Do you know what she said?"

I shook my head. "What?"

"She said, 'I get them in the door with the yard eggs because the housewives know my chickens are the best layers in the county. But while they're here, I take my time ringing up their purchases, and what do you

THE BARK OF ZORRO

know but they will find a quilt they like or maybe see some fabric or thread they need. And of course, I've always got coffee in the coffeepot.'" Ken paused to smile. "That lady was the best salesperson I've ever met, bar none."

"I remember my abuela loved to buy her eggs from Ursula. Grandpa bought chickens for her thinking it might help their budget, but Ursula swore they laid inferior eggs." I paused. "I recall we ate a lot of fried chicken that summer."

"See, the ladies loved that place. Delia wants to buy it and reopen the quilting part of it. She draws the line at selling eggs. Something about not liking chickens because they're noisy or some such thing. Anyway, I'm considering it."

We were far off the topic, but I was getting to see a side of Ken Venable I had never thought existed. "I'm with her on the chickens," I admitted. "They kind of creep me out."

He chuckled. "I don't care one way or the other, but I'd do anything to make my wife happy."

We stood in silence for a moment before I decided it was time to go. "I need to get back to the clinic. I handed him my card. "Would you mind contacting me with the information on Ursula?"

"No problem." He paused. "And you know what? If that dog isn't Ursula's or if she can't care for him anymore, I'd be glad to give him a home."

"Thank you, Ken," I said. "I'll let you know."

I thought about the tattoo and wondered for a moment whether Spot would indeed turn out to belong to the old lady who lived—or used to live—down the road. It did seem possible. It still didn't explain how he ended up behind that locked fence, but it would explain why he was in the area.

That was a whole other mystery.

CHAPTER TWENTY

On my way back to the office, I debated whether to call Jason and tell him what I'd done. No, that kind of conversation was always better in person.

I still wasn't sure where Jason stood on his uncle's guilt or innocence in this matter. However, I'd been unexpectedly swayed in my opinion.

Now to hope the facts backed up my thoughts.

I arrived at the clinic a few minutes after hanging up with Nora. Parker met me in the parking lot to help unload the supplies I'd picked up. When he spied the paint can in my trunk, he shook his head.

"That didn't come from the clinic's storage unit. Hang on a minute."

He went into the clinic, then returned wearing a pair of gloves. Parker then retrieved the can and looked closely at the white paint on it.

"Where did you get this?" When I told him, his eyes widened. "That's very near where you found Spot."

"The Venables are renovating their home, and the front is painted this same color," I said. "So there could be a good reason for these cans being discarded there."

"Yes," Parker said, his blue eyes still studying the paint. "There could be all sorts of reasons that someone who lives across the street from where a painted dog was found would have that same paint in front of their house."

"When you say it like that. . ."

"It sounds suspicious?" he said. "That's because it is. You know that."

"I do," I said. "And honestly, I thought he'd be guilty. My recollection of the Venables does not include a well-tended home with beautiful landscaping and a pretty wife. It's pretty much the opposite."

"Things change and people change," Parker said, returning the empty can to the bag.

"Ken Venable sure seems to have changed," I told him as I took the can from Parker and returned it to my trunk.

His grin faded. "Okay, so this might be more complicated than it looks. If you don't think he did it, that is."

"I don't know," I said. "I kind of don't want it to be him. He even said he'd adopt Spot if he was available. I mean, that's nice, you know? Plus he's got this sweet wife and a baby on the way. It's surprising me how much I want Ken to not be our bad guy."

"Okay," Parker said, reaching around me to close the trunk. "I get all of that, but you've got to look at all the evidence and follow all the leads. That's what you always tell Mari and me when we're trying to puzzle out something."

"True."

Thursday, February 23

The next morning the headline on the front page was THE BARK OF ZORRO. Even better, Mollie's article had been picked up by the *Houston Chronicle* and the *Austin American Statesman*. Thank goodness she left out the specifics of the rescue and limited the details to that night's stormy weather and the pup's smear of paint when I found him.

After getting dressed and doing my hair and makeup, I logged on to my accounts while the coffee brewed. A topical search showed that hundreds of people were commenting on the article. I took screenshots of the pages of comments on the newspaper's website and then saved them to a file I called Bark of Zorro.

Because my name was mentioned several times in the story, I also found that my social media accounts were inundated with messages. Rather than try to read all of that in the few minutes remaining before I had to leave for work, I decided to save that activity for my lunch break.

Creating a few memes that mentioned calling the rescue with any information on the name of the creep who painted Spot would be a good idea. Maybe I'd come up with a contest.

My phone rang with a number I didn't recognize. I was tempted to ignore the call but also curious.

"Cassidy, this is Bryce Robinson, your real estate agent. The owner got back to me and has accepted the offer the two of you made on the properties. So," he said slowly, "congratulations."

"Oh wow," I managed. I'd gone over to Bryce's office on Saturday to sign paperwork making an offer even lower than the asking price. "Now what?"

"Since you're renting before you're closing, you'll forgo a rental deposit but will need to sign a month-to-month lease at the price we agreed upon."

"When do I need to do all of that?" I said, still trying to wrap my brain around what I was hearing.

Bryce chuckled. "How about now?"

"Oh my gosh, really?" I blurted out before tamping down my enthusiasm. It was Thursday, and Thursday mornings were always crazy because I had invoices to handle before the end of the day. "How long would all of that take?"

"I suggest giving yourself at least half an hour in my office. We'll have papers to sign and there are things to go over. It's not usual for a lease-to-purchase situation to come along, so we've got extra documents to complete."

I sighed. "Okay, this morning is out. Can I text you if I see that my afternoon is clearing up? If not, I can make time tomorrow."

Bryce laughed. "Tomorrow will be fine."

"But today would be better," I said, anxious to get the keys and move in.

I sent Mari a text. THE LOFT IS MINE!

She responded with smiley faces and party hats. Then she added, CONGRATULATIONS! HOUSEWARMING PARTY SOON!

My answer was swift. FIRST LET'S CONTEMPLATE THE MOVING PARTY. THEN WE CAN TALK ABOUT A HOUSEWARMING.

Ten minutes later, I was headed out the door when an idea popped into my head. Getting results with social media means striking while the topic is still hot. I hurried back to my computer to create a new email account, then put out a simple post on my social media:

Anyone who recognizes this dog or knows anything about how he came to have the letter Z painted on him, please contact me.

I added the email address to the post, then closed my laptop, grabbed my things, and whistled for Spot. After he had spent the weekend with me, I felt like it was time to bring him along to the clinic.

The staff often brought their dogs with them, so showing up with Spot was not surprising to anyone except Aggie, the office cat. The old girl hissed and spat at him for a good three minutes, then climbed off the reception desk to inspect the trespasser in her domain close up. Spot endured her sniffing and staring like a champ, his tail thumping against the desk as the pair came nose to nose.

"Looks like Aggie approves," Brianna said, reaching for a dog treat from the jar on the counter. "Good boy, Spot. She's cranky, but you've got to earn her friendship if you're going to hang around here."

She reached over the counter to dangle the treat within Spot's view. On cue, he jumped for it, catching the bone-shaped deliciousness neatly between his teeth.

"Come on, boy," I told Spot, gently tugging his leash. "You can enjoy that in my office. I've got lots to do this morning."

"You've got some messages," Brianna said. "When I got here, your voice mailbox was full. I also had some calls this morning from people who wanted to talk to 'that lady in the Zorro story.' I put those messages on your desk. Beware. . .there are a bunch of them."

I glanced at the clock behind Brianna's head. Thanks to the addition of Dr. Cameron, the clinic now opened at half past seven on Mondays while I didn't start my workday until nine.

"From the time stamps on the voice mails," Brianna continued, "it sounds like the calls began after the paper came out yesterday."

I led Spot to my office and dropped my things on my desk while the pup circled the dog bed that was nestled into the corner of the room. Twice he stopped to sniff the bed, then stare over at me as if he was horrified that another dog had napped here. All the while, he held a tight grip on his treat.

"Sorry, buddy," I told him. "That bed gets a lot of use. If you're going to hang out at Lone Star Vet Clinic, you're going to have to get used to sharing your space with other pets."

Between dogs belonging to the staff and the occasional rescue that joined us in the office, the bed had indeed been well loved. It never seemed to matter to the pups that it was washed regularly. Somehow they all seemed to know this was not theirs alone. Still, not one of them had turned down a chance to snuggle into the plush bed.

"Don't look at me like that," I said as Spot once again cast a glance in my direction. "I know. I forgot your bed. But we're all friends around here, so take it or leave it."

At that, the persnickety canine made one more turn around the bed, then settled down to enjoy his treat. I had just opened my laptop when the office phone buzzed.

"It's Maggie Jamison," Brianna said. "She asked to speak to you specifically."

Maggie was a longtime client of the clinic and a strong supporter of the Second Chance Ranch Dog Rescue. Before Mari was given the building on her aunt's property, Maggie loaned the rescue a building on her property and took a turn at watching over any rescues that might be on the site.

"Thanks, Brianna. Put her through," I said as I reached for pen and paper in case I needed to take notes on the conversation.

"Well, aren't you the little superstar?" the older lady said with a chuckle when I answered the phone. "That story in the paper was a doozy. I was just down at the Curl Up and Dye getting my roots touched up, and all the ladies were talking about it."

"Really?" I said, pleased that there was a buzz about the topic that went beyond social media. "What were they saying? Did any of them have any information on who the culprit might be or who Spot belongs to?"

"There was a lot of chatter, but I didn't hear much of anything with substance. To be fair, Essie Spooner had just left, and apparently she didn't understand that owning a Medicare card and wearing a miniskirt just don't mix."

"Now that's an image," I whispered as Maggie continued.

"Anyway, it was all just the usual beauty shop chitchat until Hetty Bertram blamed the dog painting on the Democrats and Lyla Reed countered with a bold statement that she was absolutely sure it was the Republicans behind it all. And while they both conceded it could have been the Independents, the conversation ended with the latest version of Elvis the dog barking and the two ladies fussing on the sidewalk outside with their hair still up in foil."

"Oh no."

"Oh yes, it did," Maggie said. "They only have themselves to blame. Everybody knows there are two things Miss Loretta will not allow in her beauty shop: arguing about politics and saying anything negative about Elvis."

Elvis, being the king of rock and roll, and not any one of the many dogs that Miss Loretta has owned with the same name. She'd complain about whichever one was currently living with her as if he—or she—was an old troublesome roommate instead of a canine companion.

As fond as Miss Loretta was of the singer, she was also fond of keeping her rules. Thus, I could imagine how swiftly the arguing ladies were sent outside, likely with Elvis IV—or was it Elvis V?—yipping at them all the way to the door. Miss Loretta trained all her dogs to interrupt an argument with a loud bark fest until she gave them the signal to hush.

"It all ended well, though," Maggie continued. "Hetty and Lyla made peace, and by the time they came back in, they'd decided it could have been just about anyone who did that awful thing to your Spot."

"Well, that's good."

"It was. Until Hetty said it might have been aliens. That's where Lyla's opinion differed, and they were off again. This time Miss Loretta just turned up the music and let 'Jailhouse Rock' drown out the argument."

"Unfortunately, at this point I've come to the same conclusion as Hetty and Lyla."

"Surely not the aliens," Maggie said.

"No, sorry, I mean that it could be anyone at this point. I would love to narrow it down to just one person." I looked over at the blinking light on my phone indicating voice mails and the stack of messages Brianna had taken this morning. "Or just a half dozen suspects," I added with a sigh.

"Well, I might be able to help a little with that," Maggie said. "As you can imagine, I had that story about poor Spot on my mind as I drove home a little while ago. Tell me again what kind of paint was on that poor dog and what it looked like."

"Plain old white paint," I told her. "At least that's what I assumed it was before I cleaned it off of him. It had dried and smeared the letter, but there was definitely a Z that you could make out up close on his side."

"And it was house paint," she said. "Not fancy artist paint?"

I thought a moment. "Honestly, I don't know the difference. So, it could be either one, I suppose. Why?"

"Well," Maggie said slowly, "I saw the darndest thing when I was pulling into my driveway just now."

"Okay," I said, beginning to get impatient. "What did you see?"

"There was a fellow practically in the road. He had one of those artist easels set up right there on the edge of the asphalt. I almost ran right into him. You know there's that curve where that record producer fellow's property ends, and I didn't see him until it was nearly too late to swerve. We could have both died, Cassidy."

I said the first thing that came to mind. "I'm glad everything turned out all right. Did you speak to the painter?"

"You better believe I did," Maggie said. "Once I picked him up out of the ditch, that is. And before you ask, he jumped out of my way and landed wrong on one foot and just flat went down right there on the side of the road. From there, he just rolled into the ditch. It's a steep incline over there, and someone had left some construction supplies from that blasted never-ending house Sticks is building, so he needed some help getting out. I think he might have sprained something."

"So, Maggie?" I said, trying hard to keep the irritation out of my voice. "What does all of this have to do with the paint on Spot? Other than the fact you almost killed a painter who was standing on the edge of the road."

"I didn't almost kill him," she protested. "I just scared him a little, but honestly, anybody who thinks it's okay to paint practically in the middle of the road like that. . . I mean, he actually claimed that since he put up one of those orange cones, that I should have. . ." Maggie sighed. "Sorry, I get carried away. Anyway, after I got Henry out of the ditch—that's his name, Henry Hughes—and I fed him a slice of pie and a cup of coffee, I found out that Henry has been hired by that record producer fellow across the way to do some painting for him."

"What kind of painting?"

"That's where Henry got a little squirrelly. All he would say is Mr. Styler wanted to make a big splash with an album cover and something special for this band he's working with. You'll never guess the name of the band, Cassidy."

"You'd better tell me, then," I said.

"The name of the band is Zed."

After a few more minutes of conversation, mostly about Maggie's trip to Amarillo to see her sister, we hung up. I sat back and let out a long breath. Then I dialed Jason's number and left a message about Maggie, the painter, and Zed when the call went to voice mail.

Before I could put my phone down, it rang again.

I glanced down to see my real estate agent's name on the screen. "Bryce," I said, "what's wrong?"

"There's nothing wrong," he said. "But something has come up, and I'm going to need you to wait until Monday. Does nine o'clock work for you?"

"Sure," I said, trying not to be disappointed that I had to wait so long. "See you then."

"And Cassidy?" he said.

"Yes?"

"Congratulations."

I hung up smiling. Monday morning at nine o'clock I'd be a homeowner. Or, rather, a loft owner.

Tears shimmered as I closed my eyes right then and sent up a prayer of thanks. "As for me and my house, we will serve the Lord," I said. "Oh Father, thank You."

CHAPTER TWENTY-ONE

Monday, February 27

At ten minutes after nine this morning, I became a homeowner—well, an almost owner. I asked Mari to go with me, and she beamed as I signed paper after paper. Finally, the stack of to-be-executed documents emptied and there was nothing else I had to autograph.

"That's it," Bryce said as he reached into the file folder and pulled out a manila envelope. "Here are the keys as well as some information the owner thought you might need."

"Who is the owner?" Mari asked. "Or *was*, rather. I only saw a trust listed."

Bryce shrugged. "A trust owns the property. The signature on the paperwork will be done by the trustee of the trust. If I remember right, that's a local bank trustee."

"Really?" I gave Mari a sideways look, then returned my attention to Bryce. "That's kind of weird, isn't it?"

"We get this occasionally. There's nothing illegal or weird about it. It's just an owner who has chosen to put assets into a trust for tax purposes or possibly has become the beneficiary of a trust that was set up by someone else."

"So if I call the bank, I can speak to the trustee of this trust and ask questions?"

"You can try, but I can't guarantee that he or she will speak to you." Bryce let out a long breath as he gathered up the papers. "All I know is either the trustee or the owner was eager to get this deal done, and that's always good for my buyers."

Mari's eyes narrowed. "Is he hiding something?"

"You mean about the building?" Bryce asked. "Honestly, I'm always skeptical when an owner wants to offload a property quickly. However, in this case, I doubt it. The property has been owned by the trust for several decades, so they'll make a profit over the price they paid to purchase it back then. Also, and most important, the inspection came out great. The terms are excellent, and he's working with you to do the lease until the building can close so you can move in now. That's a buyer's dream deal."

"And you're right about the inspection. Also, both my dad and my grandfather went over the place and gave their approval." I let out a long breath. "I feel like I'm in a dream."

"Well, it's all very real." Bryce paused as his expression went serious. "However, if you're not sure, then just say so. You do not have to sign the papers today."

"No," I said. "I'm sure. The first time I stepped inside the loft, it felt like the home I've been praying for."

Bryce nodded, then shook my hand. "Then congratulations. It's your home."

"It's my home," I echoed as I tucked the folder with the transaction paperwork and the envelope from the owner into my bag. Then I accepted the keys from Bryce and held them to my chest.

"Okay, I guess that's it, then."

Bryce nodded. "All the utilities will transfer to your name when the property is actually sold. In the meantime, they will be paid by the trust. Look for the information on that in your email inbox in a few hours."

"Thank you for handling that," I told Bryce. "I guess I'm all set."

Bryce bid us goodbye, and then I walked toward the door with Mari. My best friend hugged me, then stepped back to offer a broad grin. "I have a little housewarming gift for you."

"Mari! I told you we weren't going to think about a housewarming until I've moved in. And you absolutely did not have to get me a gift."

She retrieved a box from her purse and handed it to me. Inside was a beautiful silver key chain with a simple engraving: Joshua 24:15. The same verse I'd been praying.

Tears shimmered as I hugged Mari. "As for me and my house, we will serve the Lord," I said. "Oh honey, thank you."

"You're welcome," she said. "Now let's go see your new loft."

We walked the short distance to the Mercer Building. Nora's future restaurant sat dark and silent, but it wouldn't always be that way.

I slid the key into the lock and turned it. The door opened with a click. "Mari," I said under my breath. "I can't believe this is mine."

"Believe it," she said. "Now let's go look around. I don't have to be at work for another twenty minutes. And since you only live five minutes from work, I've got time."

We walked over every inch of my loft, chattering and making notes about furniture placement and coverings for the three floor-to-ceiling windows. Then Mari grinned and raised one of the windows and stepped outside onto the iron balcony. Of course, I followed.

"Cassidy, this is the coolest place ever," she said. "I'm so happy for you."

I rested my elbows on the black iron railing and looked out over the downtown buildings and the street below. "It really is, isn't it?"

Mari slid me a sideways look. "We certainly prayed for a home for you for a while. Now about that husband?"

My phone rang. "Too bad we can't talk about that one," I said, rolling my eyes as I retrieved my cell from my purse.

Jason. "I need to take this."

"Jason?" She gave me a knowing look. "We'll definitely talk later. In the meantime, I'll get started organizing a moving party for Saturday. Now I've got to get back to work. The Woof Gang will be giving Parker a hard time by now. He's way too soft with some of those furry scoundrels."

"Thank you," I called as she hurried to the exit, then disappeared down the stairs. Then I answered the phone.

"Cassidy," the game warden said. "I've got some bad news. A call just came in from LaGrange. There's been an incident with a dog. It's Suzy."

My heart sunk as I thought of the high-energy dog. It was easy to imagine her running right into danger. "Oh Jason."

I hurried down the stairs to see if I could catch Mari before she disappeared around the corner. Unfortunately, I was too late.

"Where is Suzy?" I demanded, my focus returning to the rescue dog. "Is her new family with her? She just went home with the Bakers on Saturday."

"She's fine, and she's back in LaGrange. The rest I'll answer on the way." He paused. "If you'd agree to ride along with me. I mean, if you have to work or whatever, then that's okay. But it would help if you'd be there. But with the cameras and all, if you want to pass, I get it."

"I'm off today, actually." I paused. "And we already talked about the cameras. I'm fine with them. Where can I meet you?"

"Tell me where you are, and I'll pick you up," he said.

I gave him the address of the Mercer Building. "I'll meet you on the sidewalk out front."

"Thank you," he said. "My ETA is four minutes."

The familiar green truck pulled up in three. Behind it was a black SUV with darkened windows. I jumped in and buckled my seat belt.

"I assume your entourage is following us."

"Yes. I convinced them we wouldn't say anything worth filming using a cameraman. However, we do have a couple of cameras in the truck, as you can see. If you'd like to say hello to Camille or the sound crew, feel free."

I took note of the three small portable video cameras attached to the visors and rearview mirror. "Hello Camille."

"Cassidy," she said, her voice a purr. "So glad to see you. And I mean that literally. You look fabulous."

Okay, weird.

I gave Jason a look. "Thank you."

"You two get back to discussing this case," Camille said. "Just act like we're not here."

Jason rolled his eyes. I grinned.

"About Suzy. Thank you for doing this," Jason said. "You've probably got better things to do on your day off, but you're the only one who saw the paint on Spot. It'll be helpful if you can determine if this is the same."

"I wouldn't miss this," I told him. "After she was rescued, I watched Suzy go from a street dog to a sweet girl who was ready for a forever home. I hope she's going to be okay. Oh, and the family! They've only just brought her home, so this must be terrible for them."

"The family is upset, of course, but they're fine otherwise," Jason said as he signaled to merge onto Highway 290. "They weren't involved. Last night Suzy went missing from their yard. After a search, their vet reported her missing to the APB. They found her, but that's just the beginning of the story."

"No, he put out an APB. It's a communication notice, not a group, Jason," a familiar voice corrected from the back seat. "Hey, Cass!"

I swiveled around to see that Jason had another passenger. His brother. "Dr. Cameron?"

Jason slid me a sideways look. "He offered to join us. Camille told him he looks good on camera too."

"Hey now, I do. Don't I, Camille?"

"Stop talking to the camera, Cameron," she said through the speaker. "Remember what I told you? No looking at or talking to the camera."

"Right." He paused. "So, okay, where was I? Right. It was either that or stay behind and finish my banana pudding pancakes alone," he said with a shrug.

"And pay the bill," Jason quipped as he changed lanes, then accelerated to pass slow-moving traffic.

"Hey now," Dr. Cameron said. "To be fair, it was your turn."

"Hold on," I said, incredulous. "You two have breakfast together? I thought you. . ." I searched for the right word.

"Didn't like each other?" Dr. Cameron supplied with a twinkle in his eye. "We don't. We argue all the time. He's bullheaded, irritating, and beats me at golf even though he hates the game. He's younger, taller, and that stupid uniform has ladies fawning all over him when we are out together."

"And you talk too much," Jason said. "Which is why you're so lousy at golf."

"He's not wrong about the golf," Dr. Cameron said with a shrug. "You're probably wondering why we bother spending time together if we're so different."

No way I was going to answer that. Instead, I slid a covert glance at Jason, whose attention seemed to be strictly on the road ahead.

"Because we're family," Jason supplied.

Dr. Cameron nodded. "That's it exactly. He's my brother, and I love him. And truthfully, he's not bad. In small doses, anyway. Sometimes I actually like hanging out with him." He paused. "And I'm proud of him for what he's done with himself."

Jason looked into the rearview mirror. The men shared a grin with matching smiles they must have inherited from their father. "Ditto, dude," was his brief response.

The remainder of the drive to LaGrange consisted of bantering between the brothers—with Dr. Cameron doing most of the talking. Knowing I was being watched and heard by a car full of strangers made me extremely reluctant to say anything.

When we turned into the parking lot of a vet clinic, I realized I had not yet been told the rest of the story about Suzy.

"Jason, what's the full story with Suzy? I feel like we've been talking about everything but her accident," I said.

"That would be on purpose," Dr. Cameron said. "Jason figured it would be better for you not to have to worry about Suzy all the way here. He told me to keep the conversation going."

"Which he has no trouble doing, I'd like to point out," Jason said with a grin.

"You're welcome," the elder Saye brother said.

Jason parked the truck, then looked over at me. "Okay, Cassidy, here's the full story. Suzy didn't have an accident. She had an *incident*."

"Meaning?" I asked.

"Meaning she shouldn't have been where she was found. There's no explanation for it."

"Oh," came out on a rush of breath. "And where was she found?"

He glanced over at Dr. Cameron, then back at me. "Downtown Brenham on the square at the gazebo."

"How did she get forty miles away from her new home? Suzy has lots of energy, but there's no way she crossed that distance on her own."

"We agree," Dr. Cameron said, releasing his seat belt. "Which is why the game warden is on the case. Well, that and. . .well, you tell her, Jason."

Jason blew out a long breath. "When she was found, there was a letter Z painted on her in white paint."

My phone rang. I looked down to see it was the clinic calling. "I should probably get this."

Before I could say hello, Mari's voice came out in a rush of words. "There's been another painted dog incident in Brenham."

CHAPTER TWENTY-TWO

M ari, I'm with Jason and Dr. Cameron. I'm going to put you on speaker so you can tell them what you just told me."

"Okay," Mari said. "This morning we got a Jack Russell terrier with a Z painted on the side. The owner blames her neighbor." She repeated the details of the incident. "So the owner called the cops. The officer just left. He thinks that it's just a prank. He actually blamed the newspaper article. In his opinion, the publicity from the article has caused copycat incidents."

I looked at Jason. "That's not the first time I've heard that opinion. And remember Suzy?"

"Our crazy girl who got adopted?" she asked.

"Yes. I'm with Jason and Dr. Cameron in LaGrange. She was found in Brenham in the same condition."

"She's fast, but no way could she make it to Brenham, don't you think?" Mari offered.

"The working theory is someone took her from the Baker family's yard and transported her there," Jason said. "Is the terrier still at your clinic?"

"She is."

"Can you keep her there until I can stop by and examine her? Have you cleaned off the paint?"

"No," Mari said. "Dr. Tyler said we shouldn't do anything until Cassidy could come in and see if the letter she saw on Spot looks like the one on Muffin. That's the dog's name."

"Okay, I'll have her at the clinic in an hour. We'll head that way once we leave here." He looked up at me. "If that's okay with you, Cassidy."

"Of course," I said.

We said our goodbyes, and then I returned my phone to my bag. "That's two incidents in one night. This is escalating."

"I don't like that at all," Dr. Cameron said. "Jason, do you think these are pranks, or are they something more?"

Jason removed the keys from the ignition and reached for his hat. "I don't know yet, but either way, I don't like it."

Once the film crew climbed out of the vehicle, I followed Jason into the small veterinarian clinic. Apparently Camille had called ahead to get permission to film, because there were already signs up warning of cameras.

We were quickly ushered into the back room where the dogs were kenneled. There I immediately spied Suzy. She was turning circles in her kennel and yipping furiously, likely her version of "Get me out of here!"

The vet tech opened the kennel door, and Suzy leaped out into my arms. Between nuzzling my neck and trying to lick my face, she was squirming so much that it was difficult to examine her. Finally, I sat down on the floor and held her against me.

"All right, Suzy," I told her. "Since you can't tell me about your adventure in Brenham, we're going to have to examine you and try to figure it out. All you need to do is be still for a minute."

Of course she ignored the request. Still, I was able to hold her so that Jason could get photos and a hair sample of the painted Z. Then I turned her around to scratch her behind the ear so I could see her side. Spot's fur had been matted with smeared paint while Suzy's lettering was clear and precise.

"Well?" Jason asked me as he tucked the evidence bag with the hair sample into his pocket.

"The paint looks the same," I told him. "That much I can say with no doubt, but it's impossible to tell whether this was done by the same person. Who found her?"

"Some skateboarder," Jason said. "I'd have to check for a name."

"Ben Tanner?" I asked.

He thought a moment. "That actually sounds right, but again, I would have to confirm that."

"Right. Well, Ben is the person who I had thought might end up with Suzy."

"Why?" Jason asked.

I shrugged as Suzy began to wiggle in my arms. "Her high energy and his skateboarding seemed like a good fit. He came over to the rescue a couple of times and played with her."

"Why didn't he take her?" Dr. Cameron asked.

"He submitted an application but wasn't chosen," I said. "We decided Suzy would be better suited to a family home with a yard and kids to play with. Ben is a single guy with a business designing and building skateboards."

Once Jason and I had our turns with Suzy, Dr. Cameron picked her up to check her over. He pronounced her fit and unaffected by whatever had taken place while she was away from her family.

"Okay, so we've got the family reunion to film," Camille announced. "They've given permission and will be waiting outside when you drive up. I'm thinking Cassidy will hand the dog over with Jason sort of following a step behind."

"What about me?" Dr. Cameron said.

"Right." Camille smiled. "We're saving your part for Brenham, okay?" Then she turned back to Jason and me. "I'd like to film this more than once if you don't mind. Then we can get on the road to Brenham and do this all over again with the other dog."

All I wanted to do was to take the sweet pup home and reunite her with the boys who'd been missing her. Jason seemed to know what I was thinking.

He gave Camille his most gentlemanly smile along with a tip of his hat. Then he helped me into his truck and closed the door.

The crew scrambled to climb into their vehicle before Jason headed away from the clinic. Suzy settled into my lap for the ride to her new forever home.

"I'm going to guess you aren't trying to ditch us but rather just forgot that we drive away at the same time," Camille said through the speakers.

"Sorry, ma'am," he said. "I figured you'd know where I was going. We'll be there in just a minute. Do you want to call the family, or should I?"

"It's all arranged. Just remember what we planned."

Jason slid me a sideways glance and shook his head. When we pulled into the driveway, three boys came running toward us. Suzy practically went through the window trying to get to her people.

I climbed out with the wiggling pup in my arms and then knelt down to let her run to the boys. The oldest of the quartet gathered her into his arms and walked into the fenced yard, followed closely by his siblings. Jason strolled over to the parents and spoke to them.

"Cute kids," Dr. Cameron said. "I'm glad it all turned out okay, but I sure wish that dog could talk so she could tell us how she got to Brenham."

"Me too," I said.

Jason handed them his business card and returned to the truck. "They don't have a clue how she ended up in Brenham. I told them I would keep them informed."

A few minutes later, we were back in the truck headed to Brenham. Then Jason glanced over at me.

"I appreciate the message you left me," he said. "I'll be following up on your tip."

I nodded. "Good," was all I said. I didn't add that I'd be following up on it as well.

We rode back in silence until Dr. Cameron spoke up. "Hey Jason, you and I are invited to a party on Saturday."

Jason shook his head. "Not interested."

Dr. Cameron chuckled. "I think you will be when you find out the details."

Again he shook his head. "Nope."

"He's not much of a party guy," Dr. Cameron said. "In college, he'd be the one back at his dorm studying while I was out having a good time."

"And your grades showed it," Jason said.

"He's not wrong," Dr. Cameron told me. "Before I changed my ways, I was not the wonderful man you see before you."

Jason snorted but said nothing.

"Anyway," Dr. Cameron continued, "the party."

"No party," Jason muttered.

"The party," Dr. Cameron said, ignoring his brother, "starts at nine on Saturday morning. Plan to stay all day. Drinks and food provided by Lone Star Vet Clinic. Muscles and pickup trucks or trailers appreciated."

I frowned. "What kind of party is that?"

Dr. Cameron laughed. "You should know, Cass. It's a moving party. For you."

Jason's brows rose. "You didn't tell me you closed on the loft." He slapped his forehead with his hand. "I'm sorry. I get kind of hyper-focused when I'm working on a case."

"Where is your new place?" Dr. Cameron asked.

"It's downtown, so not far from the clinic. Mari said she would organize a moving party. I didn't expect an actual party," I said. "And not so quick. I just got my keys an hour ago."

"That's cool," Dr. Cameron said. "Which building?"

"The top floor of the Mercer Building," I told him. "My friend Nora Hernandez will be opening a farm-to-table restaurant downstairs called Simply Eat. You'd remember Nora. She used to be our pet food sales rep."

"Oh sure, I remember her," Dr. Cameron said. "I liked Nora a lot. She used to bring us breakfast at the clinic where I worked. Sometimes she would prank me, though."

With the veterinarian still telling stories about Nora and her antics, we pulled into the parking lot of Lone Star Vet Clinic a few minutes later. I released my seat belt and snatched up my bag before opening the door to climb out. Dr. Cameron marched ahead toward the door, but Jason lagged a step behind me.

The camera crew, now wise to Jason's swift moves, had already jumped into position behind us and was filming when we opened the door. The only occupant of the waiting room was a young woman of about thirty wearing yoga pants, an oversized T-shirt, and an angry expression that didn't change when she spied the camera crew. She had to be the terrier's owner.

I scooted past without making eye contact and hurried toward the kennel room. Though the space was generally filled with at least a few barking pups, only the terrier was in residence today.

"The paint has dried on Muffin," Mari said as she retrieved the dog from her kennel. "So I was able to get a hair sample for you, Jason. Kelly Miller has filed a police report. The officer in charge said he would copy you on it since you've got an ongoing investigation."

Jason nodded. "Thank you. Do you have anything to add to the report?"

"Just that the dog seemed fine when she came in. She didn't seem to be bothered by the paint. However, Mrs. Miller is furious. She's blaming her neighbors. Apparently Muffin tends to get out of the fence and get into mischief."

"Okay," he said. "I'll examine the dog and take photos first. Then I'll go speak to the owner and get her side of the story."

I stood back and watched as Jason efficiently did his work. Then he handed the dog back to Mari and left the kennel room. With Jason went his entourage, leaving Mari and me alone.

"Which neighbors specifically is she blaming?" I asked Mari.

Mari's brows rose. "Well, she lives next door to Sticks Styler's recording studio and, in her words, his 'never-ending construction zone.'"

"Interesting."

"So," Mari said, placing Muffin back into a kennel, "you've had a busy morning since I left you."

"About that," I said. "Jason called just as you were leaving. I tried to catch you, but you drove off too fast."

"So do tell," Mari said. "And I mean that. I want all the details."

CHAPTER TWENTY-THREE

I finished catching Mari up on my morning just as Dr. Cameron walked into the kennel room. "Where's our painted pup?" he asked. "I'd like a look at her before she goes home."

Mari opened the kennel and handed the dog to the vet. "Do you need me to assist, Dr. Cameron?"

"No need," he said as he headed for an exam room with Muffin in his arms.

Mari waited until we were alone to turn back to me. "Okay, so Jason. Still in the friend zone?"

"Well. . ."

Mari's attention went from me to a spot behind me. I turned to see that Jason was now standing in the door. "To be continued."

"Where's the dog?" he asked.

"Dr. Cameron is examining her. How's Mrs. Miller?" Mari asked. "She was super angry when she brought Muffin in."

"Cut," Camille called. "We need better lighting in here. Can we take this from the top after I get some spots in place?"

Jason ignored her. "Mrs. Miller is still angry. And she believes she knows who did it."

"Sticks Styler," Mari supplied. "She mentioned that when I was doing intake."

"And you ladies know this man." A statement, not a question.

"We do," I said. "Mari's aunt is the country singer Trina Potter. Sticks is her record producer. He moved to Brenham to open a satellite studio here so she could record close to home instead of flying to Nashville."

"Cut," Camille called again. "Cassidy, your friend's aunt is Trina Potter? Someone get a spot on her. Mari is your name?"

"Camille," Jason said evenly, "please let me do my job. There are plenty of other things you can film. What about a B-reel of the clinic?"

She let out a long breath, then nodded. "Sure. Okay. There isn't much going on in here, anyway. But don't try to leave without us."

Once they were gone, Jason continued with his questions. "In your opinion, is Styler capable of doing something like this?" Jason asked us.

Mari seemed to consider the question. Then she shrugged. "My instinct says no because he's adopted Honey, one of our rescues, and seems to be treating her very well, so he's definitely a dog lover. But honestly I cannot say for sure."

"Jason," I said, "don't forget he had that painter working for him. The one Maggie Jamison told me about. I mentioned him in the voice mail I left for you. I think we need to consider Henry Hughes as a possible suspect too."

He gave me a terse nod. "Definitely. I've been trying to track down the Hughes fellow, but I think his boss isn't keen on me finding him. And as for Maggie Jamison, I haven't ruled her out."

"Why her?" I asked, surprised.

"She had opportunity. And if the dog was getting on Styler's place, she might also have been bothering Jamison or her animals," Jason said. "Sometimes the person who calls in a tip is trying to deflect from their crimes."

Dr. Cameron came back in holding Muffin. "She's ready to go."

Mari took the wiggling dog. "I'll just go see if Mrs. Miller wants me to try to get this paint off."

"Dr. Kristin recommends olive oil," I told her.

"I'll come with you," Dr. Cameron said, following Mari out of the room.

Now that we were alone, I turned my attention to Jason. "Maggie didn't do this."

"You seem certain of this."

"I am. She may have had proximity, and I'll even allow that she might have had motive. But of all the ways she could have expressed her displeasure at having that dog on her property, why paint a *Z* on her? And if we're looking to tie the three instances together, there's no way she could be associated with Spot or Suzy. At least no way I can figure."

Jason leaned against the doorframe. He appeared to be deep in thought. Finally, he nodded. "I see your point. However, I'm not ruling her out just yet. I still need to speak with her."

"I'll be happy to go with you," I said.

He studied me for a minute. "I think I can handle it."

"Right, okay." I paused. "Speaking of suspects, did you ever speak with Ken Venable?"

His expression hardened. "Cassidy, I'm not going to tell you about every potential suspect I have or have not yet spoken to. That's not how this works."

So we were back to that again. My guess was he had not. That just made me want to drive over and do it myself.

"Right. Of course," I said. "Sticks is kind of hard to get a hold of. If you have any problem with that, let me know."

"I will, and hey, Cassidy, congratulations on your new home."

I upped my smile, then adjusted my bag on my shoulder. "Thank you."

I waited to see if Jason would say anything else. Instead, he just stood there.

Okay. Time to leave.

I nodded toward the door. "So anyway, I guess I'll just go and enjoy the rest of my day off. Good luck with the investigation."

I tried to press past him, but he stopped me. "Cassidy," he said softly, "the cameras aren't here right now."

I looked up at him and smiled. And this time I kissed him first. He didn't seem to mind.

Reluctantly, I stepped out into the hall a few minutes later. As I did, I realized two things. First, my car was over at the real estate office. And second, the gazebo where Suzy was found was on the way to my car.

As I made my way down the hall toward the lobby, I saw that Mari was deep in conversation with Mrs. Miller. Knowing Mari, she'd be doing her own investigating about now and would report back to me if she discovered anything new in regard to Muffin's paint job.

"Where's the film crew?" I asked.

"Out front," she said.

"See you tomorrow," Brianna called from the desk. I waved in return and stepped out into the midday sunshine.

Soon it would be March, and with March came spring and the bluebonnets. Although autumn was my favorite time of year, there was something about spying the state flower—be it a small clump on a roadside ditch or a field that stretched to the horizon—that reached me to the core. Silly, I know, but we Texans are awfully proud of our state and our bluebonnets.

I'd just reached the edge of the parking lot when Jason pulled his truck up beside me and lowered the window. He'd donned the ever-present aviator shades and was watching me intently. "Need a ride?"

"Depends on where we're going," I said.

A grin rose, reminding me why I first called him Jason the Gorgeous Game Warden. "I thought I'd let you choose. Either I can take you to your car or we can skip that and go straight to the gazebo. I figure that's where you'll end up either way."

I stifled a laugh. "Gazebo. But I can walk. It's just over there."

He nodded to the passenger side. "Get in."

I walked behind the truck and around to the other side. After climbing in, I closed the door, tossed my bag on the floor, and secured my seat belt. I was beginning to get used to this.

"What are you grinning for?" Jason said, giving me a look.

I swiveled to face him. "Like I said, it's a beautiful day."

Jason looked at me over the rims of his aviators for a long moment. "Beautiful indeed," he said on an exhale of breath.

I shouldn't have felt flustered, but I did. Something about kissing this man did that to me.

A few minutes later, Jason parked, and we walked toward the gazebo with the crew. The six-sided structure had a wooden railing that filled the space on five sides, leaving the sixth side open with wide steps leading into it. Beneath the roof, the center of the gazebo was painted the same pale blue that older homes in town painted their porch ceilings.

"Let me go first," he said.

I decided not to argue. Instead, I followed him as he made his way toward the spot where Suzy was found. Since this was a public space, and also painted white, it was unlikely there would be much evidence to gather.

Jason walked up the steps and into the gazebo while I glanced around. It was easier to ignore the camera folks out here in the open. Still, we seemed to be getting some attention from passersby.

I focused my mind on the issue at hand: finding clues as to what happened to that sweet dog. Suzy might have been found here, but it was more likely she'd run up into the structure rather than been left there. Because if I knew anything about that high-energy pup, she never stayed where anyone put her.

Instead of joining Jason, I walked around the gazebo to the side opposite the courthouse. If anyone wanted to drop off a dog, they'd do it in the least visible spot, right? And with cameras all over the courthouse, the place least visible to cameras was right here.

I stopped and glanced around. The only flaw in my theory was the streetlight I was now staring at just a few yards away. Even if the person escaped the view of the courthouse cameras, he or she would be highly visible to anyone who might be in the vicinity.

So much for that theory.

Jason leaned over the rail of the gazebo. "Did you find anything?"

I shook my head. "Did you?"

"Nothing."

"Oh well," I said. "It was worth a try."

Jason looked to be about to say something when his phone rang. Without looking away, Jason answered. "Game warden." A pause while he listened to the caller then, "Yeah. On my way."

He tucked his phone into his pocket. Before he could speak, I said, "Go handle whatever that's about. My car isn't far from here. And it really is a beautiful day. And take your entourage with you."

"If you're sure," he said with a chuckle.

"Oh, believe me. I am."

CHAPTER TWENTY-FOUR

I watched Jason and the film crew disappear in the direction of the parking lot, then turned back toward the gazebo. In my mind, I ran through what I knew about the discovery of Suzy in the gazebo and realized it wasn't much.

Then something occurred to me, and I retrieved my phone. Officer Todd Dennison picked up on the second ring. Not only was he a police officer here in Brenham, but he was also a great supporter of the rescue and had personally adopted one of our pups as his own.

"Todd, this is Cassidy with Second Chance Ranch. I'm wondering if you'd have a minute to check on something for me. No hurry on it if you're busy."

"Sure, Cassidy," he said. "Tell me what you need, and I'll check on it when I get a minute."

"I'm looking into an issue with of one of our former rescue dogs. I was told that Ben Tanner found her at the gazebo. I wonder if you could provide more information on that. Specifically I'm looking for the time that Ben called in the report and whatever statement he gave. Also, if there's any video taken during that time by the courthouse cameras or any of the businesses that are in view of the gazebo, I'd love to know about that."

"No problem," Todd said. "How about I text you a copy of the report? If we got video, I can email a link. What's your preferred email address?"

"That would be perfect." I gave him my personal email address. "Thank you, Todd."

I hung up and tucked my phone away, then began a careful walk around the gazebo. With no idea of what I was looking for, I looked for anything that might be out of place.

Unfortunately, all I found were a few candy wrappers and a scrap of sandpaper. I tossed the wrappers into the trash receptacle and then tucked the sandpaper into my bag. It probably had no value to the investigation, but it did seem out of place on a courthouse lawn.

When I reached the stairs, I climbed up into the gazebo and looked all around. Nothing here either. I climbed back down and sat on the steps, then retrieved my phone.

Ben Tanner was easy to find. I went online and looked up the number for Tanner Designs, then called the number. While I waited for an answer, I scrolled through their website that featured high-end skateboard designs.

"Tanner Designs," a male voice said.

I moved the phone closer to my ear. "This is Cassidy Carter. I'm looking for Ben Tanner."

"Cassidy? With the pet rescue?"

"Yes, that's me. Is this Ben?"

"It is." He paused, and I could hear the sound of tires on gravel. Or perhaps his skateboard on a road. "What's up?"

"Do you have some time to spare today? I'd like to talk to you about finding Suzy."

More road noise. Then the sound stopped abruptly. "Would you happen to be at the gazebo right now?"

"Yes." I glanced around the perimeter and spied someone waving at me across the street. I returned the wave.

"I'm grabbing an orange soda. Want anything?"

I realized I hadn't eaten since breakfast early that morning. And even then, with the closing looming, I'd only picked at a slice of toast.

"Sure, an orange soda would be great."

A few minutes later, Ben crossed the street wearing a backpack with a skateboard attached to it and carrying a bottle of orange soda in each hand. We exchanged greetings as he sat the bottles on the step next to me.

Then he slung his backpack off his shoulder and lowered it to the ground at his feet.

Ben's shaggy hair, baggy jeans, and skateboard-themed T-shirt belied the fact that he was a business owner at the age of twenty-three. To me, he looked like a twenty-first-century Shaggy from the *Scooby-Doo* cartoons.

Ben grinned as he retrieved a bottle opener from his backpack and opened both our drinks. "I guess you're thinking it was quite a coincidence that I'm the one who found Suzy."

He'd never complained about coming in second to a family with kids and a yard. Now I wondered how he felt about losing out on the rescue dog.

"I was surprised," I admitted. "But I figured you of all people would recognize her if you saw her. Would you mind telling me how you happened to find her?"

Ben leaned back against the step behind him and rested one elbow there. Then he took a long drink of orange soda. Finally, he placed the bottle beside him.

"I do some night skating sometimes," he said. "I'm always testing out new gear, and it's a whole lot easier to get an idea of how fast something will go if there are no cars on the road."

"What were you testing when you saw Suzy?"

One sandy brow lifted. "Why?"

"Just curious."

"Okay, well, nothing actually. I'd run into a snag on a design I'm doing for a skate pro. He's got requirements that I'm having trouble getting to work. I'd been at it awhile and kept hitting dead ends. So, I grabbed my gear and headed out to clear my head."

"On your skateboard?"

"Yeah." He took another drink, this time studying the bottle rather than returning it to its place on the step. "I'd been trying out some tricks over at the parking lot on Commerce. When I got tired of that, I decided to do a loop around the courthouse. They have cameras, so sometimes it's fun to do a loop and wave at the folks."

"And you were doing the loop when you saw Suzy?"

"I heard her first," he said. "Usually I've got in my ear pods, but I wasn't in the mood for music. I heard a dog. It sounded excited."

"Excited how? Angry, scared, hurt?"

"None of those," he said. "More like it was yipping at another dog. Not a real bark. More like a growling noise. Anyway, I thought it was odd that there would be dogs out here at that time of night. And I'm not too fond of skating past dogs that might chase me. So, I put my board in my backpack and figured I would just walk quietly past them and be on my way."

"But?"

"But when I got to a place where I could see where the noise was coming from, all I saw was Suzy."

"And she was in the gazebo?"

"No," he said with a laugh. "Does that sound like Suzy? She was running around in circles outside the gazebo. I think she had something in her mouth, but it was dark, and I couldn't see what it was."

"I found some candy wrappers when I was looking around," I offered. "She was always fond of her snacks and not above stealing the human treats if she wasn't fed quickly enough."

"I guess it's possible she was eating something." He shook his head. "Anyway, the short version is that when I realized it was Suzy, I called her, and she ran to me. I carried her to the gazebo and blocked her exit by sitting there so I could use my phone to call a friend to bring me a rope I could use as a leash. That's when I noticed the letter *Z* had been painted on her side. I checked out my hands and didn't have any on me, so it had to be dry paint."

Ben leaned around to gesture toward the opening at the top of the stairs. The scenario that he described sounded accurate.

"And you didn't see anyone around?"

"Well," he said slowly, "I didn't see any cars go by. I guess it's possible someone could have been there before I got there, but I never saw anyone."

"How did the police get involved?"

"Brenham PD came up on me while I was sitting there. I told the officer I was familiar with the dog and I'd just found her. She took my statement,

made some calls, and then took Suzy into custody and sent me on my way."
He paused. "I guess she's home with her family now."

"She is," I said.

"And she's okay?"

I nodded. "She was checked out thoroughly."

"That's good." He let out a long breath, then finished the rest of his
orange soda. Then he slid me a sideways glance. "I thought that dog's crazy
running around was going to be fun if I got to take her home. I see now
that it wasn't a good idea for me to have a dog like that. Would you let me
know next time you get a rescue that's more chill? Maybe one that would
ride on my board with me or at least hang out in my backpack while I'm
skateboarding."

"Definitely," I said, thinking of Buster, the sweet basset hound that still
needed a forever home. I could imagine his oversize ears flapping in the
breeze as he and Ben rolled down the road on a skateboard.

But before I could recommend Ben Tanner as a pet dad, I needed to
make sure he wasn't the person who'd been painting dogs. And right now,
I wasn't certain at all.

So, his name would stay on my list until I could find proof he wasn't
the one.

"Thank you for speaking with me, Ben," I said. "And for the orange
soda. Do you want cash, or would you rather I sent you a payment through
my phone?"

He grinned. "My treat. You can get the next ones."

I matched his smile. "It's a deal."

Ben donned his backpack and skated away. I reached into my bag and
retrieved a pen, then dug deeper for something I could write on. Snatching
up an envelope, I turned it over and made a list of anyone who I thought
might be involved in the Bark of Zorro mark on the three dogs.

Instead of going by instinct, I decided to record only the names that
had been mentioned since I tackled this mystery. When I was done, I had
Ken Venable, Henry Hughes, and Ben Tanner on the list. Unlike Jason, I
just didn't believe Maggie Jamison belonged on the list, so I skipped her

name. Because of proximity to Mrs. Miller's home, Sticks Styler would have to be added, at least until I could prove he didn't belong there.

I sat back against the step just like Ben had done. Who else could I add? I let out a long breath. No, that was all for now.

Now what?

I had intended to spend the afternoon doing things to get ready for my move over the weekend. There were boxes to fill and errands to run. However, with two new incidents of painted dogs, I decided to follow up on at least one of my leads that afternoon. If time allowed, I might even follow up with two of them.

Then I figured out a way to get information on two possible suspects with just one interview. I'd have to go hunting for a phone number, but I knew exactly where to look.

But first I was going home. Well, to what was now my new home.

I might not live there until Saturday, but it was all mine.

CHAPTER TWENTY-FIVE

Once I made sure the key fit in the lock and the loft was just as amazing as I recalled, I went to retrieve my car. Driving over to the clinic, I parked in the employee lot and slipped in the back door undetected.

A moment later, I was in my office with the client database open in front of me. What I was about to do might not earn me any points with my employers, but I was doing it for a good cause.

I found Sticks Styler's number in the records. Sticks had adopted Honey, a liver-and-white spaniel mix, from the rescue. She was now a patient of Lone Star Vet Clinic and a frequent flyer on Sticks' private jet as the pair split their time between here and Tennessee.

I debated whether to call from my office or go back to my car. Because I didn't want to have to explain what I was doing to anyone who might hear me talking in my office when I should be elsewhere, I tucked my phone in my bag and returned to my car. Then I drove a block away, parked, and dialed the record producer's number.

Sticks picked up on the third ring. After a quick hello, I said, "I hope I'm not bothering you. I just had something I wanted to ask you about."

"Actually, I'm in the car. I always use the hands-free option to answer, but I don't really like to talk much on it. I was just about to grab some lunch at the Dairy Bar. How about you meet me there? Is ten minutes too soon? I'm a fast eater, so don't expect me to linger long."

My stomach reminded me of the hunger I'd begun to feel while I was speaking with Ben Tanner. I was seriously starving.

"That's fine. I'll see you then."

I pulled into a parking space at the hole-in-the-wall burger joint right on time. Sticks Styler would have stood out anywhere, but here at the Dairy Bar the Englishman with the platinum ponytail was easy to spot.

I ordered a Frito chili pie without onions and then settled across from Sticks at his corner table in the well-worn but well-loved burger joint. I was about to greet him when his phone rang.

"Sorry," he said as he answered. "I have to take this one."

"Sure," I told him. "Go ahead." I retrieved my phone and scrolled through the messages I'd been getting since I put out the posts on Spot and on Buster.

Within the span of a few minutes, my food arrived and someone on the other side of the record producer's conversation got fired. I took a sip of sweet tea and waited for him to tuck his phone back into his shirt pocket.

"Sorry about that," he said. "I usually don't take calls when I'm with someone, but that situation needed to be handled."

"Sounded pretty intense," I said. "And hello, by the way. Thank you for agreeing to meet with me so soon. I know you're busy."

He took a sip of his soda and placed the glass back on the table. "I am, but I don't need much of an excuse to have a Dairy Bar burger." He paused as if studying me. "Anyway, you mentioned on the phone that you had some questions. I hope you've changed your mind about recording with me."

Ever since he heard me sing at church, Sticks had been after me to consider recording for him. Convincing him I was much more comfortable out of the spotlight had been an ongoing battle.

"Oh, goodness no," I said, laughing.

Sticks shrugged. "So if you're not here to ask me to make you a star, which I absolutely could do, then to what do I owe the pleasure of your company?"

"Actually, it has to do with the painter you hired," I began.

"The one that gorgeous creature across the street nearly ran over?" He chuckled. "I tell Maggie all the time that she should slow down on that corner, and her response is always that it doesn't matter because there's never anyone on the road but her."

I toyed with my napkin as I tried to work out his meaning. "So you stationed your painter there because you knew she'd be coming back from her hair appointment at that time, and you wanted to prove a point?"

"Of course not," he protested. "But I can't say that I'm unhappy that artist accidentally proved my point."

"Emphasis on accident," I said.

Sticks cringed. "Yes, he's fortunate that nothing was broken, poor chap. I sent him back to his hotel to recuperate. Told him to work from there for a couple of days. Can't have my temperamental album cover creator upset."

"Cover creator?"

"Yes, that's what I hired him for, although he's taken on a few other duties. Henry is handy to have around, although I do get frustrated with him." He doused his fries with the bottle of vinegar that the owners of the Dairy Bar kept just for him, then regarded me with a serious expression. "What did you want to know about Henry? And more importantly, why are you asking?"

The intense expression on the record producer's face startled me. I'd never seen this side of him. Not that I knew the man all that well, but he always seemed so cordial when he brought his pup to the vet or when we attended the same social events.

A moment later, he offered a smile that held no humor. "I'm sorry. I shouldn't have spoken so harshly. It's this conversation I just had on the phone. I don't like having to fire anyone, but it couldn't be helped. There are just things I will not tolerate."

"Right," I said, trying not to feel so curious about whatever unpardonable crime his employee had committed. Like perhaps painting a dog.

Stop it, I told myself.

"Anyway, recently I rescued a dog that had paint smudged on him," I said. "When Maggie told me about the painter, I felt like I should speak with him to see if he might have come in contact with the dog. Or, if perhaps the dog somehow got into his paints."

One pale brow arched. "And painted a *Z* on himself?"

"Well, no." My logic faltered and so did my words. "I guess you saw the article."

"The Bark of Zorro," he said. "Yes, I did. Nice write-up, but they should have featured you more."

"The idea was to feature the dog," I told him. "I wish they hadn't mentioned me at all."

He shrugged. "The writer generally gets the last word on that."

"Anyway," I said, moving the topic back in the direction of the painter, "I doubt anything will come of this lead, but a stranger in town who happens to be a painter sends up a red flag for me. I would just like to eliminate him as a suspect. And I'll ask him if he's missing a dog or has seen Spot since he arrived. I would really love to reunite Spot with his owner."

"Okay, that makes sense." He reached for his burger. "Normally I put my people up at the ranch, but I've got a boy band rehearsing there, and no one is supposed to know, so he's at the Ant Inn." A grin arose. "And don't ask me which boy band, okay?"

Was the boy band the mysterious Zed that Henry told Maggie about? I wanted to ask Sticks, but timing was everything. And this did not feel like the time to ask.

"Okay. And while I'm at it, I'd also ask why the diversion from country to pop. Are you reliving memories?"

Before his career as a record producer took off, Sticks had been the drummer in a boy band. Mari's aunt Trina told me all about it.

"Actually I just recorded an album with the ATF Angels. It's in post-production now."

"Really?" I said. "That's great."

The ATF Angels were a Miranda Lambert tribute band that consisted of female agents from the Department of Alcohol, Tobacco, and Firearms. Last year they had participated in a stakeout and arrest disguised as a party at Wyatt Chastain's home, and they'd been amazing.

"Eat your lunch. It's getting cold, Cassidy. And no, I am perfectly happy staying on the other side of the stage, so to speak," he quipped. "However, if you'd like to sing a duet with me, I might come out of retirement."

Sticks was ten years older than me and absolutely not boyfriend material. For his part, I was so not his type. However, we'd struck up a friendship that was based on jokes like this.

"If I said yes, you'd find a way to get out of it," I told him. "So let's save both of us the embarrassment and talk about something else. What's the latest on your dream home?"

Grinning, I enjoyed my chili pie while Sticks alternated between devouring his burger and fries and entertaining me with stories of his adventures in building the home that was still not quite finished. The ranch he purchased last summer across the road from Maggie came with a small home and a number of outbuildings, including a barn that had been converted into a state-of-the-art recording studio. As of now, Sticks had made a temporary home in the tiny cottage that came with the property.

When he paused to take a bite of his vinegary fries, I asked him when the place would be finished. His first reaction was to frown.

"The contractor said spring, but I guess I should have asked spring of what year?" Sticks shook his head. "Something's got to light a fire under those guys, because what I'm doing is not working."

"And what are you doing?" I asked, reaching for my tea glass.

"Firing people," he said on an exhale of breath. "Although it remains to be seen if axing this one will make a difference. I'm hoping so."

"I'm sure you and Honey are ready to have the ranch to yourselves."

He nodded. "She's good around the construction; keeps away mostly. But she's a sweet girl and she loves to play fetch, so I sometimes go looking for her and find her trying to get one of the contractors to play with her. Or succeeding, which means that guy is now working for my dog instead of me. The worst was when she kept stealing pipes from the plumbers and hiding them, thinking they were bones."

"Have you seen any other dogs around?" I asked casually.

Once again Sticks' expression went sour. "No. But my guess is you've heard about that Jack Russell terrier with the painting on it. Apparently the owner thinks I'm to blame."

"What do you say to that?"

"The same thing I told that game warden when he came to see me last night. My construction crews have never complained about strays on the property, but that doesn't mean they aren't there from time to time. It's not like I'm out walking around to check."

"Right," I said.

Jason had paid him a visit. Good.

"So if Mrs. Miller says she found that dog on my land, then she likely did. If she says I did it, then she's wrong." He shrugged. "Does that answer your question?"

"It does, but it also brings up another one. Back to Henry. How well do you know him?"

Sticks studied me a moment. "You mean, do I think he could be using his paints and brushes to paint dogs? It's possible. He's an artist, and artists are temperamental and sometimes downright nuts when it comes to their work." He paused. "But do I think he did it? No."

"Why?" I asked.

"What reason would he have?"

I shrugged. "That's where I reach a dead end on every person on my suspect list."

"Including me." A statement, not a question. "It's all right. I'm not taking it personally. The odd Englishman is always the first suspect."

"Stop teasing me, Sticks," I said.

"Who said I'm teasing?"

"Okay, then, where were you last night?" I asked, lifting one brow.

"With Trina and Wyatt for dinner, then home around nine and working on takes with the band until three in the morning." He glanced down at the remains of the food. "This was breakfast."

I shook my head. "Just one more question, please. Is there anyone on your property, either working at the studio or on the house or whatever, who you think might be guilty of dog painting? It could be Mrs. Miller's Jack Russell terrier or one of the other two dogs that have been painted in this area."

"No. Not a one. The boy band is doing nonstop recording, and everyone else is busy. As I said before, however, I don't police them all or make a point of surveying the property regularly, so I could be wrong." He paused and let out a long breath. "Now, can I buy you an ice cream for dessert? I don't know what's in that Blue Bell ice cream that you Texans make, but I'm hooked."

"It's a secret," I said, "but if you believe the television commercials, it's because the cows think Brenham is heaven."

We shared a laugh, and then I glanced down at my watch and sobered. "I wish I could stay longer, Sticks, but I've got to get going."

Actually, I was now focused on trying to find the painter over at the inn. However, I'd keep that information to myself.

CHAPTER TWENTY-SIX

ticks walked with me toward my car, stopping just long enough to say hello to Bubba and his mother. I immediately thought of Maggie's comment, though from my vantage point, I couldn't tell if she was still wearing her miniskirt.

When we reached my car, he offered a smile. "I hope you solve your mystery. Seems like you always do."

"Thanks, Sticks," I told him. "I hope you solve your contractor issues."

"It's my Trina Potter issues I'm more concerned about. She's giving me trouble with that Christmas album again."

We bid each other goodbye, and I left the Dairy Bar to drive the short distance to the historic Ant Inn on Brenham's downtown square. Built in 1899 at the corner of South Commerce and East Park Streets, the beautifully decorated inn was a favorite place for tourists to stay in Brenham.

And, it appeared, painters.

It didn't take long to find Henry the painter. He was seated in the restaurant next door to the hotel lobby with a plate of pancakes and a cup of coffee in front of him. It was the bandage on his forehead and the wrap on his right arm that gave him away. No one else in the room looked as if they'd tangled with a bear or, in this case, Maggie Jamison's new pickup truck.

"Join me?" he asked when I inquired as to whether he was the man hired by Sticks Styler to paint.

After a meal of Frito chili pie, I'd determined I'd never eat again. I glanced at the plethora of plates in front of Henry, then shook my head. "I just ate, but thank you. Go ahead and enjoy your meal, though."

He nodded and shoveled a forkful of pancakes dripping with syrup and dotted with chocolate chips into his mouth. Apparently the run-in with Maggie hadn't caused him to lose his appetite.

"I was just following up on a conversation I had with Maggie Jamison," I said, deciding to go with the Maggie angle rather than the Sticks angle in questioning him. While he might feel too intimidated to talk about his boss, he appeared to have spoken freely with Maggie.

"Nice lady," he commented, his mouth still full. "Good brakes on that truck of hers too."

"Right, well, I'm sure she didn't expect you'd be standing there when she came around the corner."

He shrugged one broad shoulder, then stabbed a strawberry with his fork. "Speed limit on that road is twenty-five. Between that and the cone, I should have been safe."

This was the point where my father would have interjected something like, "You ain't from around here, are you?" I decided to go with a less confrontational statement.

"That seems to be more of a suggestion than a speed limit among the locals."

He swallowed the strawberry, nodding. "I've got bruised ribs that would agree with you, but at least I only got hurt." Another shrug. "I'll live, and that's what matters. Are you sure you don't want something to eat? I haven't had such good pancakes since, well, I don't know when. I don't always eat well on my gigs."

"I'm surprised Sticks doesn't feed you," I told him, thinking of the record producer's well-known spare-no-expense attitude.

"Oh, he has, but I've been busy."

"Doing what?" I asked casually.

"Things I'm paid to do but not talk about," he said. "Next question."

I deliberated my response. Finally, I decided to just ask him bluntly without any more chatting up. "So, Henry, what do you know about dogs painted with a *Z*? Is that part of your gig? I'm thinking the *Z* might stand for Zed, but what I can't figure out is how and why the letter ended up on the dogs. Or why the dogs ended up where they were found."

I watched several emotions cross Henry's face.

Henry placed his fork on the table and then leaned back in his chair. He was a handsome guy, probably midtwenties, with a nice smile and beautiful green eyes. With close-cropped hair and a button-down shirt tucked into faded jeans, he wasn't at all what I thought a painter would look like.

"Nothing. No. I don't know." He gave me a broad smile. "I'm not one to mince words. What did you say your name was?"

"Cassidy," I told him.

"And Mr. Styler knows you're here?"

"He's the one who told me where I could find you," I said.

A nod. "Well, Cassidy, I've answered your questions. Now I'm going to finish my food because I am not often given the run of a nice hotel like this and a tab at the restaurant. After I finish my food, I'm going to take a pain pill and a nap. Those ribs I told you about aren't happy, and I figure I owe it to them to get a few hours of sleep."

"Okay," I said slowly. "I understand, and I'm sorry you're hurting."

"Thank you." His expression softened. "Look, I hope you find your dog."

"I did find the dog," I told him. "I'm looking for the owner. And if I happen to catch whoever painted him, that'd be a bonus."

Henry's brows rose. "Oh, okay. I get it now. You think because I'm a painter that I might have tried my skills on the side of your dog." He held up his hand as if stopping me from saying anything. "Sorry, the dog whose owner is missing."

"I think I'm following up on all leads. And I think since you're a painter, you might have heard or seen something that might help."

"I haven't," he said, reaching for a buttered biscuit. "I will if I do, though."

I nodded and reached into my purse to retrieve a business card from the clinic. On the back, I wrote my name, the email address I'd created for the dog search, and my cell phone number.

He picked up the card, looked at it, and then sat it atop the cell phone he'd situated beside his coffee cup and went back to eating. I gathered up my purse and stood. "Just one more question, Henry."

Out on Commerce Street a horn honked. He looked up at me but said nothing.

"Why were you painting in the road?"

Just before a bite of bacon went into his mouth, Henry said, "The light was better there."

CHAPTER TWENTY-SEVEN

I am determined not to leave the office today until I have gone through all of these messages and emails," I said as I looked at the number of unread emails. "Plus I need to write copy for the clinic posts I need to schedule."

I shifted positions, then glanced over at my Word of the Day calendar. I'd been so busy I hadn't managed to turn the page and see what today's word was.

Remedying this, I had to laugh when I spied the word: *leviathan*. "Meaning something large or formidable." I sighed. "That one's easy to use in a sentence. Getting all this done is going to be a leviathan task."

And it was. I was still working well after the rest of the staff left, including Mari, who had had taken Spot home with her.

Gathering up my purse and cell phone, I locked the door behind me and stepped into the parking lot. Darkness blanketed the area, and the chill air made me shiver.

"I forgot to call about that burned-out streetlight," I said with a groan.

I paused to record a voice reminder on my phone. "Call city hall tomorrow about the dark parking lot."

Then a pair of headlights blazed on, blinding me.

The vehicle's door opened, and a man stepped out. I found the pepper spray on my key chain and aimed it at the stranger. "Stay right where you are, or I'll use this."

"Hey, it's me. Jason."

"Jason?" Irritation flared. "What are you doing here? And where's your film crew?"

"It's their night off."

"You scared me to death! Turn off those headlights. You're blinding me."

He leaned inside the truck. A moment later, the lights dimmed.

"I didn't mean to frighten you," he said. "I just happened to notice that you were walking to your car alone and thought I'd stop and make sure you were safe."

"I'm fine, or will be as soon as I get over the fright you gave me," I told him. "How did you know it was me?"

He didn't answer immediately. Finally, he nodded toward a spot behind me. "I passed by a little while ago and noticed you were still here. I don't know how often you stay here alone after dark, but if it's frequent, you might want to consider getting some kind of curtains or blinds. You're way too visible."

I glanced behind me. I'd never considered that anyone would notice if I worked after dark.

"I hope you at least kept the doors locked," Jason added.

"This is Brenham. Nothing ever happens here," I said. "You know that. I'm perfectly safe."

Though I couldn't see his face in the darkness, Jason's stance didn't change. "I'm going to have to disagree with you, Cassidy."

"I figured you would," I said, clicking the remote to unlock my car. "So thanks for making sure I got to my car safely."

His radio squawked to life. While I couldn't understand everything the dispatcher said, I did get the words *dog* and *paint*.

"Ten-four. I'll check it out," he said, then returned the radio's microphone to its place on his shirt.

I took advantage of his conversation with the dispatcher to hit the Lock button on my key fob. Then I jumped into Jason's truck and closed the door while he was climbing into the driver's seat.

He looked over at me, eyes narrowed. "No. Absolutely not. You cannot go with me."

"Did she just tell you that there was a report of a dog with paint on it?" I asked, clutching my purse. "Because that's what I heard."

"No. I mean, yes, that's what she said, but no, you cannot go on a call with me."

"Civilians ride along with law enforcement all the time. It's good for public relations." I placed my purse at my feet and buckled my seat belt. "Come on, Jason. Just let me ride along on this one. I won't be in the way, and I will do whatever you tell me to do." I held up three fingers imitating the Boy Scout pledge. "I promise."

"No. And put your hand down. I'm pretty sure you were never a Boy Scout."

"I was a Girl Scout. That's close enough." I paused. "Jason, I'll stay out of your way. Don't you believe me?"

His expression softened. "Oh, I believe you. But I also believe that you have the potential to get out in the field and forget your promise as soon as you think you can help. You won't intend to do it, but you'll do it all the same."

I pressed down the lock on the passenger door. "Look, Jason. I'm a good citizen, completely honest, and a rules follower."

"Except for that time you trespassed and broke a lock to get inside a secured fence? Oh, and the times you drove without a valid driver's license?"

He wasn't wrong, but he also sounded more amused than angry. "I now have a valid license, thank you very much. As to the rest? Extenuating circumstances. A dog's life was at stake." I paused for effect. "Just like now. Shouldn't we be going?"

"You're not helping your case, Cassidy," he said.

I sighed. "Okay, look. What if I promise to try to stay in the truck?"

"Don't think I didn't notice that you inserted the word *try* into that question."

He looked away, both hands gripping the steering wheel. One minute went by, then another. I kept quiet, prepared to continue the argument if he came back with another no.

Finally, Jason shook his head. "I'm probably going to regret this, but sit still and remember that you are just an observer. Now hang on."

I imitated zipping my mouth and throwing away the key. A moment later, Jason turned on the lights and siren, and we were off.

"Who was the caller?" I asked after a few minutes of silence.

He ignored me, intent on maneuvering around vehicles that had pulled over to let him pass. "Mrs. Jamison," he finally said when we were on a less-traveled road.

"Maggie Jamison? I just spoke with her this morning. She nearly ran over a painter in the middle of the road on her way back from the beauty shop. He was fine. Well, except for the part where he rolled into the ditch. It's deep there, and he had a few minor injuries from that."

Jason jerked his head toward me. "My informant is a woman who hit a man with her car this morning?"

"Well," I said slowly. "Not quite. The car didn't actually hit him. And the man was a painter."

He returned his attention to the road, both hands on the wheel. "You said he landed in the ditch and sustained injuries."

"Rolled," I corrected. "Out of surprise and not because she hit him. Anyway, he's fine. His boss, Sticks Styler, paid to have him checked out. I spoke with him at the Ant Inn. He was definitely enjoying his afternoon off."

Jason reached for the radio and summoned the dispatcher to request a records check on Maggie. I remained silent although I certainly could have told him she was a good woman and an upstanding citizen of Washington County.

Instead, he had to hear it from the dispatcher.

Once he confirmed that Maggie wasn't some sort of criminal, he asked me the name of the man who was hit. "Henry Hughes," I supplied.

"I've got more than one subject with that name," the dispatcher said. "All but one is clear, but I've also got one with warrants out of Harris County."

Jason signed off, then replaced the microphone again. We drove in silence for a few minutes. Then he glanced over at me.

"Do you know this Hughes fellow?"

"Never met him until today," I said. "I didn't spend much time with him, but he doesn't seem like someone who would have warrants out for his arrest."

"They rarely do," he said.

A few minutes later, he brought the truck to a stop in front of Maggie's house. The land where her sprawling ranch home was situated belonged to her late husband's family. After her husband's death, Maggie was granted the right to live there for the remainder of her lifetime. Once Maggie was gone, the family would reclaim the house and surrounding property.

"What's that back there?" Jason motioned to a much larger home off in the distance.

I explained the situation with Maggie and her in-laws. "She claims they can't wait to get their hands on her house."

"Has she had any trouble with them?" he asked as he reached for the door handle.

"Not that I know of."

Maggie confirmed the statement a few minutes later when she met us under the harsh glow of the security lights that encircled her home and illuminated the driveway. Midnight, her rescue dog, paced circles around us until Jason finally knelt down to pet him.

"Cassidy, honey, I have seen you more times today than I usually see you in a month," she declared. "What are you doing here with our game warden?"

"I'm just here to observe," I told her, diverting my attention to Jason to be sure he heard me following the rules he'd set down for the ride-along.

"Tell me what you saw tonight," he said as he scratched the dog behind his ear, causing the pup to melt into a puddle of canine happiness on the concrete.

"I saw a dog run across my driveway about twenty minutes ago. Normally I'm not in the front of the house at that time of day, but I had forgotten to close the curtains, so I'd gone to do that. Just about the time I reached the window, all my lights out here came on."

"Are they motion sensitive?" Jason asked, standing.

"All but the porch light. I leave that on all the time."

He glanced around, then looked back at Maggie. "You're out in the country, so it wouldn't be out of the ordinary to see an animal cross your driveway, would it?"

She gave him an exasperated look. "Well, of course not. Honey, I was raised in the country and have lived on this property for almost as long as you've been alive. I know this because I knew your mama. She was a good woman, rest her soul. I wish she'd raised you here in Washington County, but I guess it couldn't be helped."

"Yes ma'am," he said, his tone respectful. "Thank you. I appreciate hearing that." He paused, ignoring Midnight's nudges against his hand. "Go on with your story, please."

"I know what I saw, and I saw a dog with paint on it. I'm not sure of the breed, but it was short-haired and about the size of Midnight here. He came around the corner of my house and cut across the driveway headed for the road. I went and grabbed my phone after I couldn't see him anymore."

"You said you saw paint," Jason said. "Could you be more specific?"

CHAPTER TWENTY-EIGHT

S ome fool had painted a big old letter Z on that dog's side." She shook her head. "I can't say for sure that's why he was running, but wouldn't you if someone did something like that to you?"

"Yes ma'am. It's likely I would," he said. "Do you think the dog came from across the street?"

She shook her head. "No, I don't. It wasn't heading that way either. If any of them had anything to do with it, I'd be shocked. Other than Honey—she's Sticks' sweet dog—there aren't any animals over there other than farm animals and a few horses."

"I suppose you heard about the Millers' Jack Russell terrier that had a similar painted letter applied to her?" Jason said.

"I know that dog, and it might have been her. She likes to run," she said.

Jason reached into his pocket and retrieved a business card, then handed it to Maggie. "I'm going to look around, if that's all right, but I'll probably not find much evidence, if any, in the dark. Likely I'll have to come nose around more tomorrow."

"That's fine," she said, accepting the card. "But I'll warn you now. My husband's family are not the accommodating sort. If you step foot back there, be prepared for them not to be nice about it."

He grinned. "I think I can handle them."

"Well, I thought that too when I married into the family, but I guess a gun and a badge are better persuaders than a wedding ring."

Jason didn't appear to want to respond to that statement. Rather, he retrieved his flashlight, then glanced over at Maggie.

"Would you mind providing me with the names of the people who reside in that home?" he asked.

"I'll try," she said. "But last I heard, the inmates were running the asylum."

"I don't understand," Jason said. "Who are the inmates?"

"The grandchildren," she said. "My father-in-law wasn't one to sit and grieve after his first wife—my husband's mother—passed on. He got himself a second and then a third. Not at the same time, mind you."

"Is your father-in-law still alive?"

"Oh no, he's long gone, but his last wife is still up there. At least I think she is. Anyway, I'll do what I can."

"That's all I'll need from you tonight, Mrs. Jamison. I'll let you know if I require a statement. In the meantime, if you see the dog again, just call dispatch, okay?"

"I'll do that." As Jason walked away, Maggie turned her attention to me. "It was good to see you again, Cassidy. Did you find that painter fellow?"

"I did. He's spending the night at the Ant Inn courtesy of your neighbor across the street. When I saw him, he had a few bandages and complained of sore ribs but otherwise seemed fine. I know he had a good appetite because he had quite the spread in front of him."

"Starving artists and all that, I guess," Maggie said with a chuckle. "I'm glad I didn't scare him too bad." She shook her head. "Oh goodness. I almost forgot. After Henry left, I saw he'd dropped something in the ditch. I went over to give it to Sticks, but he wasn't home, so I kept it. Midnight and I are going on a road trip to Amarillo to see my sister in the morning, and I doubt the innkeepers will be up at the time I intend to leave. Do you mind dropping it off at the inn tomorrow since you work close by?"

"I'd be glad to," I told her.

"Okay, just a minute. I'll go get it."

She hurried inside, then returned a moment later with a small paper sack. When she handed it to me, the contents shifted.

"What is this?"

"He told me it was his proudest possession. I'd appreciate it if you'd give it only to him. If the game warden sees it, he may confiscate it."

"Maggie," I said slowly, "it's not something illegal, is it?"

"No. Nothing like that."

"Okay, then. I'll do it."

Maggie smiled. "You're a dear. Now, if you don't mind, I need to go see if my lasagna is done. I wouldn't want to burn it. I'm bringing it with me tomorrow to my sister's place. She loves Mama's lasagna. It'd be easier to give her the recipe, but Mama made me promise not to."

"No, of course. You go take care of the lasagna. I'll be fine." I glanced over to spy Jason's flashlight heading toward us. "See, there he is now. I'm going to go sit in the truck and wait for him. And I'll get this back to Henry."

"Thank you, honey."

I gave Maggie a hug and headed to the truck in time to tuck the sack into my purse before Jason returned. "Find anything?" I asked when he climbed into the driver's seat.

"No, did you?" he asked, eyeing me suspiciously.

"No, I did not find anything," I said, only feeling slightly guilty that I might be skirting the actual truth.

But I didn't find anything. Maggie did. And Jason hadn't asked me if I'd put anything Maggie found into my purse. Thus, I was answering truthfully.

"You sure?" he said, lifting one dark brow.

I snapped my seat belt and offered my most innocent smile. "Positive."

We drove back to the office in silence. I was thinking about what might be in the bag, and Jason seemed intent on keeping his attention focused on the road. We'd just reached the edge of downtown when he looked over at me.

"Are you hungry?"

I was starving, but if I said yes, then likely he'd invite me to dinner. That meant I'd have to continue speculating about what was inside the bag in my purse even longer.

The sound of the dispatcher's voice rang out, relieving me of my duty to answer. Apparently someone was hunting after dark without landowner permission and might also have been shooting from the road.

These, apparently, were horrific transgressions in the state of Texas.

Jason's expression turned grim. He accelerated around the square and came to a screeching stop in the clinic parking lot. "I'll stick around until you're in the car. Be sure to lock your doors."

I was about to remind him of how safe Brenham was, but I thought better of it. "Thank you for letting me ride along," I said instead, grasping my purse.

Once I was safely in my car, he offered a quick wave, then took off at high speed with lights flashing. I started the car and was about to shift into REVERSE when my curiosity got the better of me.

I retrieved the bag from my purse. Just before I could open it, someone knocked on the window. The bag went flying and landed on the floorboard.

I swiveled around to see Henry Hughes standing there. "I think you've got something of mine."

After glancing down to make sure the door locks were in use, I looked back up at the painter and shook my head. "Sorry, can't hear you."

"Roll down the window," he said, never taking his eyes off me. "And give me that bag. It's mine."

I shifted the car into REVERSE. "Back up, I'm leaving."

He lifted a fist to pound on my window. Before Henry could say anything, however, Jason yanked him back away from the window and threw him down on the ground.

CHAPTER TWENTY-NINE

I turned off the car's engine and opened the door, then climbed out.
With handcuffs in place, Jason hauled Henry to his feet. Then he looked over at me. "Are you okay?"

"I'm fine." I glared at Henry. "What is wrong with you?"

"You have something of mine," he snarled. "And you refused to return it."

"You didn't give me time," I said. "Nor did you ask nicely. Seriously, to just jump up and pound on my window? What were you thinking? That I'd open that window? Hardly."

"I need an ID, Henry," Jason said.

"You're the game warden. I haven't been shooting anything or fishing, so you've got no jurisdiction here."

"I'm state police, Henry," he said, his tone much less cordial. "And the lady you've threatened is a friend of mine. I witnessed it, so there's that." He paused. "You've been told to produce ID by a licensed peace officer of the State of Texas. If you do not, that will cause an immediate arrest."

"Okay. Okay. Let me go, and I'll get it," he demanded.

"Not happening," Jason said. "You tried to scare the wrong lady. If I let you go, there's no telling what she'll do. I'm just here to keep you safe."

Henry gave me a dubious look. Nothing I'd learned in my self-defense class came to mind, so I stared back at him as if I actually had any idea of how to be a threat.

"ID's in my back pocket," he said. "Help yourself, boss."

Jason found the wallet and showed it to Henry. "Is this yours?"

At the painter's nod, the game warden opened the wallet and retrieved the ID, then radioed the dispatcher. Just as before, I couldn't understand much of the radio communications, but I did understand one word: warrants.

Jason held on to Henry with one hand and called in a report to Brenham PD with the other. "Don't move. Your ride will be here in a minute." He paused. "In the meantime, you want to tell me what's so important that you've got to scare this woman to get it back?"

Henry's attention went from me to Jason. "It's my keys, that's all. See for yourself. They're in the bag she's got in her car. Mrs. Maggie, she's a nice lady, she told me she gave them to her."

Jason met my gaze. "Is that right?"

I nodded, guilt twisting inside me. "Maggie handed them to me. I should have told you."

"Why didn't you?" he asked.

"She told me it was nothing illegal and asked me not to let you confiscate it." I shrugged. "I know. I trust Maggie, and I didn't think it was a big deal."

I walked over to the passenger side of my car and retrieved the bag, then handed it to Jason. "I haven't opened it."

He nodded. "Put it on the hood of your car." Then he turned to Henry. "I'm going to let go of you. If you're smart, you won't move. If you're stupid and try to run, you'll be looking at more than just warrants."

Jason walked over to the car and opened the bag, then dumped the contents. A key ring with three keys on it fell onto the hood.

"See, I told you," Henry said.

"What are these for?" Jason demanded.

"My car and the place I just bought," he said. "I hope this isn't the kind of welcome I can expect once I take care of those warrants. They're bogus, by the way."

"Of course they are," Jason said. "And for the record, Brenham welcomes all law-abiding citizens." The wail of a siren coming near sounded. "And that's how we welcome the others."

After Henry had been loaded into the back of the police cruiser and driven away, Jason gave me a look. "Nothing happens in Brenham?"

"Okay, maybe I was wrong." I paused. "About that and about doing Maggie that favor. She's an old friend of my family, and I never thought for a moment that I was doing something I wasn't supposed to do."

Jason studied me a minute. "I believe you."

"While I'm admitting to things, I should tell you that I talked to your uncle Ken and his wife, Delia. I went on an errand for the clinic to pick up supplies from our storage unit."

"The one my uncle owns."

"Yes. Thought while I was out there I would have a conversation with Ken to see if he saw anything on Valentine's night. Delia answered the door, and we chatted. Then I met up with Ken."

I watched for any sign of how he felt about this news. His expression remained neutral, so I continued. "They're really nice, Jason. I don't want to think they could be suspects."

There it was. The beginning of a smile. "Yeah, they are."

"Ken is willing to take Spot if no one claims him, which is really sweet." I paused. "But..."

All evidence of humor disappeared. "But?"

"But I found empty paint cans with their labels removed hidden behind their trash cans. A lot of them, Jason. The paint was dried, but I could see from the drips down the sides..." I paused. "It was white."

"There are plenty of explanations for that, Cassidy. Uncle Ken owns several businesses."

"And Wyatt helped him out with something that had to do with paint," I said. "I know. And I've already said it, but I'll say it again. I don't want to point the finger at either of them. I took one of the cans with me when I left."

"Where is it?"

"I gave it to Parker," I said. "He was going to put it somewhere safe. You can ask him, or I can."

"I will. Is that all?"

I lifted my eyebrows. "Have I mentioned how much I like them?"

Was that a dimple I spied? "You might have."

"Okay good," I told him. "Well, I guess I'll get going. I need to stop by my loft on the way home to take some window measurements."

He leaned against my car and looked down at me. "Ken told me you were there."

"Oh. So you already knew, then."

"Yeah." He paused. "I was wondering when you were going to tell me."

"It's not like I waited that long," I said. "And neither my conversation with Delia nor with Ken gave me any reason to think they're involved. If I'd thought they were, I would have said so."

"Okay. That's fair." He paused. "So, about that new place of yours. If you're done confessing things, that is."

"I am."

"Need help with anything?"

"Sure," I said. "With you there, I won't have to climb a ladder to measure the tall stuff."

Jason shrugged. "That's me. I can reach the tall stuff." He reached out to grasp my hand. "When I saw that guy threatening you. . ." His face darkened. "It was all I could do to keep from hurting him."

I patted his hand. "Thank you."

"Let's get out of here." He leaned down to give me a quick kiss on the cheek. "Before I stop by the Mercer Building, I need to check out the address on this tag for the keys. I told the officer I'd run that down before I turned them in, and it looks like it's downtown too."

"Sounds good." I climbed into my car and started the engine, then rolled the window down. "I'm curious. What's the address?"

He told me, and I shook my head. "That can't be right."

"Why not? That's what it says right here." Jason offered me the key chain as proof.

"Because that's *my* new address."

We drove the short distance to my place with Jason following me. I jumped out of my car, collected my bag, and then waited for him at my door.

"This is how you get up there?" he said as he approached. "That's cool."

"It is," I said. "But not if I'm sharing it with some guy who has warrants out of Harris County."

Jason retrieved the key chain and tried keys until one of them fit in the lock. He looked over at me, then turned his attention to the doorknob where the key opened the door.

"Jason," I said as my heart sunk. "What's going on here?"

"That's what I intend to find out." He hit the switch to turn on the light over the staircase, then closed the door behind me and locked it. "There's a deadbolt that can only be locked from the inside, so that should reassure you that no one can get in while you're here."

"You mean, if someone else has keys?" I let out a long breath. "Have I walked into a scam? I asked Bryce if it was weird that the home was owned by a trust and managed by a bank, but he said it wasn't unusual."

"Cassidy, don't jump to conclusions just yet. You used a reputable real estate agent and title company, right?"

I nodded. "I've known Bryce and his brother—his whole family, actually—for ages. We haven't done an actual closing yet because I'm renting while I'm waiting for financing to go through, but a title company is definitely involved in my transaction and Nora's downstairs."

"Okay," he said on an exhale of breath. "So you haven't closed. That means no money has changed hands beyond a deposit?"

I nodded.

"It also means that someone could have sold Henry this place, then turned around and rented it to you without filing a deed." Jason paused. "Again, that's speculation. I'll see what I can dig up when I get back to the office. In the meantime, let's go upstairs and see what we find."

"We'd better not find anything," I said. "I don't want to believe that anyone else has been in here but me. And you know what?"

"What?" he said.

"I'm really glad that Camille and her crew aren't here right now because I'm so angry and I'm trying really hard not to cry."

"Honey," he said, gathering me into his arms. "It's going to be fine. You haven't lost anything. Let's go upstairs, then you can call your real estate agent and leave him a message about what has happened. Likely he'll hear about it from the seller."

"About the seller," I said. "There's a trustee at a bank who has to sign everything. That's a person we need to speak to."

Jason nodded. "Tomorrow. Right now we're going to go upstairs and make sure everything is okay. Then we're going out to the hardware store to buy new locks for you."

"And pick up pizza?" I offered. "My treat."

Jason led the way up the stairs, stopping just inside the loft's entrance. "Stay right here," he said as he scanned the perimeter, then went into the bathroom to make sure no one else was there.

"It's clear." Jason hit the lights in the kitchen, flooding the space with light. "Wow," he said softly. "This place is great."

"It is," I said. "Which is why I fell in love with it."

I unlocked one of the windows and stepped out onto the balcony. Downstairs the sounds of laughter drifted up along with something that smelled delicious.

"Living close to whatever that is will be hazardous," I told Jason when he joined me on the balcony.

"This is nice," he said.

The warmth of the afternoon had quickly gave way to the cool night air. I shivered, and he drew me close. "We'll figure this out," he said.

CHAPTER THIRTY

We stood there for a bit, then Jason let out a long breath. "Okay, if we want to get to the hardware store before it closes at six, we need to get going."

"Thank you," I told him.

"For what?" he said.

"For everything," I told him. "And for just being you. You make me feel safe."

He chuckled. "That's my job. But I will say that it's not everyone who gets the special lock-changing service."

"Okay," I said. "Let's go. I'll call Bryce on the way. And I should call Nora too. Since she bought the downstairs part of this building, there's no telling who might have keys to her place."

To my surprise, Bryce picked up on the second ring. "I was working late and saw it was you," he said.

I filled him in on the situation. Silence fell between us.

"Whoa," he finally said. "That's a new one."

"I thought so."

"Put me on speaker," Jason said, and I complied.

"Bryce, this is Jason Saye. He's a good friend of mine and also a game warden, so he's state police. He's got some questions for you."

"Sure," Bryce said. "Fire away."

"Can you get me any paperwork you've got on the seller and this transaction, then do a search for any deeds that have been filed on this building? I realize that's in the title company's purview, but if you're preparing this for closing, they should have already done this."

"Absolutely," he said. "I'll send the name of the title company rep as well. That way you can contact her directly if you need to." He paused. "I'm still processing this. You're saying someone else had keys to the loft and told you he owned the place?"

"He said he had recently purchased it. But yes, he had a ring with three keys. One is for his car, and we've determined the other is for Cassidy's loft. I didn't think of it until now, but it's possible the third would be for the downstairs space."

"I'm about to call Nora," I interjected. "I figure she's going to want to have her locks changed as well so that no one but her can have access. Jason is about to do that for me."

"That's a good idea, Cassidy." Another pause. "Look, I'm sorry this is happening. You have my word that I had no idea someone else was representing themselves as the owner of the building. And you also have my word that this will get fixed. The title search showed none of this. I promise we'll get to the bottom of it."

"Thank you, Bryce," I said.

"Is that all you need, Jason?" he asked.

"For now," he said. "I'll be watching for the information from you. After I change Cassidy's door locks, that is."

He hung up and looked over at me. "I'd like you to not move into that loft until we've got this all figured out."

"I agree," I said. "I don't want to get all my things in there and then find out there's an issue with the sale or whatever."

"I'm more concerned about an issue with the former owners. Or someone else who thinks they're the new owners."

I blew out a long breath. "You know, I am really glad we're not on camera right now."

"Me too," he said.

I waited to call Nora until Jason had gone into the hardware store to pick up new locks. After I told her the situation, she was silent.

"Nora?"

"Sorry," she hurried to say. "I'm just stunned."

"I was too," I said. "But I've spoken to Bryce, and he's on it. He swears the title search came up clean and our transactions were legal. Between him, the title company, and Jason, we should get this figured out."

"Jason," she said. "As in that game warden you've been dating?"

"That's the one," I told her.

"And you're with him now?" I told her where he was. "We got a new lock for your place as well. If you don't want it, it can be returned."

"No, I definitely want it. Thank you. I can come by and pick it up. Just let me know when you're back at your place."

"I will," I said.

Silence fell. Then she spoke again.

"I'm sorry. I'm just sort of in shock. This was going to be my dream restaurant. I hadn't had a chance to tell you, but I've finalized the interior design and ordered the tables and chairs. The kitchen is next. I've been negotiating with a guy in Austin who deals in slightly used industrial kitchen equipment. That's close too."

I let out a long breath. "It's still going to happen, Nora. Jason will fix this." I looked up to see him heading toward me across the parking lot. "I need to go. We're going to be back at the loft in about ten minutes if you want to stop by. Oh, and we're ordering pizza if you want to join us."

She laughed. "Oh sure, let me be the third wheel, please."

"It's not like that," I said. "He's changing the locks, not taking me on a romantic date. Stop by. I would like you to meet him."

"Okay, then," she said. "I'll do that, but hey, since you bought the locks, let me bring the pizza."

I grinned. "Sure, why not."

Jason stowed the hardware bag behind his seat and then climbed into the truck. His expression was grim.

"What's wrong?"

"I was just told there's another painted dog incident. The cashier's son sent her a picture of a dog running around downtown Brenham with the letter Z painted on its side."

He retrieved his phone and showed me the screen Sure enough, there was a short-haired brown mutt wearing a blue collar with the same paint on his side as the other incidents.

"Did he catch the dog?"

"No," Jason said as he started the truck. "Unless the situation has changed in the last five minutes, it's still running around downtown." He buckled his seat belt, then looked over at me. "Hold on."

I was about to ask why when he hit the lights and siren. Suffice it to say, this was the quickest I ever arrived anywhere. He parked in front of my loft, which was just a block from the square, and turned off the noise and light show.

"I'd like to tell you to stay put," he said, "but I know you better than that. So stick with me until we get to the square. Then we can divide up and go hunting this dog, okay?"

I sent a quick text to Nora letting her know we had a change of plan and were now searching downtown for a painted dog. HEADING THAT WAY IN A FEW MINUTES was her response.

Jason and I reached the gazebo next to the courthouse. The night was lovely, and a few couples were strolling on the sidewalks on either side of the little park. Down the road, the sound of cheering, likely from one of the restaurants, filled the air.

I hadn't dressed for running around outdoors, but I wasn't about to complain. Not when there was a dog to rescue.

After making a turn around the park and searching the gazebo, Jason and I split up. He walked toward the restaurant and bars on the east side, and I headed to the shops on the west side. I'd just about reached the end when I spied Ben Tanner walking around the corner.

He greeted me with a wave. Tonight he was dressed in what I would call business casual. In khakis and a button-down shirt, Ben looked like the businessman he was instead of the skateboarder he also was.

After exchanging greetings, I said, "Hey, have you seen this dog?"

Ben looked at the photo that Jason had texted to me. Then he returned his attention to me and shook his head. "Never seen it before. Are you looking for a rescue?"

"It's got a collar," I said, "but there's a report that it's running around downtown, so I'm thinking it may be lost."

"Yeah, I recognize the collar," Ben said.

"You do?" I glanced down at the photo again, then enlarged it with my hands. There was some kind of design on it, but I couldn't see it clearly.

"I should. I designed it."

I shook my head. "You design dog collars?"

He laughed. "And a lot of other things, Cassidy. Before I owned my company, I was a graphic designer. That's what I got my degree in. When I came into some money, I chucked it all and opened the skateboard company. I still dabble for friends, though, but it has to be a project I like."

"And you liked this one?"

Ben nodded. "I figured I'd do something nice for Suzy." He let the silence fall between us for a moment. "But that didn't work out. I do the occasional custom collar sometimes."

"I'm sorry, Ben," I said.

"Yeah, me too. Or I was. But when I found her in the park and got a taste of how crazy she is—in a good way—I knew that Mari had made the right decision in placing her with a family that had a fenced yard for her to run in. Hey, did they ever figure out how she got from LaGrange to Brenham? She's fast but not that fast."

I shared a chuckle with him, then sobered. "Not yet, but it's an active investigation. I'm sure that's going to be figured out soon."

He nodded. "I hope so. It's one thing to mess with a person who can defend himself, but it's a whole other thing to mess with a defenseless animal."

"I agree." Then a thought occurred. "So Ben, are you still interested in adopting a rescue?"

"I am," he said. "If it's the right one."

"We've got a sweet boy that needs a home. He's a basset hound with a pretty laid-back disposition. We've searched for family and had no leads, and he's not chipped. We've been calling him Buster."

Ben seemed to consider what I'd said. Then he smiled. "I'd love to meet Buster."

"Great," I said. "Just call Mari when you're ready to do that, and she'll make it happen."

He nodded. "Thank you." Then he looked at his watch and sobered. "Oops, I'm going to be late. I've got a business meeting, and I don't want to look unprofessional to the investors."

"Oh, absolutely," I said. Another thought occurred. "Ben, who were you designing that dog collar for? Maybe we can identify the mystery dog by that information."

Ben frowned. "I'd have to look up the company. It's been a while. Can I text you the name tomorrow?"

"Absolutely," I said. "Go knock 'em dead."

He grinned and gave me a mock salute. "I'd rather take their money. I've got great plans for Tanner Designs."

"Then, in that case, I hope it works out like you're hoping."

I continued to walk around the block, eventually meeting Jason at the gazebo back where we started. "No luck at all," I told him.

"If the dog was here, it is gone now," Jason said. "I couldn't find anyone who'd even seen it."

"Me either, but I did speak with Ben Tanner. He was on his way to a business meeting. He looked at the photo and said he was the one who designed that dog's collar. Not only that, but he'd done it a while ago as a side job while he was building his skateboard business."

"Who ordered the collar?"

"He couldn't recall off hand, but he said he would look that up and send me the information tomorrow."

Jason nodded. "Okay, so we've got a random dog running around downtown wearing a collar designed by Ben Tanner."

"I wonder if that's the other dog Ben heard the night that he captured Suzy in the gazebo," I said. "He told me Suzy was barking at another dog. He thought he heard it but never saw that dog."

"It's not unusual for a stray to frequent an area and have a hideout. Dogs like that are usually afraid of human contact."

"I'd be afraid too if someone painted a big *Z* on me," I said.

Jason shook his head. "No danger of that. I guess we'll make one more pass around downtown together, then go back to the Mercer Building to rekey the doors."

When we got to the building, I spied Nora's van. She jumped out when she saw us and hurried to greet me. "And you're Jason," she said, smiling.

"And you're Nora," he responded. "Pleased to meet you."

"Same," she said. "Since I don't see a dog with you, I guess you haven't found your painted pup."

"We have not," Jason said.

Nora grinned. "Have you tried the new outdoor place on South Jackson? They're advertising as pet friendly and they've got a big outdoor area and even a play place for dogs."

"You're kidding," I said. "Bring-your-dog-to-a-playdate kind of play place? Like McDonald's or Chick-fil-A when we were kids?"

Nora scrunched up her nose. "Sort of. Minus the play equipment and anxious parents. Wait, scratch that. Add back in the anxious pet parents, for there are some."

"And how do you know about this?" Jason asked.

"When you're writing a business plan for a restaurant, you must know what's around you that's similar and what's around you that's different. An outdoor place for pet parents? Yeah, *very* different."

"I've never seen one," I agreed. "But it might be fun."

Jason looked away. I could tell he wasn't as impressed as I was.

"It's called Down on the Corner. They have food trucks instead of a full on-site kitchen, so the rules are different," Nora continued. "And most of the seating is outdoors. It'll cut down on sales in cold months, but the fact that the venue is unique in that you can bring little Princess or Pancho with you to a meal is a plus."

"Princess or Pancho?" I said, chuckling.

"Hey now," Nora protested. "I'm just trying out some names in case I ever settle down long enough to take home one of your rescues."

"So I'll just get started on changing these locks," Jason said. "Nora, now that you're here, I'm going to use this third key that we retrieved from a suspect to see if it opens your door."

It did.

Nora's face fell as Jason turned the knob and opened the door just a tiny bit. I was about to say something when Jason silenced us.

Then he leaned toward me. "You and Nora get into her van and lock the doors. Keep a low profile. No lights on and no phones to give anyone a visual that the van is occupied."

"What's going on in there?" Nora asked.

"Don't know yet." Jason turned his attention to me. "Someone's in here, and I don't want either of you to become a hostage, got it?"

Much as I wanted to argue, I nodded. We'd had lengthy conversations about having divided attention at a crime scene. Jason trying to discern who was inside that building, and having to worry about keeping me safe at the same time was the absolute definition of divided attention.

"Go somewhere safe behind a locked door," Jason said. "Text me when you get there. I'll call when I can."

"Do you want me to call 911?" I whispered.

"I am 911, Cassidy," he said. "But if I'm not back out on the sidewalk in five minutes or you get an absolute visual on trouble, then make the call."

In any other situation I would have teased that he *was* the absolute visual of trouble. However, this was not a time for teasing. I nodded, then gave him a kiss on the cheek. "Be safe, please."

"Always," he said softly. "Now go. Quickly."

CHAPTER THIRTY-ONE

I hurried to the van with Nora and sat there with my attention glued to the front doors of the future site of Simply Eat. Jason waited until we were in place and then opened the door just enough to slip inside.

"What in the world have we gotten into?" Nora whispered.

"I don't know," I said, "but this is bigger than anything I've ever seen on *Scooby-Doo*."

Nora gave me a look. Then she smiled. "I loved that cartoon. I always thought of myself as Daphne."

I scrunched up my face. My friend, a gorgeous Latina, petite and curvy with glossy black hair and gorgeous olive skin. Her big brown eyes lit up a room, and she'd never lost that energy she'd had when she was head cheerleader at Brenham High School.

However, she was absolutely in no way a Daphne.

"No," I said. "I don't see it at all. You're way too smart and so much prettier. Plus, your boyfriend is cuter."

"I'm joking," she told me. "Velma rocks. I don't know why she put up with those clowns, especially Fred and Daphne. Now, Shaggy and Scooby, I like those two. They were foodies like us. I mean, since when does a Scooby Snack not help a girl think better?"

I studied her a moment. Was that a joke? I was about to ask when the double doors burst open and Jason walked out. He motioned to us, and Nora unlocked the doors.

"I was kidding about the Scooby Snacks," she said. "But only because a nice green salad with a clean protein does a better job of helping me think. Although a Scooby Snack, or the human equivalent, does help with stress and grows brain cells. I'm pretty sure, anyway."

"Right," I told her, shaking my head.

"Apparently I babble when I'm terrified," she said, climbing out of the van.

"You didn't already know this?" I asked as I closed the van door.

"No," she told me, eyes wide. "Nothing ever happens in Brenham."

I looked at Jason, who was shaking his head. "There's no one here. Come see what I found. Just follow behind me and don't touch anything."

I followed Jason inside with Nora a step behind. The lights blazed on, making me blink until I could see clearly again. There on the back wall of the building, a giant Z had been slashed from floor to ceiling in white paint.

Jason motioned for us to stop. Then he reached for the radio and called in the situation.

"Lovely," Nora said. "I think I need a Scooby Snack."

"Ladies," Jason said, "time to walk back out the same way you came in and don't touch anything. Crime scene team will be here soon."

"Great," Nora said. "Simply Eats is a crime scene."

"We're going to find out who did this, Nora," I said.

Jason looked up sharply. "Cassidy, can I have a word with you, please?"

"Sure."

We all walked outside. While Nora went to her van to retrieve her phone, I waited behind with Jason.

I leaned against the brick wall between the windows. Jason moved in to stand close to me. In the distance I heard the sound of sirens.

"Two things," he said. "First, this isn't an episode of *Scooby-Doo* anymore, Cassidy. This is real life. We have no idea why that wall got painted like it did or who did it. We don't know why Henry had those keys, and we have no idea whether whatever's going on is limited to only Nora's portion of this property. This is serious and potentially dangerous. I need you to take this seriously."

I gulped. "I am," came out on a rush of breath. "And the second thing?"

"Related to the first," he said. "I want you to stop investigating the painted dogs. Leave that to the professionals."

Not at all what I expected him to say. "But I think we're close, Jason. Ben is going to tell me who he designed that collar for, and Lane is going to send me the name of Spot's owner soon. There are so many clues. Plus this building belongs to Nora and me. This is personal now."

He gathered me close. "It's personal for me too. I want to protect you from whoever is doing this. Please let me do that."

"But—"

"No, Cassidy," he said as the sirens grew nearer. "Don't argue, please. Just let this go. It's the only way." He traced the curve of my jaw with his palm. "Remember when we talked about divided attention?"

I looked up into his beautiful brown eyes and my heart sunk. "That's not fair, Jason."

He leaned closer. "Never said it was, Cassidy."

"We're going to need lighting to get to work fast," a familiar female voice shouted. "If this town had some decent streetlights we'd be filming right now."

Jason groaned. "What is she doing here?"

"They," I corrected as I spied Camille marching toward us on the sidewalk with her crew trailing behind.

"Guess who listens to the scanner, Jason? That would be me," Camille called. "Now, don't you and Cassidy move a muscle until we can get the lights set up. You two are absolutely adorable."

"That's it," Jason muttered as he returned his attention to me. "Cassidy, please. Just let this go and leave it to the professionals. No more investigating the mystery. I'll take it from here."

"Oh, that's perfect," Camille said. "Well, actually, Cassie, could you just turn your head a little more toward us?"

"It's Cassidy," Jason said. "And no, she can't. We're busy right now. Give us a minute, please." Then he looked down at me. "Everything in me wants to protect you. I know you're a strong and independent woman and don't need protecting most of the time. But considering what we just saw in there, this is not most of the time."

"Well, that's true," I said. "I didn't think Nora's place would come with an art wall, and I sure didn't think I'd be sharing keys with a stranger."

"A stranger who is a painter," Jason said.

"And who is in custody," I countered. "All I'm doing is looking into the situation with the dogs."

"Cassidy," he said, his tone low and his expression serious. "I need you to—"

The police cars were now in sight. I lifted up on my tiptoes and kissed Jason on the cheek.

His radio squawked, and he made a face. "Sorry."

"Go handle this, Jason. We'll change locks and have pizza another day. Can I bring you something to eat later?"

"No. I don't know how long I'll be here," he said, regret etching his features. "But thank you. And the building will be secure before law enforcement leaves for the night."

Three police cars screeched to a halt, and the officers were piling out. Camille ordered her people to change their focus to where the real action was happening. Jason took advantage of the brief moment out of the spotlight to reach for my wrist. Then he leaned toward me again.

"Kiss me," he said. "Then go home, okay? Or to Nora's. They may need you and Nora to make a statement."

I nodded. Then he kissed me. A moment later, he was walking away. I stood watching him go, all the while turning over our conversation in my mind.

Nora touched my shoulder. "Come on. Let's go grab dinner."

Jason had joined a cluster of officers and appeared to be briefing them. Camille's crew circled them, capturing the moment.

"Okay," I said. "Sure. Dinner."

Nora slid me a sideways look. "Everything okay with you and Officer Handsome over there?"

"Of course," I said, then shook my head. "Sort of."

"Come on, honey," Nora insisted. "We've got some talking to do, and by *we* I mean *you*. What's close by? I'm starving and I don't feel like making a drive somewhere when there's got to be places to eat here."

I glanced over at Jason once more, then smiled at Nora. "What about that pet-friendly place on the corner?"

Nora started to nod. Then she shook her head instead. "Cassidy, what are you up to?" She paused, then quickly continued. "Not that I was trying to listen to what you and Jason were saying, but didn't I hear him ask you to back off the investigation into the painted dog mystery?"

"You might have," I admitted.

"Okay, because didn't we just talk about how that was a place where people bring their dogs and it just might be possible that the dog you and Officer Handsome were tracking tonight could be there?"

I shrugged. "We might have."

"Well come on, Velma. Let's go get a Scooby snack."

"You're ridiculous," I said, then caught Jason watching me. I smiled, and he winked. There went my heart.

A few minutes later, Nora and I were seated at a table on the patio. On the way there, I called Marigold. Between the two of us, we managed to convince her to join us for dinner.

The place was packed. People ambled around under the canopy of white lights overhead while servers rushed from table to table almost in time to the loud Caribbean music. There were at least a half dozen dogs in the Bark Park, the designated area for canines, although their barking made it sound like more.

From where I sat, I could see the courthouse and part of the gazebo's railing. We were minutes away from the Mercer Building, but there was no sign here of any trouble.

"I'm going to go check out the Bark Park to see if I see that dog," I said. "Order an iced tea for me if the waiter gets here before I come back, please."

"Sure," Nora said. "But be careful. I don't want your boyfriend mad at me because I let something happen to you."

"Since you were listening," I said, "you'll note that he called me strong and independent. So don't worry. I can handle this."

Nora shook her head. "Just hurry, okay? We have no idea who might be watching us."

As soon as I stepped away from the table, I knew exactly who was watching us. At a table almost hidden behind large potted palm trees, Ben Tanner was in conversation with the men who I assumed were his would-be investors. While I couldn't see the person to whom Ben was speaking, the other one was waving at me.

I walked over and offered Sticks Styler a smile.

"Fancy seeing you here, Cassidy," he said. "And with no chili pie on the menu. How do you stand it?"

"Hello, Sticks," I told him.

Ben glanced over at me in surprise, revealing the identity of his companion. Ken Venable? These two were Ben's possible investors? Or were there three? There was a half-full glass of iced tea situated within reach of the empty chair. Someone else had joined them and either left before I arrived or was still here.

A covert glance didn't turn up any other familiar faces. I returned my attention to the table and upped my smile as we exchanged greetings.

"I thought you were out looking for a dog with that game warden," Ben said.

"I was, but he got called away, so I'm having dinner with my friend Nora." I looked over toward our table, and she waved. "Anyway, I don't want to disturb you. I'll just go."

"We haven't started yet," Ben said. "We're waiting on someone to join us."

So the mystery person would return. Considering where the iced tea was situated, I thought it might belong to Ken's wife Delia. But did pregnant women drink iced tea? Wasn't there an issue of caffeine to be considered?

"Actually, I'm glad I saw you," Sticks said. "I understand your boyfriend locked up my painter. Should I bail him out or leave him there?"

"Henry had warrants in Harris County, so you can blame them and not Jason," I said. "You'd have to go to Houston to discuss bail, I think."

Sticks made a face. "I don't think I'll do that."

"I wouldn't," Ben said. "If you can't trust an employee to tell you who he is, then he's gone. That's my opinion, anyway. I've had to fire good workers who just didn't understand that they have to play by my rules."

"I'm usually a good judge of character, but I got Henry all wrong, I suppose." Sticks shrugged. "Same story with my general contractor, though. I guess I'm slipping in my old age."

Ken laughed. "You're as sharp as ever. That's why you've hired me. I'll get everything back on track in no time. You'll be having Christmas dinner in front of that fireplace."

"I'd rather have Thanksgiving dinner in the dining room," Sticks said. "Or, better yet, Fourth of July poolside. St. Patrick's Day in—"

"Okay, I get it." Ken shrugged. "Don't worry. It'll get done. I always do what I say." He paused to direct his attention to me. "Where's my nephew tonight?"

"He's working," I said, keeping the explanation brief. I spied the waiter returning to our table with our drink order and waved to Nora. "I should go. It was nice to see all of you. Enjoy your meal."

After saying my goodbyes, I continued on toward the Bark Park to casually look over the assortment of dogs running and playing, then walked back to the table. I found Nora scrolling on her phone. She looked up as I sat down.

"Mari is parking. She'll be here shortly. Any luck?"

I shook my head, reaching for the glass of iced tea. "None looked like the photo."

"Oh well. And those guys at the table—it seemed like you knew all of them. I thought I recognized Ben Tanner. He's a downtown merchant. Skateboard design and accessories, I think. I had him listed on my business plan as someone with a storefront in my neighborhood."

I nodded. "Yes, that's Ben. I saw him earlier when he was on his way here. He said he was meeting investors. I wished him luck. But the men he's with don't strike me as investors in a skateboard design company."

"Who are they?"

"The guy with the white-blond ponytail is Sticks Styler."

"The record producer?" Nora asked.

"That's the one. And the man across from him is Ken Venable." I took another sip of iced tea and then placed the glass on the table. "Jason's uncle."

"I don't know him. What does he do?"

"He owns storage buildings. He also does construction work. Something to do with paint." I paused. "That's another story. He and Sticks were talking about him doing work on a home. So maybe he's a contractor now? I don't know."

"Someone with access to white paint?" Nora asked.

"Yes." I told her about the paint can that Parker had put in a safe place for me. "So he's had opportunity. Oh, and he lives very near the old pump site."

"Cassidy," Nora said. "Jason's uncle could be our guy."

"It's possible," I said. "But when I met him, he was so nice. And his wife Delia is just darling. Not at all like people who paint pups, you know? And besides, what would be the motive?"

"That's where most of our suspects fall short. Opportunity but no motive."

"Undiscovered motive," Mari corrected as she pulled out a chair and joined us. "We just need to discover it. So, start at the beginning. What have I missed and who are our suspects?"

CHAPTER THIRTY-TWO

Nora reached into her bag and retrieved her day planner. "Hold on. I'll take notes."

Mari shook her head. "Your level of organization is impressive, Nora."

"Thank you." She grinned as she turned to a blank page in the Notes section and retrieved her pen. At the top of the page she wrote: SUSPECTS.

In the time it took to bring Mari up to speed on what she'd missed tonight at the Mercer Building, the fourth person had rejoined the group at Ben's table. *Now if I could just see around those big palm trees to figure out who it was.*

"Before we start listing suspects, are you two okay? I mean, the duplicate keys and the letter *Z* graffiti? That's a lot."

It was a lot. "I'm okay," I said. "The more I think about all of this, the more I just get mad. And more determined. How about you, Nora?"

"Oh, I agree. Simply Eat was going to be the thing I did that made me not care if Lane ever asked me to marry him. It's me standing on my own two feet and making my own way. And yes, I know I've been doing that with my sales job, but this is about working for me." Nora paused as if collecting her thoughts. "Anyway, we need to find this guy and make all these issues go away. I've got a restaurant to open. Plus it makes me mad that someone is painting these dogs. I hope they got bit in the process."

"Okay," Mari said to me. "Who's on our suspect list?"

"Henry the painter had our keys, so he belongs on there. Ken Venable has proximity and white paint, so I have to include him even though I don't want to."

Mari nodded. "Parker showed me the paint can. That's definitely incriminating. What about that college kid you went to see?"

"Gavin Welch," I said. "I guess so, but the weird thing is there was no sign of a dog at his house. And when I caught up with him, he was mucking out a stall at the veterinary college. There was just something about him that made me think he didn't do it."

"Do the painting on Spot?" Nora said.

"No," I responded as I thought over my impression of our conversation. "I'm not convinced he painted that bulldog. I'm not even convinced he owns a bulldog."

"But the dog was chipped and he's the owner."

"I know," I said. "I can't explain it. There's just something off there."

"So keep him on the list or take him off?" Nora asked.

"On," Mari and I said in unison.

"What about Ben Tanner?" I asked, glancing over at the table where the group was now speaking with a waiter. "He's the one who found Suzy. Do you think that was a coincidence, or was he the one who put her there?"

Mari sat back in her chair. "Okay, I see what you're saying, but let's ask why he would do something like that."

"Because he wanted her," I said. "So he goes to LaGrange and waits for his opportunity to get her back."

"I'm not saying he's capable of that," Mari said, "but I can see where it's something that a person who really wanted a dog that went to someone else would do. So, yes, he can go on the list. However, this is where it comes to the question of undiscovered motive. What would Ben's motive be in painting Suzy and calling the authorities?"

"Oh," Nora said. "I know! He wants to discredit the adoptive family so he can jump in and take Suzy for himself when they are forced to give her up."

"Right," I said, "except he didn't demand they give her up. He could have made a fuss about how the adoptive family wasn't watching the dog, how they are unfit, or whatever. But he didn't."

"True," Mari said. "And remember, Suzy was the second dog to be painted. Does Ben have any connection to Spot?"

We fell silent as the waiter brought our meals. Once he was gone, I said, "I'm searching my brain for anything to connect him with the pump site, and there's nothing." I paused. "Unless he's got some sort of connection to Spot's owners, I'm at a loss."

"I wish it wasn't taking Lane so long to get a response on that tattoo," Nora said.

"He said it might be a week or more. Something about the database owners moving slow."

"Barring any relation to the owners of Spot, are we saying we can rule Ben Tanner out?" Mari said.

"I think so," I said.

Nora put her pen down. "Hold on. As you know, I have done research on downtown businesses as a part of my plans for Simply Eat. Ben Tanner's storefront sells skateboards and skateboard accessories. His foot traffic isn't as significant as his online presence, which raises a flag with me."

"What do you mean?" Mari asked.

"He doesn't repair skateboards. He creates them and sells accessories for them."

"Right," I said. "We know this. What's your point?"

"Why does he need a storefront?" She shrugged. "The guy does everything online. If you check out his website, all design consults are done by Zoom or FaceTime. He has an online store. Why does he need a brick-and-mortar building?"

"Maybe he lives above the store," Mari offered.

"It's possible," Nora said. "I didn't go into that much detail with any of the businesses I researched."

"But it is still odd, isn't it?" I said, glancing over at the subject of our discussion. "He's young and single. Maybe he lives with his parents and needs a place to go to work uninterrupted."

"Maybe," Nora said.

"But we do have unanswered questions," Mari said. "So leave him on the list."

I nodded. "I agree. Now what about Sticks Styler?"

"Why him?" Nora asked as she reached for a carrot stick off her vegan charcuterie plate.

"Several reasons," I said. "First, Mrs. Miller, the owner of the third dog to be painted, is alleging he or someone on his property is responsible. Second, Maggie Jamison claims she saw a painted dog running through the front of her property. Sticks lives across the street from the front of her property."

"True," Mari said. "And he employed Henry Hughes, the guy who had your keys and had warrants in Harris County."

"Right," Nora said. "But again, why? I don't see motive here."

"I do," I said. "Sort of, anyway. Maggie said Henry told her that Sticks was producing an album for a boy band out at his studio on the property. The name of that band is Zed."

"Okay," Mari said. "So a band name that starts with Z and dogs painted with Z. Why?"

"And that's where it all falls apart," I said. "I have no idea why. Getting painted dogs in the news is one thing, but connecting them to a boy band? I can't see it."

"No," I said. "Me either. And even if there is a connection—like, for example, Zed's new album is called Bark of Zorro or something—why do this in Brenham? Wouldn't it make more sense in a bigger city?"

"Brenham and College Station," Mari corrected. "And yes, I agree. Why here?"

"I'm with you on the promotional angle," Nora said. "I've looked at ways to get word of mouth started on my restaurant once it's open but never did I consider painting a dog—or four—and setting any of them loose to sell seats at the table."

My phone buzzed with a text. Normally I wouldn't interrupt a meal to check it, but considering what happened over at the Mercer Building earlier, I figured I'd better take a look.

It was from Jason. WHERE ARE YOU?

"Sorry," I told them. "I need to answer Jason's question. Keep discussing."

HAVING DINNER WITH NORA AND MARI AT DOWN ON THE CORNER.

Three dots appeared, alerting me to the fact he was typing a response. Then they disappeared. Then the dots were back.

YOU SAID YOU WERE GOING HOME.

I AM. RIGHT AFTER THIS. JOIN US? OR I CAN TEXT YOU WHEN I GET HOME.

"Something wrong?" Mari asked.

I glanced over at her. "Why do you ask?"

"That face you're making," she said.

Nora shook her head. "He caught you, didn't he?"

"I don't know what you mean," I said, returning my attention to the screen as I plotted my response.

"Yes you do. Officer Handsome asked you to go home and lock the doors and let him know when you did all of that." She turned to Mari. "Not that I was listening to their conversation."

"Which she was," I said.

"Which I was," Nora agreed. "But anyway, he told her, and I quote, 'Go somewhere safe behind a locked door. Text me when you get there. I'll call when I can.' End of quote."

"Great. You not only eavesdrop, but you've got complete recall of the conversation."

"Not all of it," Nora said. "I got distracted when the film crew showed up. That lady really knows her camera angles and production value."

"That lady!" I said. "I just thought of something. Is it crazy to consider that Camille Finley might be involved in all of this?"

"The woman filming for the lawman show?" Mari asked. "I'll entertain the idea. What's your reason for putting her on the list?"

"Nothing ever happens in Brenham," I said.

Nora made a face. "But now it does, apparently."

"Right. And since when?"

"Since the film crew came to town?" Mari said. "I can't disagree with the timing. But has she filmed any scenes with painted dogs?"

"The day we returned Suzy, they followed us to LaGrange to get the reunion on camera, and then they were with us when we got back to the clinic after we'd been told Mrs. Miller's dog had been painted."

"Okay, so one day of filming and two painted dogs." Nora paused. "How did she know to show up at the Mercer Building? Do you buy her excuse that she was listening to police scanners?"

"Before Grandma Peach married the pastor, she listened to police scanners to help her fall asleep," Mari said.

"Because nothing ever happens in Brenham," Mari and Nora said in unison.

"That might explain the painted dogs, but what about the situation with our keys? I can't see where that fits in," I said.

"I guess we need to do some research into Colleen Finley," Nora said.

"Camille," I corrected. "And yes, I would love to know why she chose Brenham for her show."

"She might not have had a choice," Mari offered. "It could be she's just the producer and someone else is choosing the filming locations."

"True," I said as my phone dinged with another text. "Sorry. Jason again." I'm outside.

Why not just come inside? Join us. There's room for one more. I would rather speak to you out here.

"Uh-oh, there's that expression again," Nora said. "Officer Handsome isn't happy with her for not going straight home and locking the door."

Much as I thought she was right, I didn't answer. Instead, I placed my napkin on the table and stood. "I'm just going to go out and speak to him for a minute. You two keep talking, and I can catch up when I come back in."

I made my way through the crowd and out into the street. There were plenty of folks out there walking around or standing in clusters talking, but my game warden was impossible to miss.

Jason was leaning against the front of his truck with one booted foot resting on the bumper. The streetlights cast a shadow on his face, but there was no missing the fact his lips were set in a grim line.

I'd done nothing wrong. Taking a detour to grab a quick dinner with Nora and Mari was perfectly safe. After all, we'd been talking about ordering pizza before the stupid Z on the wall ruined everything.

So why did I feel like a kid on her way to the principal's office?

His expression never changed, even as I closed the distance between us. It didn't take a genius to realize he was upset with me.

"Is everything settled over at the Mercer Building?" I said as casually as I could manage.

"BPD is wrapping things up. The scene is under their control, and they're aware there could be keys out there other than yours and Nora's. They'll see that both properties are secured."

"Well, that's a relief." I reached over to touch his sleeve. "Why don't you come in and join us? We were just getting started on our meal, so there's plenty of time to order something You must be starved."

Jason let out a long breath, his attention never leaving my face. "Why didn't you just go home like we agreed?"

"I am," I protested. "As soon as I leave here." I glanced around, then back at Jason. "Hey, where's your entourage?"

"They stuck a camera in my face one too many times. I told them I was done."

"For tonight or just done?" I said gently.

"Not sure yet." He shook his head. "Look, Cassidy, there's only one thing I want to talk about right now, and that's you."

I knew perfectly well that he wasn't happy with my choice of stopping there for dinner instead of racing home to hide behind a locked door. I also knew that I was a grown woman who could make choices for herself without a grumpy game warden deciding what was best for her. So I decided I would not help him with this line of questioning.

"What about me?"

"When you didn't text me? I was worried," he said. "Like it or not, you're involved in a criminal investigation now."

"I don't like it, actually," I said. "But I seriously doubt that whoever painted that Z cares one flip for what I'm doing. There's been no threat against me, and other than having a key to my loft, there's no connection to me either."

"Until we catch whoever is behind this, you're not safe, and neither is your friend Nora." A muscle worked in his jaw. "You're not taking this seriously. We don't know what they're capable of."

"Painting dogs, apparently," I snapped, my temper starting to rise. "Oh, and one wall in a building that doesn't belong to them. I'm taking it as seriously as something like that requires."

"No. You're not. You're enjoying a meetup with your friends at a restaurant that has no walls and has high visibility from a dozen buildings in the vicinity."

"Oh come on, Jason," I said. "Do you really think there's some sniper looking for me while I eat my Cobb salad? That's ridiculous. I'm just an office manager at a vet clinic."

"Stop being sarcastic, Cassidy." His voice rose. "You're much more than that, especially to me."

I looked up into his eyes. If I wasn't furious at Jason's overprotectiveness, I'd be smiling right now and telling him he was much more than that to me too. But I was furious, and I was also deciding just how much of what I wanted to say I would actually say.

So I almost missed the fact that his attention had gone from me to someone else in the crowd. I followed his line of vision but couldn't tell which of the many people standing around he was watching so closely.

"Go back to your table inside. I'll be there in a minute," he barked and then took off running through the crowd.

Of course I followed him.

Until I lost him in the crowd.

CHAPTER THIRTY-THREE

I sighed and retraced my steps, slightly regretting my decision to ignore him again. That certainly wouldn't help me win the argument.

Maybe Jason wouldn't know I'd ignored him. Unfortunately, he saw me before I could duck inside Down on the Corner.

He caught up to me and then stopped. "Are we going to work, Cassidy? I need to know."

"What do you mean?" I asked.

"I wasn't looking for a relationship when I met you, but I've fallen hard in a very short time." Jason paused. "Do you trust me?"

"Yes," I said.

"No," he said. "You don't. You just proved it."

"You weren't chasing anyone, were you?" I said, my eyes narrowing. "You did that to test me."

Jason barely blinked. "If it had been a test, you would have failed, Cassidy."

If it had been.

I fumed. And yet he wasn't wrong.

"I'm going back inside," I told him. "I would like it very much if you'd join us. Before I came out here, we were putting together our suspect list."

His expression told me exactly what he thought of my invitation. "No, Cassidy. Stop this. Don't chase suspects. Don't follow me when I ask you to stay put. I told you this was not just a case of painting dogs anymore. It's dangerous business and no place for amateurs."

I opened my mouth to respond and then thought better of it. Anything I might say short of an apology would just make things worse. And I absolutely was not ready to apologize. I hadn't done anything wrong.

At least not in my estimation.

So I straightened my spine, turned my back on Jason, and walked back into the restaurant. I hoped Jason was following me, but realistically I knew he wouldn't be.

When I got back to the table, Nora and Mari ceased talking to look up at me. "Okay," Nora said. "Whatever happened with Officer Handsome, it wasn't good."

"No, it wasn't." I said.

"Are you okay?" Mari asked. "Because you don't look okay."

I waved away her comment with a sweep of my hand. "I'm fine. Let's get back to what we were discussing. Where were we?"

"We were talking about Camille Finley," Nora said. "I've got a note here that says her motive might be to create something interesting to film with the painted dog situation."

"I can see how she would be able to find some dogs and paint them, but how does the Mercer Building fit with that plan?" I asked, trying to keep my mind off the man I left standing outside. "She would need an accomplice to get access to that building."

"Which brings us to Bryce Robinson," Mari said. "Nora, you've said you've known him a long time."

"Since junior high. So has Cassidy, but I grew up next door to him and his younger brother."

I nodded my agreement. "But you're right. He's got a connection that we can't ignore."

"What's the motivation?" I asked.

"Money?" Mari said. "Someone paid him to look away while the property got sold twice?"

"Okay, I can see that," Nora said, "but he's not stupid. He had to know he would get caught if he arranged two closings for the same property."

"What if he didn't sell it twice?" Mari said. "He just sold it once for real and the other had faked paperwork."

"Or both were faked," I said. "Either way, I'm afraid I may not own a loft anymore."

I felt tears sting my eyes. Nora reached across the table to pat my hand. Mari scooted closer and placed her arm around me.

"It's all going to work out," Mari said. "You haven't paid anyone anything yet, right?"

"We put down deposits," Nora said. "But it was just a few hundred dollars to pay for the credit report for each of us, so it could have been a lot worse."

"Cassidy," Mari said. "Are you okay?"

"I'm fine," I managed. And I was. About losing the loft, anyway. Sure, I would have loved living there, but I'd get over losing it.

It was losing Jason Saye that I wasn't sure I'd get over.

"Moving on," I said. "I agree Bryce stays on the list. But he's either someone's accomplice or he had an accomplice. I don't see how painting dogs or risking his reputation as a real estate agent with shady transactions helps him at all."

Mari and Nora both nodded.

"Care to guess who he would be in collusion with?" I asked.

"It could be any of them," Nora said. "Oh, wait. What about the person who signed our documents on behalf of that mysterious trust, Mari? Who was that?"

"There was no name on the paperwork we got, remember? He was going to send our documents to the bank for the trustee's signature," I told her.

"Right," Nora said. "But Bryce was having conversations with someone. He had to send our offer to the trustee, and then he had to relay the trustee's response to us. So there's a real person, and Bryce knows who it is."

"Okay," I said. "Since you know Bryce better than I do, Nora, will you contact him and see what you can find out?"

"Absolutely," she said, making a note in her day planner.

Mari sat back in her chair and let out a long breath. "So, are there any others we haven't put on the list but should?"

"Jason thought Maggie might be involved. Or someone in her husband's family. But I don't think so."

"Me either," Mari said. "She was one of the first supporters of Second Chance Ranch. And I haven't seen anything that would indicate her husband's family is involved. What would be the point? They want Maggie off the land, but painting dogs isn't going to do that."

We all looked at each other and shook our heads.

"Okay," Nora said, closing the book. "We've got our suspect list. Now we just have to rule them all out one by one."

"Agreed," Mari said.

"I'll see what I can find out about Bryce," Nora said. "And I'll call my contact at the bank to see if I can get any information about the trust that owns the Mercer Building and the trustee in charge of that trust."

"Cassidy and I will divide up the rest of the list and start digging," Mari said.

I nodded. While Mari and Nora continued to chat, I glanced around. The table where Ben and his investors were seated was now empty. I looked beyond their table to the buildings that surrounded this corner establishment.

Jason was right. This was a high-visibility place, and there were a dozen places someone could be watching from.

Or more.

I reached for my purse. "Has the waiter brought the bill yet?"

"Already handled," Mari said.

"How much do I owe, and who do I give it to?" I asked.

"None and neither of us," Nora said as Mari nodded. "Our treat."

"Thank you," I said, rising. "I'm just going to go now."

"Hold on," Mari said. "Nora and I will walk you to your car."

I was glad for the company, but we walked in silence. Nora and Mari seemed to know I wasn't in the mood for chatting. When we got back to my car, I spied the crime scene tape stretched across the doors to both properties, and tears sprang to my eyes.

"Good night, ladies," I said, hurrying to my car before either of them could catch me crying.

When I got home, I locked the door behind me and reached for my phone. I wanted so badly to text Jason. Or, better yet, to call him and talk until we were both so sleepy we couldn't form complete sentences anymore.

But I didn't. Okay, so I might have actually typed out a text once, but I didn't send it. I could be just as stubborn as Jason Saye.

CHAPTER THIRTY-FOUR

Tuesday, February 28

The next morning at work, I stayed busy. True enough, I had plenty to do. But even if I hadn't I still would have found something to keep me occupied. Anything to keep me from going over and over last night's conversation with Jason in my head.

My phone buzzed with a text, and I snatched it up. It was Lane, not Jason.

Got a match on the tattoo. Owner's name is Ursula Schneider. Address is on the same road as the dog was found. Name is Guenther, not Spot, though.

I smiled. Ken Venable was right. Spot belonged to my grandmother's friend Ursula.

Another text came through with contact information for Ursula and a daughter who lived in Chappell Hill. After trying both phone numbers Lane gave me, I was still no closer to speaking with Spot's owner. The first had been disconnected, and the second had no voice mail set up.

Maybe my grandmother would have updated information for her. I'd make that call after work because there was never a way to have a quick conversation with my abuela. I wrote myself a note to do that, then moved on to the next item on my task list.

Camille Finley's card was still in my purse. I called her, figuring I would probably get her voice mail. Instead, Camille answered.

"Cassidy," she said cheerfully. "I'm glad you called. I would love to meet up with you and get some recollection shots."

"Recollection shots?" I said, temporarily derailed from my mission.

"That's what I call them. It's that part in a show where someone who's been in a high-action scene answers post-scene interview questions. Sort of giving the viewer a glimpse into that person's thoughts as they were going through the scene. I like to use it as a wrap-up technique when I'm filming. So are you free at some point today?"

"Actually," I said, "I was calling for another reason. I have a question about the choice of Brenham as a film site for the show. Was that your call or did someone else make that decision?"

There was a pause, and then Camille laughed. "Okay, well, no. I did not choose Brenham. Nothing ever happens here."

Another pause.

"I was given no say in the matter. My paycheck comes from a production company owned by some trust fund kid. There are several layers between me and that person, whose name I don't know, so I couldn't speak to whether there was any interest in this city particularly. For all I know, he threw a dart at a map of Texas and here we are."

"One more question," I said. "Are you or any of your crew painting dogs to create crimes to film?"

There was silence on the other end of the line. Then I heard laughter that held no humor.

"Sorry," Camille said. "I'm just stunned you would even ask that. No. Absolutely not. I would quit this production company before I manufactured situations that would be sold to viewers as live-action footage. In fact, I have quit over this very thing before. Do an online search for my name, and you'll see I quit a well-known television show three years ago because they wanted me to fake scenes."

I believed her. I would absolutely follow this call with an online search. But I did believe her.

"Thank you, Camille," I said. "I'm sorry if I offended you with my question, but I had to ask."

"No, you're trying to find out who's doing this. I understand," she said. "And I hope you find the person who is painting these dogs. I'm an animal lover, and if I found that someone had painted one of my pets for whatever reason this idiot is doing that, I'd be furious."

I thought of Mrs. Miller's face as I passed her, camera crew in tow, and wondered if anyone had followed up with her.

"Thank you for speaking with me, Camille."

"Of course," she said. "And while I've got you on the phone, I need to apologize to you."

"Oh?"

"When I'm in the moment and the cameras are rolling, I tend to be a little intense." She paused. "If anything I said or did yesterday was the cause for you and the game warden to stop filming with us, then I want to say I'm sorry for that."

I smiled. "No, Camille, it wasn't you or the film crew. Jason and I just had a little disagreement. If he's not filming, you'd have to ask him why. I wouldn't know."

"Yes, I'll do that," she said. "And in the meantime, if you want to consider doing those recollection shots, the offer stands."

"Thank you."

After we said goodbye, I found Kelly Miller's number in our client database. When she picked up, I greeted her warmly.

"I'm just calling to check on you and your dog," I told her. "And to follow up."

"I appreciate that," Kelly said. "To be honest, you're the only one who seems to care that my precious Muffin was subjected to such trauma."

"I'm sorry," I said. "Is there anything I can do to help?"

"Well, I don't know. Do you have any pull with whatever department it is that revokes building permits? Because the constant noise next door has us both suffering with migraines."

"Oh no," I said. "I'm sorry you and Mr. Miller are having headaches, but I'm—"

"There is no Mr. Miller anymore," she said. "I'm a widow. The 'us' I'm talking about is Muffin and me."

I wasn't certain that a dog could have a migraine, but then I'm no vet, so I wouldn't dare to contradict her. "I'm sorry about your husband," was the best I could do. "And your headaches. But no, I don't have any influence with anyone who could revoke a building permit. Maybe you need to get a lawyer."

"Oh, I've tried. I went to that Chastain fellow. He told me I would need medical proof that my dog suffered from migraines due to the construction next door. I was appalled."

"Wyatt is a good lawyer," I said. "So I'm sure he was just trying to present the best case."

"Well, nevertheless, he refused to go forward with my demands to that awful Englishman, so we parted ways. I'm sure he regrets not taking a case that is obviously a simple one. My dog was targeted. It's plain."

"Targeted?" I said. "Why?"

"Well, Muffin wanders. It's who she is. We can't change who we are. So, well, sometimes she will visit the neighbors."

"I see."

"Can I tell you something in confidence?" she said. "You're part of the veterinary staff, so there's a code of silence or something, isn't there?"

I wanted to explain she was either talking about confidentiality in the confession booth or HIPAA rules. Instead, I just waited for her to continue.

"So, Muffin wanders a lot. Little Mr. Miller loves to go visit Maggie Jamison's dog, Midnight. She almost got caught not too long ago when Maggie called the cops because she saw a dog running across her yard. I was able to grab Muffin and bring her home before the game warden grabbed him. That would have been a terrible trauma for Muffin."

"Kelly," I said slowly, "I can call you Kelly, right?"

"Sure," she said.

"Okay, Kelly, I was with the game warden when Maggie's call came in. He's a friend of mine. The dog she called in wasn't found."

"Of course not," Kelly said. "Because I brought her home before he got there."

"Right, well, there's just one more thing," I said. "Maggie swears the dog she saw had a *Z* painted on its side in white paint."

Kelly said nothing.

I went out on a limb and continued. "I know she's got automatic lights that come on with any movement and a porch light that stays on. I don't know what kind of security they have out there, but if she's got cameras or one of those doorbells that films things, then all the game warden will have to do is take a look and he'll know whether Muffin had a *Z* on her."

A moment went by. Kelly was still silent.

"Kelly?"

"Okay, I admit it," came out in a rush of words. "I was so mad at that stupid Styler fellow that Muffin and I concocted a scheme to try to get his construction stopped. I figured if the cops thought that Styler fellow painted dogs, they'd pull his permits and maybe even put him in jail."

Kelly paused. "But I didn't paint her. I just added an applique to one of her cute outfits that I bought from Peach Potter Nelson's puppy boutique. It was her Halloween costume. She went as an artist. Anyway, Muffin did not like the alterations to her suit, so she took off running. Usually she goes to see if Honey is out over at the Styler place. She loves that dog. But anyway, that's how she ended up at Maggie's place."

"I see," I said. "But Muffin did end up getting painted. Did you do that, Kelly?"

"I had to," she said. "Muffin was furious with me and refused to wear a costume."

"So you painted her, then drove to our clinic to make your allegations," I said. "Oh Kelly."

"I know, but I'm desperate," she said, her voice now a high-pitched whine.

"I'm going to have to let the veterinarians know," I told her. "So they can update Muffin's records."

"I suppose you have to," she said. "But they're under the same rules as you are."

I decided not to explain that her thinking on these rules wasn't quite correct. "Yes, they are," I said instead.

"Well, see if any of them has any pull with permitting, okay? Muffin and I would really appreciate the help."

I hung up thinking that was not the kind of help that Kelly Miller needed. What she really needed was a friend. A human friend. I wondered if Maggie Jamison was up to the task. She just might be, but that was a call for another day.

CHAPTER THIRTY-FIVE

I went to my notes and added the information I'd just learned. With one incident accounted for, that left unexplained only Spot, Suzy, the incident in College Station, and possibly the mystery pup we chased around Brenham last night.

Technically the painted bulldog had been explained. At least the campus police thought so. But I wasn't so sure. I also wasn't sure about the incident last night. How could a dog just disappear from a crowded street? And how could no one have seen it except the person who sent in the tip? I decided it was probably a hoax.

So that left two incidents in Brenham and one in College Station to explain.

I thought first about Gavin, the veterinary student. An idea occurred, and I picked up the phone. "Lane," I said when he answered, "you're probably not going to be able to help me, but I need some help with this painted dog case, and I have a question you might know the answer to."

"Hello, Cassidy," he said in his slow Texas drawl.

"Sorry," I told him. "That wasn't a proper greeting. Hello, Lane. How's the weather? Can you help me with something? Is that better?"

He laughed. "Of course I'll help if I can. First, are you okay? Nora told me what happened. I'm pretty ticked off right now. Unfortunately, I don't know who to be ticked off at."

"Blame whoever put us in this situation," I said. "I know the police will get to the bottom of it. I would just like to do my part if I can. And

KATHLEEN Y'BARBO

I especially want to find out who is painting these dogs. If it's connected, even better."

"Right," Lane said. "So what do you need from me?"

"It's about that incident on Kyle Field. The one you told me about."

"Right," he said. "What about it?"

"I read the police report, and I know who was responsible. Or at least who the report says claimed responsibility because he owned the dog." I paused. "I've met him. I went to the house he's renting and met his roommate. Then I visited with him at his job. And something's just off."

"Okay, how can I help?" Lane asked.

"You can give me some insight, but there's one caveat, Lane. This needs to be off the record. I don't want to mess up this student's life if he's innocent. So when we talk about this, it needs to be completely off the record."

"Because he's on a course of veterinary medicine studies?" Lane paused. "I'm guessing he is because otherwise you wouldn't be worried about talking to me."

"Lane," I said. "Off the record?"

"Yes, absolutely off the record," he said.

"What do you know about a vet student named Gavin Welch? His social media pages show he wants to specialize in equine medicine."

Lane was quiet for a moment. "The name doesn't sound familiar, but then I'm currently specializing in canine medicine, not equine. What's your impression of him, other than what you've already told me?"

"My impression is he's involved in something he either regrets or had no choice but to cooperate with. He's afraid that what he's done or agreed to will affect what matters to him, and that's his future in equine medicine."

"Okay," Lane said. "What do you think he's involved in? Because pulling a prank on Kyle Field is not exactly going to get him kicked out of college."

"That's where my theory falls short. I don't know. I mean, there are some connections to the mystery I'm trying to solve. He's from LaGrange, and one of the dogs that got painted lived with a family in LaGrange. He allegedly painted a dog with the letter Z."

"And that's what was painted on three other dogs," Lane supplied, "as well as on the wall of Nora's restaurant."

217

"Right. Although I have new information that explains the painting on one of the dogs. Apparently the owner did it to try to get revenge on a neighbor."

"I see," Lane said. "Okay, so two verified in Brenham and one in College Station."

"Yes, plus a tip yesterday that was never verified," I said. "Jason and I searched but didn't find the dog."

"And graffiti on my girlfriend's place," he added.

"Yes, but back to Gavin Welch. His place showed no evidence of a dog unless it was hiding under all the laundry and mess that was on the floor. If he painted a bulldog he owned, why wasn't that dog at his place? It certainly wasn't with him when I found him mucking out the stables."

"Did you ask?"

"Let's just say that Gavin was not receptive to my questions. He couldn't wait to get rid of me." I paused. "Not in a mean way, though. He just looked like a scared kid who was afraid I'd ruin things for him."

"What about the dog?" Lane asked. "In order for the police to connect him with the prank, the dog's chip would have to be read to determine the owner. Where was the dog taken to have that chip read? Did the report say?"

"I can look. Do you mind if I do that now?"

"No, go ahead," he said. "You've got me curious."

I went to my computer and found the photos I had taken of the report while I was at the police station. "The dog was brought to the college's small-animal hospital to be checked out and have the chip read."

"My guess is we kept the dog until the owner picked it up. The local cops are great, but they don't have a facility to keep a dog for any amount of time."

"Okay, so would there be a record of who signed for the dog?" I asked. "I'm curious if it was Gavin or someone else. I'm also curious where the dog is now, but I doubt you can help with that part."

"I may be able to do better than a record of who signed for the dog," Lane said. "There might be a digital image of the transfer from clinic to owner. I'll see what I can find."

"You're the best, Lane."

"Tell your friend Nora that," he said with a laugh. "It never hurts to have good PR when you're trying to impress your girl."

"I will," I said. "And thank you."

I went back to my list and added the notes from my conversation with Lane. So far we had one event explained and another a little closer to at least being clarified.

If only Suzy could explain how she got from LaGrange to Brenham and Spot could tell us how he ended up behind that locked fence. Before I tackled my ever-growing stack of invoices and clerical work, I decided to make one more call.

Barking was the first sound I heard. Then came the greeting from Penny Baker, barely audible above Suzy's enthusiastic chorus.

"Hi, I'm Cassidy Carter with Lone Star Vet Clinic in Brenham. Do you have a minute to talk about Suzy, the rescue you adopted from Second Chance Ranch?"

"Of course," Penny said. "We're very thankful that we have her back."

"I'm sure," I said. "She wasn't at the rescue long, but Suzy became a favorite. She's got plenty of personality. Anyway, I'm just wondering if now that you've had time to think about it, you have any idea how Suzy got from LaGrange to Brenham."

"I have no idea how she got to Brenham," Penny said, "but just this morning my husband was able to figure out how she got to College Station."

"I'm sorry. College Station?"

"Yes, crazy isn't it?" She laughed. "So my eldest plays trumpet in the junior high marching band. This morning he noticed that the AirTag that should have been attached to his trumpet case was missing. That's when our youngest admitted to putting it on Suzy's collar so he could track her."

"But Suzy didn't have a collar when she was found in Brenham," I said.

"I know. The collar was found in College Station."

"Really? Where?"

"In a trash can inside Kyle Field."

"The football stadium? Weird."

But was it? That would place two painted dogs in one place. Maybe I needed to make another trip to College Station. The question was, once I got there, where would I begin? Gavin's dog—or whoever that dog belonged to—did not live in his house. He wasn't forthcoming with any information. And unless I missed my guess, he also wasn't the person who picked the bulldog up from the small-animal clinic.

I'd just have to wait and see if there was video proof of who did pick up that dog. Once I had that, maybe the rest of the pieces would fall into place.

I hung up with Penny and went back to work. A few minutes later, Mari knocked on my office door.

"Do you have a minute? I've got Aunt Trina on the phone, and she may have an answer on why you can't reach Ursula."

"Sure, come in."

Mari put the phone on speaker. "Okay, Aunt Trina. I've got Cassidy here."

"Cassidy, Mari has been keeping me informed about the search for that poor painted dog's owner," Trina said.

"And the search for who painted on him," Mari added. "But you were going to tell her about Ursula."

"Oh, sweet Ursula. Yes, Mama Peach loved that woman. When she wasn't arguing over the price of fabric, that is. If I remember right, she retired a while back. Mama bought out the remaining inventory of fabric from there." She paused. "That would be the landslide of fabric that put her in the hospital after it fell on her last year."

"Thank goodness for Hector," Mari said with a giggle.

Hector was Mama Peach's ornery cat. Somehow he'd not only managed to accidentally call for help when his owner tripped and landed under a pile of fabric, but he'd also mastered the art of opening doors.

"I've tried to contact Ursula or her daughter," I said. "I'm not getting any response from the numbers I have."

"Well, you wouldn't," Aunt Trina said. "The two of them left to cruise around the world about six months ago. It was all Mama could talk about for a week at least."

"Wow," Mari said. "Running a quilt shop must pay well."

"No, but winning the lottery does." She sobered. "So you really think that that dog in the Bark of Zorro article is Miss Ursula's dog?"

"A vet at A&M found a registry entry that matches his identifying tattoo."

"Well, obviously they couldn't bring the dog with them, but I doubt seriously they'd just abandon him. There has to be more to that story."

"Ken Venable told me he'd take the dog if Ursula didn't want him. That tells me she didn't speak to him about it. But I wonder if it might be a good idea to let Spot live down the street from his former home, at least until Ursula and her daughter return."

"I always liked Ken Venable," Trina said. "His family was a mess and Ken got into trouble occasionally, but deep down I thought he was a good guy."

"Cassidy has a favorable impression of him and his wife," Mari told her. "They're expecting soon, and they've fixed up the place."

"I'm glad to hear it," Trina said. "Look, I would love to chat, but I've got a meeting that I'm already late to."

We exchanged goodbyes, and then Trina hung up.

"Got a second for some updates?" I asked Mari when she'd tucked her phone away.

When I told her what I'd learned, she shook her head. "So you've solved Muffin's case and managed to place Suzy and the bulldog at Kyle Field in College Station."

"Well, Suzy's collar, anyway. I think whoever took her discovered the tag and tossed it in the trash, then drove her to Brenham and let her loose downtown."

"I am with you all the way to where dog and collar part ways. But after that, why take her to Brenham? Why there?"

"No idea," I said. "Except that I'm wondering if it all has something to do with that graffiti on Nora's wall."

Mari nodded. "So we have three painted dogs and a big Z in an empty building. Two of the dogs have definitely been in Brenham, but one was out at the old pump site while the other was downtown. Two of the dogs have definitely been in College Station—if the tracking is accurate—but Spot has not."

"As far as we know," I said.

"And we can't place any of them inside Nora's place."

"I was only in there for a few minutes, but I don't remember seeing anything in there except the big *Z* on the wall. It was empty."

She shrugged. "Okay, so we keep digging. I've been busy this morning with the Woof Gang. I'm hoping to have time to tackle my list this afternoon." Mari paused. "Any news from Nora yet?"

"Not yet," I said.

"What about Jason?" Mari asked.

I gave her a look. "What about Jason?"

"Have you talked to him today? I'm just wondering if he's made any progress."

"I wouldn't know," I said.

"So he didn't call you last night?"

I shook my head. "No, but to be fair, I didn't text him either."

Parker stuck his head in. "Dr. Tyler is looking for you. He's got a question about that cat that was in surgery this morning."

"Thank you, Parker. Tell him I'll be right there." Mari stood. "I wish I had words of wisdom about how to handle your problems with Jason, but I don't."

"I know," I said. "Maybe we just weren't meant to be."

As I said the words, I hoped they weren't true. But Jason Saye was bullheaded and absolutely unreasonable. Unless he changed his ways. . .

I stopped myself. I had my faults too. Not that I wanted to admit them to Jason or anyone else.

Surely there was middle ground we could meet on.

I sighed. If Dr. Cameron was to be believed, there wasn't much middle ground when it came to the younger Saye brother.

I shrugged off the thought and went back to work. Invoices weren't interesting, but they'd never made me cry.

CHAPTER THIRTY-SIX

I t was well past lunchtime when my growling stomach forced me to step away from my desk. I hadn't packed a lunch, so I headed out to find something to eat.

I was standing in line at Smarty's on the Square when my phone rang with a call from Wyatt Chastain. After offering a greeting, he came right to the point. "You know that library dog that Ed checked out? He wants to keep him a little longer. Might even pay to take him out of circulation, but Ed's got to get back to me on that."

I laughed. "Tell Ed that's fine."

"You really shouldn't make things so easy on him, Cassidy. He already thinks he runs things around here," Wyatt drawled. "But seriously, I do appreciate the extra time. I think he's going to work out, but I want to make sure we're not too much for him."

"Remember, he was already used to a crowd."

"About that crowd," Wyatt said. "I'm in negotiations to bring him for a visit down at the nursing home. If everything works out, he ought to be seeing his old friends sometime this week. If that's okay with the rescue."

I swiped at a tear as I edged up another step in the line. "I think that would be great," I managed. "Permission granted for that too. Just one request, though. Would you send us a picture to put on the bulletin board at the rescue? I promise we won't share online it unless you give us permission."

"It's a deal." He paused and could almost hear his grin. "It's a nice day out. You ought to take those Smarty's tacos you're getting down to the gazebo."

I glanced around and spied Wyatt sitting in his truck in the parking lot. He waved and held up a bag. "I just beat you here by a few minutes. Now enjoy your lunch. Some of us have to be in court this afternoon and can't enjoy an outdoor picnic."

With one more wave, he sat the bag down and started the truck, then pulled away. I finally reached the front of the line, placed my order, and determined that it really was a nice day for the end of February. The gazebo did sound like a fine place to enjoy my tacos.

It wasn't until I was in sight of the gazebo that I realized what that sneaky lawyer was up to. The only game warden in Washington County had decided he'd be enjoying his lunch at the gazebo too.

And it looked like Jason had a bag of Smarty's tacos.

I stuttered to a halt, but it was too late to turn around. He'd already seen me.

"It looks like we both had the same idea," Jason said as he scooted over to make room on the step beside him. "Join me?"

"It's a nice day," I answered with a shrug. "The idea of going back to my desk with this didn't sound as good as the gazebo."

"Yep," was his one-syllable answer.

My stomach rumbled again. Two bites into my taco, my brain switched back on. I glanced over at Jason and decided to toss out a topic for conversation. Maybe pretending last night hadn't happened would be a good plan.

"Lane found Spot's owner. It's Ursula the quilt lady. According to my mother, she's out of the country on an extended cruise. We're looking into options."

He crumpled the empty taco wrapper and stuffed it into the bag, then retrieved another one marked Smarty's Special No Onions Extra Jalapeños. "I asked you to stay out of the investigation, Cassidy."

Of course he would say that. I let out a long breath and waited a beat before I responded, something I should have done last night.

"Finding the owner of dogs rescued by Second Chance Ranch is what I do as a volunteer, Jason. We rescue dogs and, if possible, reunite them with their owners. That has nothing to do with your precious investigation."

Silence fell between us. I finished my taco, then tossed the empty wrapper into the bag and took a drink of water.

A light breeze picked up the edge of the paper napkin he'd placed in his lap. He reached down to tuck the napkin into the bag before looking up at me. "Okay."

That was it? Just *okay*.

I let out a long breath. Meanwhile Jason shifted positions and leaned against the rail.

"Okay what?" I asked.

He gave me a sideways look. "Okay, I see the difference. You need to find Spot's owner, and it sounds like you're getting close."

"I am," I said.

Now to decide whether to tell him the rest of the things I'd learned that morning. While he wasn't looking, I took note of his somber expression and furrowed brow.

Maybe now was not the time.

Someone honked, and I looked up to see Parker driving past in the rescue van. I waved. I'm sure he'd have questions later since Mari surely updated him on the squabble I'd had with Jason last night. And I was also sure that he'd be calling Mari to report in on what he saw.

We ate in silence for a few minutes. Then Jason wrapped up his taco and shoved it back into the bag. I had plenty of my meal left, but I was no longer hungry, so I did the same.

It was time to clear the air. At least some of it.

"I got home fine," I said. "I didn't know if you wanted to hear from me, so I didn't text you. I'm telling you now instead."

He continued to stare at the road. "Okay."

Another okay? I let out a long breath.

"If anyone had bothered me, I would have zapped him with my Taser flashlight."

That did it. Jason swiveled to face me, a storm brewing in his expression.

"Cassidy," he said slowly. "Do you have any idea how much trouble you'd be in if you tased someone and they were injured? The State of Texas might not regulate those things, but if you tase someone in just the right place, you could cause serious damage. You could even kill someone."

"Goodness, Jason. You're so serious. I don't think a fake Taser is what our problem is."

"A private citizen owning a Taser is a bad idea one hundred percent of the time, and the consequences are serious. Get rid of it and buy some pepper spray."

"I have pepper spray on my key chain already. This is different, and technically it's not a real Taser, so just calm down. I would never own one of those things. This looks like a flashlight except when you push the right button, it sounds like a Taser. The noise alone would make you run. It's genius, really."

"Cassidy," he said patiently, "the best protection is situational awareness. Always know your surroundings. Look around. See if there's anyone suspicious and make eye contact with them. Find at least two exits. But most of all, call me if you feel threatened."

Jason's expression gave me the immediate impression he hadn't intended to say that last part. Instead, his passion for situational awareness and personal safety had gotten the better of him.

We sat together in silence for a few more minutes until Jason spoke again. "I drove by your place last night to make sure you were okay."

I thought of several responses but discarded them all. Instead, I nodded. Then I whispered, "Thank you."

"I saw the dots that said you were going to text me. Then they disappeared. I thought I better check to make sure nothing was wrong."

"Thank you," I said again.

He answered with a curt nod. "Look, I'm mad at you right now, Cassidy, but I had to be sure that you were safe. It's not in me to not do that."

"I'm mad at you right now too."

"That's fair."

Not at all what I thought he would say. "I'm not a puppy. You can't tell me to sit and stay and expect me to always do it. Besides, it's rude."

"It's not rude when it's keeping you safe," he snapped.

I stood. "Jason Saye, you are so busy trying to keep me safe that you do not see that you're losing me. You just need to chill out and enjoy the fact that you and I have a great time together and just might be meant for something more if we are able to stand each other without arguing about who is going to solve what mystery."

Jason looked like he'd been punched. He tossed the bag onto the step beside him and rose. The man towered over me, so I walked up three steps until we were eye level. Then I placed my hands on his shoulders.

"You're a good man, Jason Saye, and I have no doubt you're a good game warden. You work hard and you love what you do." I paused to let that sink in. "But there is no law or protocol or safety instructions that come with spending time with me. I do not have package instructions to read and follow or a map you can follow to make sense of me. You're bullheaded, and everything in your world is black and white. I am a rainbow."

A rainbow? Where had that come from? *Why is it I never know when to stop talking when I'm angry?*

He blinked twice. Then he laughed.

I let go of his shoulders and took a step back. His good humor made me even madder.

"Cassidy Carter, you are adorable. And of all the rainbows in the world, you are my favorite."

I forced myself to keep a straight face. "That's not funny. I'm still mad at you."

"You're mad at me because I acted like an idiot."

He paused as if he wanted me to agree with him. I decided to wait him out and see what else he would say.

"I treated you like a child, but it wasn't because I don't think you can take care of yourself. I recognize that you're a strong and independent woman who is fully capable of doing whatever she sets her mind to."

"Thank you," I said.

"But you are foolish when it comes to your own personal safety. If I lost you. . ."

"You were about to, Jason."

He nodded. "I know. So where do we go from here?"

"We?" I shrugged. "That depends on your definition. I'm not going to go home and hide behind locked doors."

"Point taken," he said.

"And I'm going to continue to look into why dogs are being painted, Jason. I'm curious. I want to know."

He opened his mouth to speak, then seemed to think better of it. "You know how I feel about that," he finally said.

"You're a professional, and I'm an amateur. I don't know all the safety protocols and how things are supposed to be done, and I could get myself hurt."

Relief flooded his features. "Yes, exactly."

"Did you see that case recently where law enforcement spent a fortune and used dozens of men over a two-week period to find a missing person only to have a three-man diving team of amateurs discover that the person's car had gone into a river behind some warehouses and the person drowned?"

Jason gave me his what's-your-point look.

"Sometimes the experts are so focused on doing things a certain way that they miss the clues that solve the crime."

"Or they insert themselves into an active criminal investigation, tamper with evidence, and then claim whatever reward the family has put up." He paused. "Meanwhile they could very well be the ones who committed the crime. That would certainly explain how they were able to do what the police couldn't. I saw that on the news recently too."

Of course he would make that argument. "Or," I countered, "they just looked at the situation with a fresh perspective and saw an obvious answer."

"We could debate this all day," Jason said, "but the bottom line is I am asking you to let me handle this."

"And I'm asking you to let me have a fresh perspective."

"Your 'fresh perspective' puts you in danger, Cassidy," he protested.

"So does crossing a street or, for that matter, getting behind the wheel of my car. I don't stop doing those."

He shook his head. "You're impossible."

"No," I said. "I'm not. I'm just not like you. And maybe that's going to make us a stronger team."

"So we're a team now?" he said.

"I would like to be." I paused and offered him a smile. "Especially since I have new information that you might want to have."

CHAPTER THIRTY-SEVEN

J ason's eyes narrowed. "What information?"

"First I need to know if you're still mad at me."

"You know I'm not," he said. "But you're still mad at me."

"A little bit," I admitted with a shrug. "But I'll get over it. In time. With the proper wooing."

"Wooing?" he said with a chuckle. "What exactly does that entail?"

I grinned. "It's all that stuff you were already doing minus the part where you told me to stay and sit and go hide in my apartment."

He shook his head. "You're impossible, Cassidy."

"No, I'm just improbable." I looked up at him. "That was my word of the day on my calendar. It means unlikely or unexpected."

Again, why hadn't I just stopped while I was slightly ahead?

"Unexpected," he said as he leaned toward me. "Yes, that fits you, Miss Rainbow."

Then he kissed me right there on the gazebo steps. Okay, I'll admit it. I happily kissed him back. I was still not one hundred percent certain I wasn't still mad at him, but I was sure I'd forgiven him all the same.

And yes, I am completely aware that this does not make sense.

Jason broke the kiss first. "So we're good?" he said against my ear.

Why did he have to ask that?

"Well," I said slowly, causing Jason to take a step backward.

"What is it, Cassidy?"

There was that tone again. I sat and patted the place next to me. He complied, never taking his eyes off me.

"All right," he said, his legs stretched out in front of him. "What is it now?"

"It's about the Bark of Zorro case," I said warily. "I have some new information, but since me working on the case makes you mad, I'm not sure if I should tell you or just keep it to myself."

His eyes narrowed. For a moment, he didn't say anything.

"What information?" he said. "And for the record, this is me trying not to be mad, okay?"

"Okay," I said, encouraged. "All I did was make a few calls, so it's not like I spent the morning doing something dangerous."

"And what was the result of these calls?" he said evenly.

I told him, trying not to go into too much detail while also trying to provide all the important information. When I was done, he sat very still. He shifted positions and looked out at the street in front of us.

After a minute, he retrieved his pocket notebook and then turned his attention back to me. "Good work, Cassidy," he said as he began scribbling notes.

I was temporarily speechless. When I found my voice, I said, "Thank you, Jason."

While he wrote, I sat very still next to him and pondered the crazy assortment of facts in this case. On the one hand I had Gavin and Penny Baker and Ursula the quilt lady, all owners—supposedly, in the case of Gavin—of painted dogs. And on the other hand, I had suspects with undetermined motives.

Of those suspects, I landed on Ben Tanner as the most likely. He had a business that needed money and worked out of a building even though everything he did was sold online. I really liked him but couldn't figure him out. As with the Gavin situation, something there was off.

He was young and hip and probably figured that a dog painted with a Z would get him more business. I shook my head. What was wrong with me? That made absolutely no sense.

Or did it?

Jason put his notebook away and smiled. "Really good work, Cassidy. Three phone calls and you've gone a long way toward solving this thing."

"I just asked the right questions, I guess."

"Yes, but you knew what questions to ask," Jason said. "You're really good at this."

This time I beamed. He meant it.

"There's nothing that explains Spot," I said. "That bothers me, but at least he'll be going home once I reach Ursula. It's the other side of the whole mystery that has me completely confused."

"What do you mean?" Jason asked, leaning back on one elbow.

"Okay, let's just say that someone is doing all of this Z stuff to get attention. Why? My guess is they're promoting something. What? I have no clue. Is it a product? A service? A location? It's a mystery."

"Okay, Velma," Jason said. "Let me give you a tip."

I made a face. "If it has anything to do with hiding behind a locked door or staying out of an active investigation, I will warn you now that you should probably not give me that tip."

He chuckled. "Neither, I promise. Although. . ."

"Jason!"

"Okay." Jason let out a long breath. "So here's what I do. When I have a bunch of clues that seem unrelated, I write them all down and see if I can make connections between them. Sometimes I can, and sometimes I can't. But while I'm trying to figure it out, sometimes another way to solve the case comes to me."

"I'll give it a try. But before I forget, last night at Down on the Corner, Ben Tanner was at a table with three men he was hoping to convince to invest in a business venture with him. One was Sticks Styler, and the other was your uncle Ken. I never saw the fourth one. He was gone when I came back inside."

"I may have," Jason said.

"What?" I shook my head. "How could you have since you never went inside?"

"The guy I was chasing, Cassidy. I wonder if he's your fourth."

"I thought you were just testing me," I said. "You were really chasing someone."

"Yes," he told me. "Dark hair, medium build. He was already walking out of the building faster than an average pace. Then he made eye contact with me and practically sprinted off."

"I never saw him," I said.

"Because your back was to him," he said.

"Why didn't you tell me you were really chasing someone and it wasn't just a test?"

Jason shrugged. "Because I've been told by an expert that I'm bullheaded."

"Your expert is not wrong," I said. "But this helps the case. We just need to find someone with dark hair who knows Ben or has money to fund his business."

My heart sunk. "Jason," I said slowly, "I only know one guy like that in Brenham." I paused. "Our real estate agent, Bryce Robinson."

Jason grabbed his radio and asked the dispatcher to run some kind of check on Bryce. One of these days I was going to have to learn all the shortcut terms that these guys used so I could properly eavesdrop on Jason's conversations.

After a minute, the dispatcher responded with something that sounded like the word *clear*.

"So?" I said.

Jason returned his radio to its place. "He's got a clear record. So if he's doing something wrong, he's never been caught at it before. The way I remember it, he was supposed to send me your records. I need to check on that."

"I guess never having been in trouble is good," I said.

"Better than warrants," Jason replied. "Speaking of warrants, Henry Hughes was picked up by Harris County transport officers this morning. He declined to give a detailed statement as to where he got the Mercer Building keys. All he would say is that he bought them, and if they'd let him out, he'd show them the paperwork."

"Which he might actually have somewhere," I said.

"He might, but he'll be delayed a bit in retrieving them." Jason shrugged. "It's a tangled mess, Cassidy, but eventually it's all going to straighten out."

"I think so too," I said. "I just hope I still have a loft at the end of all this."

We walked over to toss our bags into the trash, then headed toward the sidewalk. A thought occurred, and I stopped short. "Jason, I just realized I never followed up on Gavin's parents. I told him I was going to call and see if the bulldog that got painted was with them."

"Do you have a number for them?"

"No, I was hoping I could find them with an online search. He's from LaGrange, I know that much."

"If that was in the police report and he's a minor, then his parents will be listed."

"He is," I said. "That's why the police didn't release his name to the press."

"Okay, LaGrange is in my district. I'll speak to them." He paused. "I'm glad you remembered that."

"And Bryce Robinson?" I said.

"I'm going there now." He looked away, then back at me. "Would you like to go with me?"

I glanced at my watch. I'd already taken a long lunch. But I really wanted to hear what Bryce had to say.

"Let me check in at the office." I placed a call, and Brianna answered. "Anything going on that I need to be there for?"

"Mrs. Nelson brought in Hector for his dental exam."

The cat hated all of us except Dr. Kristin. "Okay, well, too bad I'm missing that. If you need me I'll be out a little longer. I've got an errand to run."

I hung up and tucked the phone into my pocket. "Okay, let's go."

Jason opened the door for me, and I walked in to find Bryce at his desk. "Got a minute, Robinson?" Jason asked as the door closed behind us.

Bryce had been slouched back in his chair with his booted feet resting on the desk. At Jason's abrupt entrance, he sat up straight and put his feet on the ground.

His office was decorated in a stark mid-century modern style with chrome and glass everywhere. In lieu of paintings, Bryce had a giant flat-screen television on the wall across from him and framed awards and diplomas behind him. Sleek cabinets painted jet black filled the remaining wall.

"Cassidy," he said. "I heard what happened at the Mercer Building. I'm so sorry you're in the middle of this."

"Thank you, Bryce. It's not how I expected my first home-buying experience would go," I said.

Jason pulled out a chair across the desk from Bryce for me, then took the seat next to me. On the way over, we had discussed how this meeting would go. It was agreed that I would ask for a copy of my paperwork and then Jason would take it from there.

Of course, both of us knew that I'd be jumping in if I had anything to say. Or, at least I figured Jason knew that.

"I came here for a copy of my paperwork that you were supposed to have sent to Jason. And, if you'll give it to me, Nora's as well. I can get her on the phone if you need her permission."

Bryce looked surprised. "Well, okay. Sure. Just give me a minute. And I'm sorry I didn't remember to send that to you, Jason."

He stood and walked over to the cabinets, then thumbed through files. "Okay, got it."

Placing the file on the desk in front of me, Bryce smiled. "There's yours. Nora will need to come in for hers. Sorry, but those are the privacy rules I have to abide by."

"Get it for me, Robinson," Jason said. "Or I can subpoena it."

I opened the file and looked down at the first page, then the second. "Bryce," I said slowly as I thumbed through the remainder of the stack, "this is blank paper, not a real estate rental and purchase contract."

"Let me see that," he said as he snatched the folder back. "That's impossible. The contracts were in here. I don't understand."

"Check Nora's file," Jason said.

Bryce nodded. "Right. Okay." He returned with Nora's file and opened it. Then he looked over at Jason. "They were here."

Jason nodded. "Okay. Then let's do this. I'd like to see the record of the deposits Cassidy and Nora paid."

"It was in the files," he said.

"There would be a deposit record," Jason said. "Give me that instead."

Bryce shook his head. "Not with these two transactions. The Mercer Building was being sold as rental first, then, once the financing went through, as a traditional sale. The checks that they wrote were being held until closing."

"So they were in the file," Jason said.

While the men continued their conversation, I went into my online banking account. "The check was cashed this morning," I told them.

Bryce let out a sharp breath. "I don't know how that's possible."

"I do." Jason looked at me. "This is the guy from last night."

"What was last night?" Bryce asked.

"You had a meeting at Down on the Corner with Ben Tanner, Sticks Styler, and Ken Venable."

"No," he said, eyes wide. "I didn't go anywhere last night. I was at home all night."

His expression made me think maybe it wasn't Bryce that I saw last night after all. "Jason," I said gently, "I might have been mistaken. I didn't get a clear look. I assumed it was him."

"Can anyone corroborate your alibi?"

Bryce sat very still. Then he shook his head.

CHAPTER THIRTY-EIGHT

Yeah," Jason said. "You are."

"Okay," he said on an exhale of breath before turning his attention from Jason to me. "I'm innocent, Cassidy, but I can't explain any of it. Whatever is going on, I'm sorry it has affected you and Nora."

"Who's your contact at the bank on this file?" Jason said. "I want to know who is making decisions for the trust that owned the building."

"Yeah, absolutely." Bryce reached for his phone and scrolled through his contacts. "I've got it here." He turned the phone around, and I leaned forward to read the screen.

"Delia Venable?" I sat back in my chair, stunned.

Then I glanced over at Jason. He had to be shocked at that news too. However, he looked completely unaffected.

Oh, he was good.

"Call her," Jason said. "Ask her to email you copies of the documents. She signed them, right?"

Bryce nodded and pushed the button to call Delia. Then he put the phone on speaker. When she picked up, he said, "Delia, this is Bryce Robinson."

"Hello, Bryce," Delia said.

"Look, I don't know if you've heard what's happened with the Mercer Building, but we've got a situation over there. And to tell you the truth, *I've* got a situation *here*. I can't find my executed copy of the contracts for rent and sale of the two properties in the building. Would you mind emailing them to me again?"

There was a pause. Then Delia said, "Of course, Bryce. I'll do that right now. Do you want to hold on while I do it?"

"Yes, please."

"Okay. Let me just put you on hold."

A soft jazz tune filled the room. Jason sat very still. Then he looked over at Bryce. "How far is the bank from here?"

"Two-minute walk," he said. "It's just across from Down on the Corner, actually."

Jason nodded, then turned to me. "I'm going to go talk to Delia. If she comes back on the phone before I get over there, don't tell her I'm paying her a visit."

I nodded.

He looked at Bryce. "I'd prefer that you not mention it either."

"Wouldn't think of it," he said. "If you cut across the alley next to the restaurant, it's even faster."

When the door closed behind Jason, I swiveled toward Bryce. "What's going on here? It's just all too weird."

"I truly don't know," he said. "I know I keep saying this, but I promise you I thought I was just getting a great deal for you and Nora. I truly did. I would never have suggested this if I'd known how it would turn out." He paused. "See, I've kind of had a crush on Nora for a while. I know she's got that soldier-turned-professor boyfriend in College Station, but he's not putting a ring on her finger, now is he? So I thought maybe I could get in her good graces with this deal and we'd somehow strike up something between us."

"Oh Bryce, I had no idea." I paused. "How long have you had this crush on Nora?"

He shook his head, smiling wistfully. "When did she move to Brenham?"

"Seventh grade," I said.

"Then the answer to that would be since seventh grade." He shook his head. "She has no idea, and I'd rather keep it that way. But hey, if she ever dumps this guy with the commitment issue, I'd appreciate it if you'd put in a good word for me." Bryce's face fell. "If I'm not in prison, that is."

"Check your emails," I said, looking for a way to change the direction of the conversation. "Maybe Delia has sent you the documents by now."

"Not yet," he said when he'd checked.

An uncomfortable silence fell between us.

"So, how's your family?" I asked to fill the quiet.

"My folks are great," he said. "Mom and Dad bought an RV last year. They peep the leaves on the East Coast in the fall, then drive south to winter in Sarasota. I expect they'll be back here in a month or less. Mom doesn't like to miss the bluebonnets."

I nodded. "That sounds fun," I said, although I couldn't think of anything worse than living in a tiny metal home with wheels with a shower that you could barely turn around in. Then there was the idea of parking in a new place every night and putting your lawn chair out to converse with whoever parked next to you. Why people wanted to do that was beyond me.

"What about your brother?" I asked. "What's he up to? I remember him as the kid who was always doing crazy tricks on his skateboard."

Bryce laughed. "He's great. You'd never believe it, but he's got an engineering degree from MIT, an MBA from Harvard, and was working on a PhD in something to do with finance at A&M but got bored. All before the age of twenty-five. I'm pushing thirty and work for a living, but he's playing games at twenty-four. Or at least that's what he was doing the last time I talked to him. Some kind of virtual reality thing."

"And remind me of his name?" Then I remembered. "Never mind, I remember. So he's into virtual reality?" I said casually.

"He's crazy about it," Bryce said with a laugh. "Me? I can't get past having to wear that thing over my eyes."

An image like dominoes falling flashed in my mind.

Like puzzle pieces fitting together.

Bryce's brother. The bank. The painted dogs.

I smiled. Of course.

"Bryce, I need to go. Please, if you want to avoid jail, do not leave this office. I really want to help you, but I will only vouch for you with Jason if you are still sitting behind that desk when I come back. Please understand that this is super important."

I headed in the direction of the bank and met Jason walking toward me in the alley. "I know who did it, Jason. I figured it out."

He shook his head. "That fast?"

I nodded. "You're going to need to make a few phone calls, but you can do that on the way."

"On the way to where?" he said.

"I'll tell you that in the truck."

We arrived in College Station just as the local police were bringing out Bryce's brother in handcuffs with his virtual reality goggles still perched on his forehead. He spied me and turned my direction.

"Did Bryce give me up?"

"Cassidy figured it out on her own," Jason told him.

"It all clicked when Bryce bragged about your education," I told him. "Engineering, an MBA, and then something in finance until you got bored and into virtual reality? That's the perfect recipe for a new business venture in the form of a video game with dogs, isn't it?"

"No comment," he said.

"But you needed financing," Jason continued. "So you went to your brother. He couldn't help you, but his files could."

"And so could his friends," I said. "It took me a minute to figure out which friends. You needed money and you weren't going to get much from the investors you'd met with. So you went to Ben Tanner. You and he went way back to your school days when you skateboarded together. He went to bat for you and presented your business plan to investors as his. I saw him at that meeting with Sticks Styler, Ken Venable, and a third person who I now know was your brother. He was pitching on your behalf, wasn't he?"

"Leave Ben out of this," he said. "He hasn't done anything wrong."

"Except be friends with you," I said. "And give you office space in his building. That was a mistake. What I don't understand is how you convinced him to fundraise for you. Why would he do that?"

He said nothing, so Jason picked up the story. "First you tried asking for money, but Ben's is all wrapped up in his trust fund. We know this because in a phone call on the drive here the trustee confirmed he lives on an allowance from the trust and the remainder is under the control of Delia Venable, the trustee. Ben has a building because his trust bought one for him. They actually bought two, but after Ben picked the one he liked, they kept the other until they eventually put it on the market."

"And that's when you managed to sell it to Henry Hughes in an under-the-table deal, but with the stipulation that you use the first floor for business purposes for a period of time. Then he could move in. Henry was already a con man, so he didn't ask many questions, and the deal he got was a quarter of the price the building should have gone for."

"And yet a deal is a deal," he said.

"Only that building wasn't yours to sell. And your brother was only the real estate agent," Jason said. "You thought you were too smart to get caught. If anyone was going down, it would be Bryce. Only it didn't work that way."

"I noticed," he said.

"Just one question," I said, "before you go. I think I understand everything else about this, but why dogs?"

"People love dogs," he said. "Happiness is a warm puppy, as Charles Schulz says. But not everyone can own a dog. Virtual dogs are the future, man."

"And yet your virtual reality couldn't be made without real dogs," I said. "You found Spot wandering around the neighborhood looking for his home after his owner sent him to live with a relative while she was on a cruise. How did you get him inside that fence? And why there?"

"Industrial looking," he said. "I liked the vibe. I would have gone back for him if someone hadn't stolen him."

I exchanged a look with Jason. He shook his head.

"Why Suzy?" I said.

"The fast one?" He shrugged. "I tried getting Gavin's parents' bulldog to move like her, but he wouldn't cooperate. Then the stadium groundskeeper found him, and I had to go into damage control. It's amazing how little cash a broke college student will settle for to lie."

"That's terrible," I said.

"It's business," he responded with a shrug. "As to that crazy dog, I was skating with Ben and he told me about this dog he wanted. I was curious. It was easy to get her in my car, but I was about ready to toss her out the window by the time we got to Kyle Field. I didn't notice her collar tag until I'd been there a while."

"So you tossed the tag instead of the dog, then headed back to Brenham to give yourself an alibi," Jason said. "What did you tell Ben?"

"Just that I thought I saw his dog in the park. He did the rest." A shrug. "Why do you care? They're just dogs. The last one didn't even make the film reel. He got loose downtown. Dumb dog went back to Ben's place. I washed off the paint and returned him to the yard where I found him. The owners never knew he'd been gone."

So that was why we couldn't find the last dog or confirm he was there.

A second College Station police officer joined us. "If that's all, Game Warden, we'll take him down and book him."

Jason turned his attention to the man in handcuffs. "You know what? Everyone we talked to on the way here was shocked that you were involved in this. That leads me to one conclusion." He paused. "You would've gotten away with all of this if you hadn't made just one mistake. You just had to brag about it, but you thought you were smarter than everyone else with all your training and degrees."

"And here I was, just the office manager at a vet clinic, and I figured it out," I told him.

Jason grinned, first at me and then at the prisoner. "Yep, she figured it out. An amateur."

I shrugged. "It was the Z that did it. The Bark of Zorro. You had twenty-six letters to choose from to make your video game and do your promotion. You should have chosen better, Zach."

Jason and I drove back to Brenham together, our fingers entwined and our conversation nonstop. By the time we returned to Brenham and delivered Spot to Jason's uncle Ken and aunt Delia's care, we'd not only decided to try again with the pasta recipe, but we also decided we just might have to continue this relationship and see where it went.

CHAPTER THIRTY-NINE

Two weeks—and a few days—later. . .

Somehow Jason managed to get the police tape removed from the Mercer Building and our keys returned to us just one week after Zach Robinson's arrest. True to her promise, Mari threw a moving-in party for me last weekend. So it was my turn to have my friends over, to thank them for all they'd done to help me settle into my beautiful loft.

I cringed considering how many trips we made up and down the staircase in the process of moving in. Though I had second-guessed giving away so many of my things to charity, I know my friends appreciated that I had.

Except for the heavy antique armoire that I was absolutely certain would look perfect against the brick wall nearest my kitchen. And I was right. But I don't want to think about how many guys it took to move that monstrosity in here.

Dr. Tyler may have actually mentioned that I could never move again. Of course, that's fine because I love living on the top floor of the Mercer Building. It's everything I hoped for and more.

Abuela commented I'd always be in shape thanks to the staircase I'm required to go up and down just to leave and return. She's a tough critic, but she pronounced my place heavenly and my kitchen exceptional. She and Mama have even promised to return next weekend to finally teach me how to make Abuela's famous tamales. Considering I have been begging her for the recipe for ages, I'm pretty excited about that.

Anyway, my first week in my new place had flown by. Between my days at the clinic and my evenings here unpacking, hanging pictures, and planning the things I'd be doing to the place, I had been exhausted.

Standing there with Nora's pasta sauce simmering on the stove, however, all of the tiredness was evaporating. I couldn't wait to see everyone and enjoy my first meal with my friends in the home the Lord provided for me.

Nora had spent all day at my place cooking—except for making the pasta—then suddenly had to run out for more supplies the minute Jason arrived. I think she knew we'd appreciate a few minutes alone together before the party started. I'd been so busy unpacking that we'd only managed to see each other once since I moved in.

"Are you going to stand there daydreaming, or are you going to help me make the pasta?"

I gave Jason a sideways glance. The Gorgeous Game Warden had donned a striped chef's apron, one of a pair we'd left the restaurant with on our second visit to cook with Alessandro last week. In one hand, Jason held a bag of flour, and in the other the cookbook he'd purchased along with the aprons.

"I'd rather watch you," I told him with a smile.

Jason deposited the cookbook and flour onto the countertop, then turned to face me, matching my smile. "No way. Making pasta is our couple's activity."

I laughed and was about to protest when he stole a quick kiss. Then he took a step back and studied me.

"What?" I asked him.

He shrugged. "I like thinking of us as a couple, Cassidy."

"Me too," I admitted.

"So get over here and let's make the pasta. They'll all be here soon."

As if on cue, the bell rang, announcing someone at the door downstairs. Jason laughed. "Okay, I'll make the pasta. You go greet your guests. But, Cassidy?"

"What?" I said, moving toward the stairs.

"Just so you know, you make me happy."

It was my turn to steal a kiss from him. "Same, Jason," I said, then hurried downstairs to open the door.

Half an hour later, almost everyone had arrived. Conversation and laughter combined to make a symphony of sound that I hoped I would always hear in this place. Nora's charcuterie board and appetizer plates certainly helped keep the party lively.

Delia, Bryce, and Ken were deep in conversation about some sort of investment portfolio something or other while Spot snoozed at Delia's feet. Dr. Kristin, Mari, and Isabel were taking turns telling Nora and Lane about something funny that happened at the clinic earlier in the week while Parker added his comments sparingly.

Meanwhile, Dr. Tyler, Dr. Cameron, and Jason were discussing the finer points of their golf swings while Dr. Kristin's rescue pup snoozed on Dr. Tyler's shoulder. I stayed out of the golf conversation, although I did return Jason's smile when he caught me watching him.

Nora had loaned me two of her long harvest tables and some of her restaurant chairs for the evening. We'd managed to squeeze lots of chairs around the table, but there was also seating at the bar or out on the balcony, if necessary.

The balcony. I hurried across the room to throw the doors open to the evening air, then lit the candles on the outside table. The evening would be chilly but the afternoon had been warm, and there was a remnant of that warmth in the air.

My phone buzzed in my pocket. I retrieved it to see a text from Ben.

Look down.

I frowned as I walked to the balcony rail and did as he asked. The streetlights illuminated an empty street. Then I heard the familiar sound of wheels on concrete.

Craning my neck, I spied someone on a skateboard coming up the road. It was Ben. When he got close enough to hear me, I called out a greeting.

"You're late," I said as he skidded to a stop on the sidewalk beneath my balcony. "But I'm very glad you're here."

"Guilty as charged," Ben said. "But only because I was finishing up my best Tanner design yet."

"What's that?" I asked.

"Check this out." He turned around to reveal that the backpack he'd been wearing contained a canine passenger.

"Buster?" I said. "You made a backpack for Buster? You've only had him a week. And is he wearing goggles?"

A few days after Zach's arrest, Ben had returned to Second Chance Ranch. His intention had been to apologize for his part in the Bark of Zorro situation, unwitting as it was. The result had been that he'd met our sweet pup Buster and immediately knew the basset hound was meant to be his.

Ben turned to face me once more. "I know, right? It took some engineering to achieve it. You might have noticed he's not exactly a small dog, and he's getting on in years, so I needed some support and comfort for him. Thanks to me, this guy has a cozy padded seat where he can ride along with me on my skateboard. And yes, those are actually standard pet store Doggles. I didn't come up with them, but they're brilliant. I may customize some for Buster eventually, but one project at a time, you know?"

"All he needs is a helmet," I teased.

"Actually, I'm working on that. So far he's rejected all the prototypes I've created, but hey, we've got time, the two of us. We'll get it right."

It figured that the trust fund genius would be turning his brain toward something that helped someone. Or in this case, helped a pup. He really was a nice guy.

"I'm sure you will," I said. "Give me a sec and I'll let you in."

By the time I reached the door, Ben had released Buster from the backpack. The pair followed me upstairs and joined the crowd of people and pets.

"The gang's all here," I called.

Then the doorbell rang again. I glanced around the room to see who was missing, but none were. Jason must have noticed my expression of confusion because he broke away from his conversation to walk toward me.

"Not expecting anyone else?"

I shook my head.

"Then how about I answer this one?" he said, going into first responder mode.

I placed my hand on his sleeve. "I'll do it."

"And I will be right behind you," he said.

Arguing with a man this stubborn is futile. So I headed toward the stairs with Jason following a step behind.

I opened the door to find Camille standing there holding a bouquet of flowers. She smiled at me, then glanced behind me. Her grin disappeared. "I'm sorry. I had thought to drop off a housewarming gift, but I can come another time."

"Don't be silly," I said. "Come in. And thank you for the flowers. They're beautiful."

"Hold on," Jason said. "You're here alone, right? No film crew?"

"No film crew," Camille said. "Just me. We've wrapped here, and I'll be leaving in a day or two. Post-production will start soon." She shook her head. "Anyway, I just didn't want to leave Brenham without thanking you for putting up with our intrusion into your life. Your Bark of Zorro story is going to be the highlight of the season."

"What about your intrusion into mine?" Jason said in what I hoped was a teasing tone.

Camille shook her head. "You knew what you were getting into, Game Warden. Cassidy didn't." Her tone was also light. Then she grinned.

I could tell by his expression that Jason wanted to argue. I wasn't about to let him.

"Well, thank you for the flowers. Now come up and meet my friends."

"I couldn't," she said. "That's intruding. Really, I—"

Dr. Cameron stepped out onto the staircase landing. "What's taking you so long?" Then he paused. "Camille Finley? Is that you? I'm ready for my close-up!"

Camille gave me a look. "You didn't tell me he was here."

"Oh, he's here all right," Jason said. "I'd tell you to ignore him, but I know from experience that it's impossible."

"I heard that," Dr. Cameron said before returning his attention to Camille. "Stay, even though he's here, okay?"

The brothers' banter continued as we made our way up the stairs and into my loft. After introductions—though most of the crew already knew who she was—Camille settled right in and became part of the group.

"She's nicer than I thought," Nora said, coming to stand beside me.

"She is," I told her. "But then most people are."

"I'm glad everything turned out all right with the painted dogs," she told me. "Maybe after I get the restaurant up and running, I'll get a dog of my own. Or two."

I smiled. "Still considering calling it Princess or Pancho?"

She shrugged. "Maybe. Or just Scooby or Shaggy. I'm kind of liking this mystery-solving thing. Maybe I'll take up sleuthing on the side."

"In your spare time?" I joked.

Jason came up beside me and wrapped his arms around my shoulders. "It's a great party, Cassidy."

Nora laughed. "You're just worried because you overheard us talking about solving mysteries. Admit it."

"I admit nothing," Jason said, though his grin gave away his mock serious tone. "Okay, maybe one thing. I'd be perfectly happy if Cassidy gave up chasing bad guys and left that to the professionals, but I'm awfully proud of her for what a great job she did in putting Zach Robinson away. This amateur did what the professionals couldn't do. That's impressive."

"I feel bad for Bryce, though," Nora said. "He had no idea that his brother was doing any of this."

"Why don't you go tell him that?" I said. "He's always enjoyed talking to you."

Nora gave me a look. "He's had a crush on me since seventh grade. It doesn't take an amateur sleuth to see that."

"You knew?" I said. "You never let on."

"He's such a sweet guy. I never wanted to ruin a friendship." She shrugged. "But yeah, I'll go talk to him."

Jason watched Nora walk away, then returned his attention to me. "So you had no idea that Bryce had a crush on your friend?"

"None," I said, watching the man's face light up when Nora settled onto the empty chair beside him. "Not until he admitted it that day in his office."

"Since seventh grade?" Jason continued.

"Not a clue," I said.

"Some amateur sleuth you are, Velma," Jason said with a chuckle.

"Hey now," I told him. "I still maintain that Velma was the reason those mysteries were solved. Okay, Shaggy and Scooby-Doo did their part, but without Velma—"

"Kiss me, Cassidy," he said. "I'm teasing."

Around us the dogs barked, and our friends chattered happily. The food was amazing, and the evening was absolutely perfect. But standing in Jason Saye's arms, all the happy chaos faded as I obliged the Gorgeous Game Warden with a kiss.

Later, after everyone had left and it was just me and the moonlight streaming through the windows, I snatched up the homemade quilt my mother and grandmother had given me as a housewarming gift and walked out onto the balcony. The night air was crisp, but the quilt, made with love, kept me warm as I settled onto a chair and looked up at the sky.

The stars overhead were twinkling, though the city lights hid most of them. Looking up, I thought of the future. There were uncountable stars up there sparkling. I couldn't see them, but I knew they were there.

I smiled. Not everyone shares the same faith I do, but I would like to think they believe in hope and a future too. I know I have both in abundance, and I am grateful.

So about that relationship between Jason and me? It's too soon to know for sure, but I think it's going to work out just fine.

I know there will be kissing. There probably will be an argument or two about my amateur sleuthing and his penchant toward being overprotective of me. Maybe I will even dust off that mystery novel I've been thinking about and start actually writing it again. I'm sure Jason would prefer I solve fictional mysteries over real ones.

Did I mention there will be kissing?

And as to exactly what the future holds, that's one mystery I'm willing to wait around to find out.

KATHLEEN Y'BARBO is a multiple Carol Award and RITA nominee and bestselling author of more than one hundred books with over two million copies of her books in print in the US and abroad. A tenth-generation Texan and certified paralegal, she is a member of the Texas Bar Association Paralegal Division, Texas A&M Association of Former Students and the Texas A&M Women Former Students (Aggie Women), Texas Historical Society, Novelists Inc., and American Christian Fiction Writers. She would also be a member of the Daughters of the American Republic, Daughters of the Republic of Texas, and a few others if she would just remember to fill out the paperwork that Great-Aunt Mary Beth has sent her more than once.

When she's not spinning modern-day tales about her wacky southern relatives, Kathleen inserts an ancestor or two into her historical and mystery novels as well. Recent book releases include: bestselling *The Pirate Bride* set in 1700s New Orleans and Galveston; its sequel *The Alamo Bride* set in 1836 Texas, which features a few well-placed folks from history; and a family tale of adventure on the high seas and on the coast of Texas. She also writes (mostly) relative-free cozy mystery novels.

Kathleen and her hero-in-combat-boots husband have their own surprise love story that unfolded on social media a few years back. They make their home just north of Houston, Texas, and are the parents and in-laws of a blended family of Texans, Okies, and three adorable Londoners.

To find out more about Kathleen or connect with her through social media, check out her website at www.kathleenybarbo.com.

GONE *to the* DOGS *Series*

Grab a lapdog to cuddle and relax into a fun small-town Texas mystery series.

OFF the CHAIN
(Book 1)
BY JANICE THOMPSON

Marigold and her coworkers at Lone Star Vet Clinic only want to help animals, but someone is determined to see them put out of business.

Paperback / 978-1-63609-313-0

DOG DAYS of SUMMER
(Book 2)
BY KATHLEEN Y'BARBO

Country music star Trina Potter is back in town to help her niece start a dog rescue, but more than one person wants to send her packing back to Nashville.

Paperback / 978-1-63609-394-9

BARKING UP the WRONG TREE
(Book 3)
BY JANICE THOMPSON

Veterinarian Kristin Keller is determined to figure out why her star patient is suddenly acting like a very different dog just days before his next big agility competition.

Paperback / 978-1-63609-451-9